SCRAPPING

Scarlett

Books by Pamela Burford

Jane Delaney Mysteries
Undertaking Irene
Uprooting Ernie
Perforating Pierre
Icing Allison
Preserving Peaches
Simmering Stu
Liquidating Larry
Scrapping Scarlett
Jane Delaney Humorous Mystery Series: Books 1-3 Box Set

Romantic Suspense
Snatched
Going Commando
Storming Meg
A Case of You
Twice Burned (Double Dare book 2)

Contemporary Romance
Rags to Bitches
In the Dark
Snowed
Too Darn Hot
The Boss's Runaway Bride (a novella)

The Wedding Ring matchmaking series:
Love's Funny That Way
I Do, But Here's the Catch
One Eager Bride To Go
Fiancé for Hire
*The Wedding Ring Matchmaker Series: Complete Four-Book
Romantic Comedy Box Set*

SCRAPPING *Scarlett*

A Jane Delaney Mystery

Book 8

Pamela Burford

RADICAL POODLE
PRESS

for the wonderful Burford sisters:
Kate, Janice, and Good Twin Pat

1

A Good First Impression

"JANE! HI!"

The sound of my name brought my head around. I saw Amy Collingwood striding toward me across the courtyard of the Americana apartment building. I wasn't surprised to run into her there. I knew several people who called the Americana home, and this young conservation scientist was one of them.

The building itself was a stodgy redbrick box, consisting of sixty-five rental units in four stories. I'd just parked in one of the guest spots and was headed for the entrance when she waylaid me. The sun had set minutes earlier, and the autumn afternoon light was rapidly fading.

I glanced at my wristwatch. Yes, I still occasionally wore one of those, particularly when promptness was important. It was 5:54 p.m.

Amy and I exchanged greetings, and she gave a little love to Sexy Beast, who occupied his usual luxurious conveyance, a straw bucket tote hanging from my shoulder. Sexy Beast (SB for short) was an apricot toy poodle and my most cherished companion—well, if you didn't count a certain yummy bartender who'd recently moved into my house.

Okay, I admit it. It wasn't actually *my* house, at least not yet. Sexy Beast had inherited the McMansion a year and a half earlier from his original owner, Irene McAuliffe. Yeah, you read that right. I lived in the fanciest doghouse on the planet. It would belong to me someday, but since that someday would be one that didn't include my beloved SB, I had no problem with my role as the landless guardian of a seven-pound good boy, thank you very much.

My name is Jane Delaney and I am a small business owner. What kind of business? Let me put it this way. There are certain necessary chores that most of us would rather not face. Many of these chores are emotionally taxing. Some might even be considered distasteful or—let's be honest here—downright disgusting.

And when I say most of *us*, I mean most of *you*. It doesn't bother me in the slightest to arrange for a human body to be composted. Or to force a funeral director to dress a body in a garish clown costume and grinning white-face makeup for the viewing, in accordance with the deceased's last wishes. Or to swipe, I mean liberate, a valuable mermaid brooch from the corpse during a wake.

Okay, that last one didn't quite go as planned, but you get the idea. People hire me to get things done. Things that involve dead folks. As you might guess, some of the assignments I'm offered are blatantly illegal. I have no problem turning those down. (What's that? You have one in mind that's not so blatant? Let's talk.)

But as for all those death-related tasks that are unspeakably gory or gooey? Hey, that's my bread and butter. And yeah, I know that's a nauseating metaphor and I don't care. 'Cause I'm the one and only Death Diva.

Yep, that's what they call me around these here parts—

which happens to be Crystal Harbor, an affluent town on the North Shore of Long Island, New York, so I don't know where that *these here parts* came from.

But I digress. I was about to tell you about the thing that happened at the Americana on Tuesday, November 4, at precisely 5:58 p.m.

A young couple entering the building held the door open for an older man with a cane who was leaving. I snuck a peek at my watch while Amy gave SB a few more scritches. It was 5:55.

The crisp breeze lifted strands of Amy's long, brown hair. She tucked her hands into her jacket pockets to warm them. "So who are you visiting here?"

"Oh, it's just a meeting with a prospective client," I said, hoping she didn't ask which of her neighbors was thinking of hiring me. I believe in protecting the privacy of those who find themselves in need of deathy services. If, on the other hand, a client chooses to tell all his friends about the spectacular job the Death Diva did in having Uncle Ed's ashes mixed into a beautiful stained-glass window, I'm not about to squawk. I mean, who turns down free publicity, right?

I asked, "Did you just get home from work?"

She nodded. "Figured I'd run out and pick up some Thai."

As we chatted, I noticed a person on the building's roof. And was that smoke? I squinted at the purpling sky. A figure in a baggy jacket was leaning with his back against the black metal railing up there, puffing on a cigar and blowing smoke rings.

Sexy Beast started acting restless. He uttered a short, polite bark. It didn't take someone fluent in Poodle to figure this one out.

"All right, all right." I set the tote on the grass, clipped the leash onto his harness, and let him hop out to take care of business. Better now than when I was in the middle of my meeting. And yes, the prospective client had granted permission to bring him along. *Oh, I love dogs. They're so much more trustworthy than people. I'm planning to get one from the animal shelter.*

Amy strolled with me as I followed my pet and his high-powered nose around the lawn abutting the concrete walkway. "Did you hear the latest?" she asked, with a scowl.

"No. What's going on?"

She flung her arm toward the building. "The Americana's being sold. Can you believe it? The new owner's planning to demolish it and put up one of those big, ugly mansions."

"Can they do that?" I asked. "Legally, I mean. Some of the tenants have multiyear leases."

"They can do it," Amy said, with a disgusted sigh. "The leases we signed allow for termination under certain circumstances."

"So it's a done deal?"

"I don't think it's *done* done," she said, "but close enough. No idea when it's going to become official."

I watched SB investigate a crepe myrtle before finally deciding it was worthy of his attention. He lifted his leg. "What will happen to all the people living here?"

"Precisely!" she said. "Some of them have been here for decades. Clover Eklund in One-D has lived here since the place was built fifty-one years ago. She's a retired math teacher. Barely squeaks by on a minuscule pension and Social Security. She has no family to take her in. Where will she go?"

"Good point," I said. "It's not like there are any other rental apartments in Crystal Harbor."

"Oh, don't get me started on that," Amy said. "The Town Council would just love to see this place torn down. Those rich so-and-sos think anyone who has to rent an apartment is someone they don't want in their precious community. Let me amend that. They don't want them *living* in their precious community. They're perfectly happy to have the riffraff commute an hour and a half from someplace else to mow their lawns and scrub their toilets."

I happened to know that Sophie Halperin, Crystal Harbor's mayor and my best friend, didn't share those snobbish views, but I wasn't prepared to get into it just then. I had to hurry things along if I didn't want to be late for my six-o'clock meeting. Isn't there some saying about having one chance to make a good first impression?

The cigar smoker was still on the roof. Probably didn't want to stink up his own apartment, or was under his spouse's strict orders not to. But then why not come downstairs and step outside onto the grass? There were even a couple of benches. He could chat with his neighbors going into and out of the building. That had to be more pleasant than a solitary smoke on the roof of an aging four-story apartment house.

I checked my watch: 5:57. Time to get a move on.

I returned Sexy Beast to his tote, hefted it onto my shoulder, and was about to excuse myself, but Amy was on a roll. "And it's the same for so many of the folks here, particularly the older ones. I mean, I'll do okay. I've saved enough for a down payment on a nice condo, and my credit is good. But most of the others, well, they'll be in trouble. I assume they'll receive some sort of relocation allowance, but how far will that take them?" Her expressive features told me how worried she was for them.

I started to move toward the entrance to the building. "I'll see what I can find out from Mayor Sophie. She always seems to know everything that's going on in town."

Her expression brightened. "Oh, that's right. You two are close. Maybe you can exert a little influence." She offered a crooked smile. "Or a lot."

"Believe me, I'll try. I'd hate to see—"

A shrill scream interrupted my words. The three of us (yes, I'm including Sexy Beast in that count) turned toward the sound and watched in horror as the cigar smoker plummeted off the roof, along with a section of the railing.

Amy and I screamed, too, and averted our eyes as the poor fellow landed on the building's concrete frontage with a sickening thud.

No, not a fellow, I belatedly realized. That scream had been decidedly feminine.

That didn't just happen. It couldn't have happened.

Amy was groaning, "No, no, no…God, no…"

Sexy Beast was whining and barking in turns, climbing out of the tote to cling to me. He didn't need to comprehend the specifics to know his alpha female was in distress. Protecting me was Job One.

A few residents drifted out of the building in response to the screams, only to recoil as they took in the tragic scene.

Amy was shaking so hard, she could barely tap 911 on her phone. As she spoke with the dispatcher, I secured SB in a firm football hold and forced myself to approach the motionless body lying faceup on the concrete. A four-foot length of the roof's metal railing lay nearby. So did the still-smoldering cigar.

Four stories was a long way to fall, but I'd heard of people surviving falls from similar heights. Even before I knelt to feel for a pulse, however, it was clear she hadn't been one of the lucky ones.

The poor thing was so young. She couldn't have been more than twenty-five or so. I rose and rejoined Amy.

"They're on the way," she said, her voice quavering. Shaking her head in disbelief, she turned away from the sight of her neighbor's broken body. "Poor Scarlett."

My gaze snapped to her face. "Scarlett Proctor?"

"Yes. Did you know her?"

"No, we only spoke on the phone," I said. "She's the one I was supposed to meet with."

2

Shout It From the Rooftops

"WHAT DID SCARLETT want to talk to you about?" Sophie asked me, as Martin slid a double Scotch across the bar to her.

I shrugged and lifted my snifter of tequila. "I wish I knew. She refused to discuss it over the phone. All I know is that she wanted to hire me for some kind of Death Diva gig."

Amy said, "Which could mean almost anything, considering the scope of your services." She was nursing a classic Tanqueray martini, straight up with a twist.

Since Amy and I had been the only witnesses to Scarlett's fatal accident, the police had questioned us at length. For obvious reasons, I was better equipped than Amy to deal with the emotional fallout (yeah, not the best choice of words), so once the cops were finished with us, I took charge. I packed Amy into my red Mazda and swung by the Thai restaurant to pick up our dinner—chicken satay, coconut shrimp, and pad Thai—then headed to my place.

Between bouts of weeping, Amy managed to put away a few bites. I admit it, I felt downright maternal toward her just then, despite the fact that at age forty, I was only eight years her senior. But then, what did I know about being maternal? I'd never been a mom, and the window of opportunity on that one was rapidly slamming shut, much as I wish it weren't.

Sexy Beast and his recently adopted sister, Layla, a large, black, mixed-breed dog, did their best to cadge some of our takeout, but in the end were forced to settle for their gourmet dog food, which cost nearly as much as our meal.

After settling the two pooches in front of the giant television in my family room and turning on SB's beloved *Cat TV* (yeah, my dog's not right), I'd taken Amy to Murray's Pub for a therapeutic cocktail or three. A historic watering hole dating from the late nineteenth century, Murray's was my favorite hangout for many reasons, not the least of which was the presence of my man, Martin McAuliffe, behind the bar.

We'd picked up my bestie, Mayor Sophie Halperin, on the way, and the three of us had claimed the corner barstools farthest from the door. The place was barely half-full on this Tuesday evening, for which I was grateful. Knowing what we'd been through, Martin managed to be attentive without hovering. Speaking of things I was grateful for, he was way up there at the top of the list. I knew he'd be even more attentive when the two of us got home later that night.

Oh, get your mind out of the gutter. I was referring to how supportive he was, how well he read my moods and knew just when I needed a little TLC. My emotional resilience when it came to all things death-related might have been buttressed by my chosen profession, but trust me when I say that nothing in my past had prepared me for the shocking tragedy I'd witnessed earlier.

There was no need to explain any of this to Martin. He knew. I read it in the way his crystal-blue gaze lingered on me even as he mixed drinks and chatted with his regulars.

He produced the bottle of fine añejo sipping tequila he

kept on hand just for me, and pulled the stopper for another pour.

I placed my palm over the snifter. "Thanks, Padre, but I'm driving."

"Why does she call you that?" Amy asked him. "Don't tell me you trained for the priesthood."

His answering grin was so preposterously sexy, it was illegal in twenty-three states. My man was tall and tasty, with an athletic build, those mesmerizing blue, blue eyes, and short, sandy hair that I never tired of running my fingers through.

It hadn't always been this way. Our relationship had gotten off to a rocky start, and it was back then when I'd bestowed the nickname.

"The first time I met Jane," he said, stoppering the bottle and returning it to its special hidey-hole behind the bar, "I was impersonating a priest."

His words made Amy snort midsip, only to grimace in the next instant as fine English gin exited via her nostrils.

Remember that mermaid brooch I'd been hired to swipe, I mean liberate from a corpse during the wake? Well, guess who beat me to it. I'd foolishly given Martin the opening he'd needed because I'd assumed he was an actual priest—of the, you know, really hot variety, but a priest nonetheless.

And yes, I do know how wrong that hot-priest thing sounds, but you didn't see him. Anyway, it turned out all right in the end—well, except for a certain murder, but we had nothing to do with that.

Sophie said, "There's just one thing I want to know. Well, there are a bunch of things I want to know, but let's start with what Scarlett was doing up on that roof. Aside from having a smoke, because there's nothing wrong with firing up a good stogie now and then."

I happened to know that Sophie herself was not averse to enjoying the occasional cigar. The mayor was a well-nourished fifty-something-year-old with chin-length salt-and-pepper hair and a closet full of colorful tunics and pants.

"It was getting dark," I said, "and I couldn't make out details from that distance. Between the short haircut, the baggy clothes, and the cigar… well, I actually thought she was a guy at first."

Scarlett's blonde hair had been cut in a feathery pixie style. When she'd died, her figure had been concealed under a brown field jacket and worn-looking jeans.

Martin addressed Amy as he filled a pitcher from the beer taps. "Do you know if she made a habit of that? Going up to the roof for a smoke?"

Amy nodded. "I'd see her up there quite often—always in that same spot. Sometimes she'd be smoking. Other times she'd have her sketchbook with her. She liked to draw up there. Winter, summer… The cold didn't seem to bother her, as long as it wasn't raining."

I said, "Was she a professional artist or was it just a hobby?"

Amy sipped her martini. "Scarlett was a cartoonist. I know she had a website, and she used to sell pieces to this online magazine."

"And she made a living at that?" Sophie asked.

Amy wagged her hand in a gesture that said, *More or less.* "She once told me she supplemented her cartoon income with freelance work through one of those task sites. You know, like if someone needed some sort of illustration, or a portrait, maybe a business logo. That sort of thing. Kind of like what her sister does, but not in the same nine-to-five way."

"Her sister?" I said.

"Yeah, her older sister lives at the Americana, too. Carolyn. She moved in four months ago after her divorce. Apparently her ex got the house, which is right here in Crystal Harbor. The girls grew up here, and apparently neither of them wanted to move away. Carolyn does graphic design for some big ad agency in the city."

"I didn't realize Scarlett had family in the building," I said. "That must've been nice for her."

Amy looked dubious. "Not really. They weren't that close. Whenever I saw them cross paths, they basically ignored each other."

"How sad. Do their parents lived nearby?"

"They're both gone. Their mom died when Scarlett was just eleven—cancer, I think—and their dad committed suicide about nine months ago, around the beginning of March."

"Oh no," I said. "Tragedy seems to follow this family."

"It gets worse," Amy said. "Their father had been embezzling from the construction company he worked for. After he was caught, he hanged himself in his attic rather than face prison."

That shut us all up for a moment. Finally Sophie said, "Any other siblings?"

"No, it's just the two sisters. Scarlett did have a boyfriend for a while, since last spring. Hal something." Amy frowned in concentration. "Last name begins with a *K*. He lives on the third floor."

Martin spoke up. "You said she *did* have a boyfriend. What happened?"

Amy shrugged. "All I know is, they split up about six

weeks ago, at the end of September. I do know he wasn't happy about the breakup. More than once I got out of the elevator on Four and saw him talking to Scarlett through her closed door, trying to get her to open up, to give him another chance."

Sophie said, "So you live on the same floor as Scarlett."

"Yep. We'd ride the elevator together sometimes. She wasn't much for gabbing, kind of kept to herself, but I have a way of drawing people out. We had a few pleasant conversations in the laundry room waiting for our wash to get done."

The padre set a bowl of salted nuts in front of us. "Sounds like Scarlett was a loner."

"She was definitely that," Amy said. "And it might sound strange to describe a young person this way, but she was a little eccentric. Maybe 'offbeat' is more accurate."

Sophie said, "Didn't keep the boyfriend from trying to get back with her, apparently. Was he that way, too? Offbeat?"

"No, Hal seems like a normal guy. Not that I know him that well. And good-looking. But then so was Scarlett. I mean, yeah, she didn't do much to enhance her looks, with those shapeless thrift-store clothes and never a drop of makeup. Not that she needed it. She was really a very pretty girl, with a nice, petite shape."

"So she bought her clothes from thrift stores?" I asked.

"Mostly, yeah," Amy said. "She made some things, too, like hand-knitted shawls and hats. She bought this sewing machine from Clover Eklund when Clover's arthritis got to where she could no longer use it. Scarlett taught herself to sew with it. She'd collect unique old textiles, like tablecloths and curtains, and turn them into funky clothing."

Sophie's eyebrows rose. "Not too many young people sew nowadays. What kind of clothes did she make?"

"Let's see… long skirts, halter tops for the summer, that sort of thing. I doubt she ever relied on a pattern. Oh, and she made a quilted comforter for Hal back when they were together."

Martin asked, "Did she do this, the thrifting, for financial reasons or was it a fashion choice?"

Amy thought about it. "Most likely both. Plus she believed in recycling things instead of sending them to the landfill and using up the earth's limited resources to replace them. That's how she put it. She didn't just buy secondhand, either, she also salvaged stuff from people's trash. She scored a beautiful old desk that way. Refinished it herself."

I said, "Somehow I can't see the Crystal Harbor constabulary letting her rummage through the citizens' trash on their curbs."

Amy smiled. "Scarlett could be pretty sly about it. Sometimes did it in the middle of the night before the truck came around in the morning. But usually she'd make her rounds in full daylight after people put their bins at the curb. She'd lift the lid and take a peek, and if she saw something she wanted, she'd simply knock on the homeowner's door and ask permission to take the old cookbook or chipped planter or whatever it was that caught her eye. She was very polite about it, and they almost always said yes. A couple of times people even invited her into their homes to offer her other items they were done with."

The padre paused while wiping down the bar. "It sounds like this loner had some people skills."

"I think that's a good way of putting it. She interacted

with other humans on her own terms. She was the most self-reliant person I ever met. Even cut her own hair, and it always looked really cute." Amy started tearing up, and I leaned over to put my arm around her. "I'm okay," she said, as Martin handed her some paper napkins.

"Next question," Sophie said. "Does the Americana allow the residents to go up to the roof?"

"No." Amy blotted her eyes. "It's supposed to be just maintenance staff that go up there. The door leading to that stairwell is kept locked. But somehow Scarlett managed. The only other person I occasionally saw up there was this old guy Nolan Whitehouse. Well, he wasn't that old—maybe sixty. He lived on the second floor. But a real curmudgeon, one of the most unlikable people I've ever met. He and Scarlett seemed to get along, though. I used to see them up there together."

"Did he move away?" I asked. "You said he *lived* on the second floor."

Amy shook her head. "He died about a month ago."

"Speaking of the Americana," I said, "you mentioned the property's about to be sold. Any idea who the buyer is?"

Sophie answered for her. "It's a developer acting on behalf of an extremely wealthy client. Don't know much more, but I'll try to find out. Most of the Town Council is thrilled, of course. They've been wanting the Americana gone for years. An eyesore, harboring undesirables, all that nonsense. There was even talk at one point of having the building condemned."

"They'd never get away with that," Amy said. "The Americana is well maintained and always has been. Sure, it's getting on in years, and it might not be the prettiest structure in Crystal Harbor, but it's sound and… well, I just can't see how it makes sense to evict sixty-five households and tear down a perfectly habitable apartment house so some developer can slap up a single-family monstrosity in its place. Scarlett was more outraged about it than anyone."

I wasn't surprised, considering how committed she'd been to preserving and conserving. Scarlett Proctor would have had some choice words for that developer.

3
Loose Ends

IT FELT KIND of sad and, yes, a little creepy to be returning so soon to the Americana apartments. I even pulled my Mazda into the same guest spot it had occupied four days earlier when Scarlett had taken her tumble off the roof.

The truth is, I'd been mentally debating how much time I should give her sister before contacting her. I was dying to know what Scarlett had wanted to hire me for, and I figured the sister might know. But I wasn't about to bother a grieving family member just to satisfy my own unquenchable curiosity.

Imagine my surprise, then, when Carolyn Proctor Bailey called me out of the blue yesterday and asked for a meeting. She said she needed to discuss something with me, but preferred to do so in person.

Just like Scarlett. Déjà vu.

Of course I agreed to the meeting, though it took every ounce of willpower I possessed to keep from blurting, *Stay off the roof!*

I knocked on the door of apartment 2J and arranged my features into a pleasant half smile for the eyeball on the other side of the peephole. After an awkward half minute or so, I heard the deadbolt slide and watched the door swing open.

Like her late sister, Carolyn was petite, about three inches shorter than my own five foot six. She looked to be about thirty and wore her long, dark-blonde hair in a casual half updo, with soft tendrils framing her face. Unlike Scarlett, her clothing choices were conventional—a lavender pullover sweater and taupe pants, plus a bit of makeup and gold hoop earrings. No thrift-store finds or handmade duds for her, not even on a Saturday morning when meeting with that weirdo Death Diva lady.

Her welcoming smile put me at ease as she ushered me into her apartment. Amy had mentioned that Carolyn had lived there for only four months, since her divorce, and indeed, the furnishings had that flat-pack "some assembly required" vibe, as if the apartment's occupant had been forced to leave her cherished Ethan Allen dining-room set and king-size sleigh bed in a center-hall Colonial she no longer called home.

She said the predictable thing. "Thank you for agreeing to meet with me on such short notice."

I gave the predictable response. "No problem. I'm so sorry about your sister, Ms. Bailey."

She acknowledged this with a little nod, and said, "Please, call me Carolyn. The police told me you were there when it happened."

This conversation was suddenly more difficult than I'd anticipated. "Yes, I was. I'm so very sorry for your loss," I repeated. "I can't imagine…" I bit my tongue to keep from saying *sorry* again.

"Where are my manners?" She gestured for me to sit. "Coffee?"

"I'd love some. Black, no sugar."

While Carolyn busied herself in the kitchen, I chose a

modern upholstered armchair that the Swedish manufacturer probably called something like *Äktenskapsskillnad*. She returned moments later with two mugs and a plate of homemade oatmeal cookies.

I was still full from breakfast, but hey, ain't nothing wrong with a pick-me-up to tide me over till lunch. I believe the British call this particular mini-meal elevenses. For the record, I'm also a fan of threeses, nineses, and middle-of-the-nightses.

As Carolyn settled herself on a matching armchair, I felt obliged to say, "You have a lovely apartment."

"Thank you. It's just a rental, but I try to keep it nice. I put together most of the furniture myself."

In truth, it was far too spare for my taste. Soulless, even. Few decorative touches, no art on the walls. The place seemed transitory, as if its occupant wasn't emotionally invested in her new home. As if she anticipated another move in the near future.

A move back to the home she'd shared with her ex? I wondered who'd initiated the divorce, and why.

Glancing around, I did spy one item that appeared out of place. A copy of *GQ* sat on top of a small stack of periodicals on a side table. A man's magazine. Maybe Carolyn had moved on from her former spouse after all.

Signaling an end to the polite small talk, she said, "You're probably wondering how I got your phone number, Jane."

Not really, considering approximately ten thousand of my business cards were circulating around town, but I played along. "I hope it wasn't too difficult."

"I found it in Scarlett's apartment. I'd never seen the place before."

Excuse me, what? During the entire four months you've been living here, you never once entered your sister's apartment? Amy had said that the sisters basically ignored each other. Until this moment, I'd assumed that was an exaggeration.

Carolyn's mouth twisted. "Turned out she was living in a hoarder's paradise. Big surprise. In any event, I found a note on her fridge with your number and the time you two were supposed to meet."

"Okay," I said, and waited for her to continue.

She said, "Can I ask what she wanted to discuss with you?"

I took a bite of a seriously delicious cookie to buy time to formulate a response. It's a policy of mine not to discuss a client's business with others, but I realized in this case there wasn't much to discuss. Finally I said, "I wish I could help you, Carolyn. I know she was interested in hiring me, but she wouldn't discuss it over the phone. To be honest, I was hoping *you* might know."

This wasn't what she'd expected to hear, I could tell. A frown tugged at her eyebrows. "Well, that's a disappointment. It feels like a, well, like a kind of loose end. I don't like loose ends."

"Could it have had something to do with a relative's death?" I asked. "Or a friend's?"

She shook her head. "We haven't lost any relatives recently. Our mother died fourteen years ago. And Scarlett didn't have friends."

Had Carolyn even known her sister well enough to make a statement like that? If it was true that Scarlett had no friends, that sad fact didn't seem to bother Carolyn, judging by her impassive expression. All she seemed to care about was the "loose end" she was trying to tie up: Why did her dead sister want to hire the Death Diva?

Scarlett might not have had friends at the time of her death, but if what Amy had told us was true, that hadn't always been the case. There was the ex-boyfriend, Hal, who lived in the building. And hadn't she said that Scarlett had been friendly with an old fellow named Nolan before he died?

"I suppose we'll never know why Scarlett called me." I set my mostly full mug on the coffee table, preparing to make my exit. "Was there anything else?"

If that was all Carolyn wanted to talk about, I could've saved myself the drive over there. What was it with the Proctor sisters and their aversion to phone conversations? Perhaps they believed, as Martin did, that there was no substitute for face-to-face communication.

She surprised me by saying, "There is something else. I was actually hoping to hire you myself, Jane."

That was more like it. I said, "It can be complicated, not to mention emotionally taxing, to arrange for a loved one's funeral and the disposition of the remains. I can help you with that, Carolyn. And if you'd rather handle it yourself, I'm happy to offer advice and contacts—at no charge, of course."

Carolyn raised her palm. "That won't be necessary. Scarlett's already been cremated. No need for a funeral. Most of our relatives live in California, and like I said, she didn't have friends."

Was this woman really that cold, or was it a defense mechanism to keep from dealing with her sudden loss? I'd seen all kinds of reactions over the years, but in my experience, even family members who hadn't gotten along with the deceased will at least put on an outward display of grief.

As for Scarlett being denied even a modest sendoff, some recognition of the life she'd lived… well, to my mind, that in itself was a tragedy.

I was just irked enough to say, "I find it hard to believe your sister had no one in her life aside from you. She must've had at least a couple of business connections where she sold her cartoons."

Carolyn shrugged. "I suppose so. I wouldn't begin to know how to contact them."

"Do you have her computer?" I asked. "Her contacts should be—"

"Yes, of course," she said, with obvious annoyance. "I retrieved her laptop when I was in that awful apartment. That's not the sort of thing you want to end up in the wrong hands. She kept her passwords on a sticky note right there on the computer, for heaven's sake. I mean, how careless can you be?"

She seemed to expect an answer, so I said, "It certainly saved you some hassle, though."

"I have her phone, too," Carolyn said. "As for searching her contacts, it turns out my sister disabled both her contact and calendar apps. Who lives like that?"

Everyone had lived like that, I wanted to remind her, before personal computers and smart phones were a thing. "Maybe she was old-school," I said. "As in a paper calendar and address book. If so, it wouldn't be that difficult for you to track down her business associates."

Correction, I thought, as I took in Carolyn's stony expression. It wouldn't be that difficult for someone who actually cared about the deceased.

I said, "I assume you've notified your relatives in California."

"Of course. But they hardly knew Scarlett and can't be expected to put their lives on hold to travel across the country for the funeral of a virtual stranger."

"Did she have any pals from her school days?" I asked.

"None that I know of. Listen, Jane, I know you mean well, but—"

"How about family friends?" I persisted. "You know, friends of your parents, folks who might've been around when you two were growing up."

Carolyn went still. She was thinking about someone. I waited, and finally she gave a resigned sigh. "My dad had this close friend from college. Robert Jernigan. The two families used to get together all the time."

"Okay," I said, "now we're getting somewhere."

"Not really. I completely lost touch with the two sons our age, and so did Scarlett. I believe Bob told me one of them is teaching in Barcelona, and the other is... an accountant? Something like that. In Chicago."

"So you're still in touch with the father?" I said.

"Well, yeah, he lives in this building. It's temporary. He moved in when he got divorced last winter."

Just like Carolyn herself, I thought. Did she consider her stay here temporary as well, just until she finds husband number two? That would explain the knockdown furniture. I imagined her poring over the cartoonish assembly instructions for this coffee table, with all the parts spread out on the floor, including that cheap little Allen wrench they always give you.

"That's nice," I said, "that Bob's your neighbor now, at least for a while."

"We don't see each other much on a day-to-day basis," she said. "Our jobs keep us busy. But we make time to meet for lunch every few weeks. And we go to the same gym. Sometimes I see him there. He likes to check up on us—" She faltered on the word *us*, but recovered quickly. "Since our father is deceased, I think Bob feels kind of responsible for our welfare. Maybe that'll change now that it's just me. I know he was worried about Scarlett. She was so… reckless in the way she lived her life."

I flashed on an image of Scarlett Proctor leaning on that roof railing four stories above the ground.

"She didn't join you and Bob for these lunches?" I asked.

"My sister wasn't the most sociable person, and she didn't care for him."

"Are you in touch with his ex-wife?" I asked.

"No, I was never that close with her," she said. "He's engaged to someone else now. I've met her a couple of times, the fiancée. April Urban. She seems nice."

"It sounds like Bob might welcome a celebration of Scarlett's life," I said.

"A what? Oh, that's your fancy way of saying a funeral. He did seem surprised I wasn't planning anything. He said I could always change my mind and arrange a memorial service at some point in the future when my grief isn't so fresh."

Grief, huh? Guess that's what they're calling apathy nowadays. "So Scarlett had opted for cremation?" I asked.

Carolyn rolled her eyes. "She wanted some woo-woo thing called a 'green burial.' I wasn't about to start in with that nonsense. Cremation is quick, cheap, and efficient, as I'm sure you'll agree."

I had to take a slow, deep breath to calm myself. Don't get me wrong. There's nothing wrong with cremation, but this woman had just shamelessly admitted she'd disregarded her sister's clearly stated wishes. "Just so you know," I said, "there's nothing woo-woo about green burial. It's simply a more natural, eco-friendly option. Any funeral home can arrange it, and it's actually much cheaper than a conventional burial."

"Well, it's done," she said, "and it's one more thing I don't need to think about."

"So if you didn't want to see me about your sister's final arrangements, what is it that I can do for you, Carolyn?"

"Scarlett's apartment is crammed to the rafters with all kinds of… well, all kinds of worthless crap, to be blunt. I'd like to just bring in one of those junk-removal companies to clear it all away, but it's possible there are some items of value mixed in with the trash. I don't have the time or inclination to go through it all myself. I researched you and spoke with a couple of your clients. They vouched for your integrity and professionalism. Is this something you'd be willing to tackle?"

I'd taken on that kind of assignment several times in the past, though I'd be lying if I said I enjoyed it. Nowadays I generally make my excuses and recommend someone else.

But Scarlett was a different matter. I'd witnessed that poor girl's final seconds on this earth, heard her terrified scream as she fell to her death. I'd thought of little else during the four days that had elapsed since then.

Perhaps if I had free rein to sift through her belongings, I could figure out what she'd wanted to hire me for. Still, the very thought of diving into a hoarding situation made me itch.

"I'll tell you what," I said. "Let me take a look at her apartment before I make a decision."

"Fair enough. The cops gave me her keys. I'll take you there after we finish our coffee. The building's owners would like the cleanup done ASAP, of course, so they can rent it out again."

"They actually said that?" I asked. "So soon after you lost your sister?"

"Oh, they pretend to care," she said, "but I can read between the lines. And also, well, her apartment is just this huge chore hanging over my head. I don't need the pressure."

"Who owns the building?" I asked, thinking of the impending sale.

"It's this married couple, Joel and Joanie Devine. They're the original owners, and as you can imagine, they're getting on in years. And getting lazy and cheap, if you ask me. Cutting corners."

"What do you mean?"

She seemed surprised I had to ask. "How about the fact that the railing on the roof failed. Obviously it wasn't properly inspected or repaired. I'm planning to file a wrongful-death lawsuit."

I must admit that when Amy mentioned how well the building had always been maintained, I did wonder about that railing.

"I can recommend a lawyer," I said, "if you need one."

"Thanks, but Bob Jernigan is a lawyer. I'm sure he'll be happy to handle it for me."

I said, "I visited Scarlett's website. She was a very talented cartoonist. I love her quirky drawing style."

"'Quirky'?" she scoffed. "Amateurish is more like it."

Believe me, there was nothing amateurish about Scarlett's drawings. They exhibited a refined artistic skill and keen sense of humor. She'd populated her cartoon world with a wide variety of human, nonhuman, and inanimate subjects. There were a few recurring characters, including a smart-mouthed baby, a time-traveling Leonardo da Vinci, an extraterrestrial alien with an inferiority complex, and a neat-freak rat with strong opinions about housekeeping.

Her website also included a short video in which she discussed her work. Scarlett had been, as Amy had rightly noted, quite pretty, with lively brown eyes and a golden-blonde pixie cut that was substantially less red than my own strawberry-blonde hair.

I asked, "What do you do for a living, Carolyn?" As if I didn't already know.

"I'm an artist, too. I work for Ainsley Media."

"The big ad agency?" I said. "I'm impressed."

"I'm proud of the work I do for our clients. But of course, I'm an anonymous cog in the machine. Countless people have seen my designs, but how many know the name Carolyn Bailey? I'll tell you how many. Precisely zero. I did better than Scarlett in all our art classes. Ask any of our teachers. She didn't have a fraction of my talent, to say nothing of a little thing called work ethic, but she's the one with her name out there."

Out there? Until four days ago, I'd never heard of Scarlett Proctor. I like to think that if her life hadn't been cut short, she might've gained wider recognition, but during her lifetime, her work was not widely known.

Carolyn's mouth thinned. "My sister did a lot of damage with those 'quirky' cartoons of hers."

I frowned. "Damage? All I saw was these really cute, slice-of-life drawings and panels. I mean, it's clear she took some inspiration from her own life—"

"Not just her own life, Jane. She didn't care whose secrets she revealed, whose trust she violated."

"Are you referring to yourself?"

Her tone was pure venom as she said, "My marriage was a casualty of my sister's so-called art."

"Are you telling me she shared, um, inappropriate details about you and your husband?" I asked.

"That's exactly what I'm saying."

"And she identified you by name?"

There was that eye-roll again. "She didn't have to. Anyone who knew Stefan and me would know immediately who was represented in those drawings of hers. And they were published in that online magazine for the world to see."

"I assume Stefan got upset when he saw these cartoons?" I said.

"Once I pointed it out to him," Carolyn said. "Like most men, he was oblivious at first. Until then, he'd actually enjoyed Scarlett's cartoons. He was *proud* to have such a talented sister-in-law, can you believe it?"

I didn't bother asking why she'd made sure her husband got good and worked up over Scarlett's unflattering depictions of his marriage. What had she hoped to gain?

She said, "Stefan blamed *me*, of course. He decided I must've filled Scarlett's head with all sorts of nonsense about our marriage, that I must've exaggerated our problems. That's when he made the decision to leave me."

I was beginning to get it. Carolyn's husband had openly admired Scarlett's artistic accomplishments. One had to wonder whether he'd had nice things to say about the advertising images his wife created for her company's clients. It would seem that her effort to turn Stefan against Scarlett had backfired.

Carolyn was on a roll. She leaned toward me, her face flushed. "But that's not the worst of it. Our father would be alive right now if it weren't for my sister's treachery."

I chose my words carefully. "I was under the impression

your father took his own life after he was caught stealing from his employer." She gave me a sharp look, and I added, "It's hardly a secret, Carolyn. Are you saying Scarlett somehow *made* him commit suicide?"

"That's not… She didn't…" She gave a frustrated huff. "She blabbed about it in those stupid cartoons of hers. About the embezzling. Where was her sense of decency? Her loyalty? She's the reason he killed himself. He couldn't take the public humiliation."

"So he did it?" I asked.

"Excuse me?"

"Your dad. He stole funds from his company?"

Her flush deepened. She sat back. "I don't see how that's any of your concern."

"Well, that seems to be what you're saying. How much did he get away with? Before they, you know, caught him at it?"

I could see her trying to decide whether to answer. Finally she said, "Almost two hundred thousand dollars."

"Wow." My tone and facial expression said I was pleasantly impressed. My tone and facial expression lied. "And his employer didn't miss it?"

She flapped her hand. "Millions of dollars flow through that company every day. It's one of the top five construction firms in the country. My dad's, um, financial transfers were done over time, and represented a drop in the bucket."

"So if Scarlett hadn't spilled the beans, your dad would've made off with a nice little nest egg. Maybe shared some of it with you."

She stared at me, clearly trying to decide how full of manure I was. "That's not really the point, is it? It's about family loyalty, like I said."

Family loyalty, huh? Clearly Carolyn didn't feel that was something she owed her dead sister, judging by how she'd spent the last few minutes trashing her.

Abruptly she stood. "I think we're done here. Let me show you that apartment."

Fine with me. I came to my feet. The sooner we got this over with, the sooner I could get away from this unpleasant woman. "Lead the way."

As we turned to leave, the apartment door swung open and a young man strolled in. He offered a dazzling smile as he tucked his key chain into the pocket of his neatly pressed chinos. "Apologies, Caro," he said. "Didn't know you had a visitor."

Far from looking apologetic, he had the relaxed, confident demeanor of a man who knew he was just too goshdarn gorgeous for words. We're talking intense dark-blue eyes and a regal bone structure. Thick, wavy, sable-brown hair that curled over the collar of his navy blazer. And a tall, sinewy physique that seemed at odds with the preppy exterior.

Carolyn, for her part, was the opposite of relaxed and confident. She appeared downright nervous. "Um, we were just on our way out," she told him. "I'll be back in a few minutes."

As she started to push past him, he extended his hand to me and introduced himself. "Hal Kazarian."

"Nice to meet you, Hal. I'm Jane Delaney." As we shook, I replayed Amy's words in my mind.

Scarlett did have a boyfriend for a while, since last spring. Hal something. Last name begins with a K. He lives on the third floor.

I felt Carolyn's watchful gaze on me. No doubt she was wondering whether I knew that this charming, handsome man—who just happened to have a key to her apartment—was her dead sister's former boyfriend.

Speaking of, you know, family loyalty and all that.

Of course, it wasn't unheard-of for the loved ones of a deceased individual to offer each other comfort, in whatever form that took. Which made this cozy scenario a big so-what.

Well, except for one minor detail.

That copy of *GQ* on the side table? It was the August issue, which had probably been purchased back in July, the same month Carolyn moved into the building. Amy had told us Scarlett broke up with Hal six weeks ago, at the end of September.

Of course, it was possible someone other than Hal had left that magazine here. It was also possible Hal had left that old August issue here sometime in the past few days. I supposed it was even possible Carolyn herself had bought that copy of *GQ*. The magazine wasn't just about men's fashion, after all. It published some pretty good articles.

But as I observed these two and the subtleties of their body language, my gut told me that magazine belonged to Hal and that he'd been making himself at home in Carolyn Bailey's apartment since well before he and Scarlett split up.

4

Cabinet of Curiosities

MARTIN TOOK TWO steps into Scarlett's living room and stopped dead. "Wow." He propped the flat bundle of unassembled cardboard cartons he was carrying against a wall.

"Did I lie?" I gave Sexy Beast a treat and lowered him to the lime-green shag rug so he could commence his olfactory inventory. I predicted he'd be at it a good long while.

"No." The padre did a slow three-sixty, gaping in wonder. "No, Jane, you did not lie."

Right about now you're probably thinking we were standing in what Scarlett's sister had termed a "hoarder's paradise." I would ask you to consider the source of that description. Carolyn lived in a barren box, furnished with a few sad pieces of knockdown furniture. Kind of a surprising way for a self-described artist to live, but hey, whatever floats your boat, right? Clearly, she and I defined *hoarding* differently.

Very simply, Scarlett's apartment was filled (notice I did not say *over*filled) with an eclectic assortment of unique objects. It was a meticulously curated cabinet of curiosities, to use a quaint old term. My gaze flitted between an African woven basket holding doll heads of every description, a cluster of quirky cookie jars (Mr. T? Really?), stacks of classic board games dating back to the Depression, and a gigantic ashtray carved from a petrified log, filled with hundreds of dice in all colors and sizes. And that's just a tiny sample of Scarlett Proctor's salvaged treasures.

In lieu of curtains, Scarlett had swagged colorful, fringed shawls and scarves over the rods. Whatever wall space wasn't taken up with shelves was covered with dozens of framed paintings, posters, and photographs representing every imaginable style and subject.

An old-fashioned Formica diner table occupied the dining area, along with two mismatched chairs. A lazy Susan in the center of the table held salt and pepper shakers in the shape of black and white mice, a pottery sugar bowl that appeared to have been made by a child, and a cut-glass bud vase containing a handful of daisies, now wilted.

The wall art in the dining area all had food themes, including a watercolor of peaches and berries, a botanical poster featuring a variety of herbs, a nineteenth-century photo of a baker kneading bread dough, and a butcher's guide with dotted lines dividing a cow into its various cuts. In French.

I'd brought a duffel bag filled with packing supplies—tape, markers, bubble wrap, newsprint—which I placed near a charming antique desk in a corner of the living room. I recalled Amy mentioning this piece of furniture that evening at Murray's. It had been destined for the landfill before Scarlett rescued and refinished it. The desktop held a printer and document scanner, as well as a stapler, paper clips, pack of sticky notes, and an assortment of pens and pencils in a ceramic mug shaped like a rattlesnake. There was a bare spot where I assumed her laptop had once resided, the only item Carolyn had bothered to remove from her dead sister's home.

Martin was examining the titles in Scarlett's bookcase, which was constructed of discarded planks and cinder blocks. The books, several hundred of them, appeared well-worn, and I'd bet real money she'd read every one of them. He turned to me. "How much time do we have to clear this place out?"

"Well, her rent is paid up through the end of the month," I said, "which is three weeks away. I'm sure the building's owners are eager to get a new tenant in here."

"Mind if I open the windows?" He didn't wait for an answer, correctly anticipating my assent. It had been only five days since Scarlett had gone up to the roof for what was to be her final cigar, but already her home was starting to feel stuffy and closed-in.

The barest sprinkling of dust was visible, representing five days of neglect. The shag rug and surrounding hardwood floors appeared clean. I already knew from my initial inspection the day before that the kitchen, bedroom, and bathroom were just as well maintained. Clearly Scarlett had taken pride in her home and possessions.

Hoarder's paradise indeed.

I welcomed the cool breeze that wafted through the window screens. It was a mild fall morning, and I suspected the physical work we were about to embark upon would keep us warm.

"So, what's the game plan?" he asked.

"Well, her sister, Carolyn, assumes none of this has any worth." I spread my arms and looked around as if to say, *Go figure.* "But to be on the safe side, she hired me to go through it all and identify anything of real value before it's carted away to the dump."

"I guess it depends on what you consider valuable." He

picked up a small bronze statue of a jackalope—yeah, that's right, a jackrabbit with antelope horns—to inspect more closely. I watched a smile spread across his face.

Yes, *valuable* can absolutely mean different things to different folks.

Including folks of the nonhuman persuasion, I thought, as I watched SB explore the old-fashioned New York phone booth that occupied one corner of the living room—complete with its original coin-operated phone in case you were wondering.

"After Carolyn showed me this place yesterday," I said, "I verified that she had no interest in keeping any of her sister's belongings—aside from anything that might be worth serious money, of course."

"Of course." He grabbed the packing tape and started assembling the first box. "Scarlett's sister sounds like a real piece of work."

"She's very judgmental," I said, "especially with respect to her dead sister."

"Amy had mentioned they weren't close," he said.

"An understatement if ever there was one." I ran my hand over a large ceramic butter churn that had been repurposed to hold a variety of antique walking sticks. "I asked if she had any objection to my selling most of this stuff and donating the proceeds to charity in Scarlett's memory. She seemed surprised that anyone would want to buy this 'crap,' as she put it, but she doesn't care as long as I make it all gone."

"So for now," he said, "we're just going to box it all up."

I nodded. "I'll rent a van when we're finished here. If you come across anything that might be worth real bucks, set it aside and I'll have it appraised. And if you find an address book or appointment calendar, or any important-looking documents—" I pointed to the desk "—set them aside. Otherwise, just try to keep similar stuff together, and log the contents of each box on this." I reached into the duffel for a legal pad and pen.

With that, we spent the next couple of hours sorting, evaluating, asking each other's opinion about this piece or that, and spending far too much time simply admiring various items and speculating on the impulse that drove Scarlett to add them to her cabinet of curiosities.

Sexy Beast exhausted himself sniffing his way through the apartment. I gave him water in an antique china bowl, one of many delightfully mismatched pieces in Scarlett's kitchen cupboard. Carolyn had already asked the super to throw away all the perishable food in the apartment, so I didn't have to worry about anything rotting while we spent the next few days there.

SB settled on the cushy pink leather sofa, a vintage piece from the 1980s, and I tucked a wool granny-square afghan around him. "You can finish up in here, Padre. I'm going to start on the bedroom."

"Check it out, Jane." He held up a vinyl record album, one of dozens filling a couple of plastic milk crates sitting next to an old-fashioned record player, the kind with a turntable and built-in speakers that unfolded out of the case. "Herman's Hermits. This album is from nineteen sixty-eight."

I went to work in Scarlett's bedroom as the old pop-rock tune "Mrs. Brown, You've Got a Lovely Daughter" started playing.

The first thing I noticed was the sewing machine positioned near a window. I recalled that Scarlett had bought it from her neighbor Clover Eklund when the older woman's arthritis forced her to stop sewing. For some reason, I wasn't expecting this gorgeous antique. It looked to be from the 1940s, a curvy black model labeled *Singer* in gold lettering, built into a wooden console on legs. Scarlett had apparently been in the middle of a sewing project: a cover for a throw pillow, by all appearances.

Next to it stood a floor lamp with a fancy, leaded-glass shade. "Hey, Padre," I called. "Do you know how to identify an authentic Tiffany lamp?"

He popped his head in. "Sorry, that one's outside my skill set."

I supposed I could look it up online, but I didn't trust myself to get it right. "Okay, this is one for the experts."

I opened the closet door and riffled through a motley assortment of clothing, everything from a mechanic's blue coveralls (originally owned by someone named *Fritz*) to a psychedelic-patterned velvet cape with a stand-up collar. A peek into Scarlett's chest of drawers revealed more of the same. I'd brokered sales to vintage clothing stores on behalf of clients in the past. This part of the job would be pretty straightforward.

Scarlett had slept in a brass-and-iron bed that looked old enough to be a genuine Victorian antique. Another one for the appraisal list. It was neatly made up with a colorful quilted comforter. I recalled Amy saying Scarlett had made something similar for Hal when they were dating. Perhaps it was meant to be a matched set, kind of a his-and-hers thing.

That thought made me sad, so I moved on, turning to the tilted drawing table set against one wall. The table was strewn with sketches and studies representing, I assumed, ideas for future cartoons. Most of the wall was covered with a thin sheet of steel, which was itself half-hidden under sketches, reference photos, and notes held in place by dozens of small magnets. The notes were cryptic for the most part and probably represented sudden flashes of inspiration she intended to come back to later: *fitted sheet hell* and *chopping onions* and *swimsuit shopping*.

So this was where the magic happened. I couldn't resist stepping closer to the table to inspect Scarlett's work in progress, a five-panel cartoon depicting an old man feeding pigeons from a park bench while the number of birds gradually swells to Hitchcockian proportions. It's clear the man and the head pigeon are conversing, but the dialogue had not yet been added. At this point, of course, it never would be.

No way was I going to leave these papers and drawings—a snapshot in time of Scarlett Proctor's creative process, if you will—to be hauled away to the landfill when I finally let the cleanout crew in. Should I bother offering them to her sister? I could imagine Carolyn's response. *Why are you bothering me with this crap? I told you to get rid of it all.*

A new Herman's Hermits tune was wafting in from the living room. I hummed along with the melodious strains of "There's a Kind of Hush All Over the World" as I glanced around the room to see if I'd missed anything.

Martin called, "Are you ready for boxes in there?"

"I guess so." I lifted the edge of the quilted bedspread to see what Scarlett had stored under her bed. It was a good bet I'd find something there because apartments this size aren't known for having a lot of storage space.

I saw only one item, some kind of large book with a leather binding. It had been pushed so far under the bed that I had to flatten myself against the braided area rug and reach way, way in, and even then my fingertips barely brushed it.

I yelped when Martin gave my jeans-clad bottom a playful smack. I hadn't heard him come in.

I pushed my hair off my face and peered up at him. "I need your long arms, Padre."

He flexed his muscles. "My long arms are at your disposal. What are you trying to do?"

I came to my feet and we swapped places. "There's something under there."

"A book. I see it." He quickly retrieved it, sprang to his feet, and handed it over. "Looks like some kind of photo album."

The book, I now saw, was navy-blue with a gold border, about twelve by fourteen inches and covered, not in leather as I'd first thought, but in a cheap imitation, what's sometimes referred to as leatherette. I set it on the bed and flipped it open to a page in the middle. Several items had been haphazardly glued to the thick, light-brown kraft paper: a canceled postage stamp, a completed crossword puzzle clipped from a newspaper, a wadded-up length of bakery string, and a convenience-store receipt for a six-pack of Budweiser and a loaf of white bread.

"Hmm…" I said.

"Hmm…" Martin said.

"Okay, I know Scarlett was… How did Amy put it?" I asked.

"Offbeat."

"But in a cool way, you know? At least that was my takeaway. This is just so…" I shook my head.

"Sad and weird." He turned the page. "Maybe more weird than sad."

Here was the paper tab from a Lipton teabag, as well as two more postage stamps, the back cover of a paperback book about conspiracy theories, and a Polaroid snapshot of four teenagers, a girl and three boys, loitering near the mailbox bank on the building's first floor. The kids stared at the picture taker with undisguised contempt. One of them offered a single-digit salute.

"Let's see something." I turned to the first page and sagged in relief. "It's not Scarlett's."

Martin read aloud the words written there in bold block letters. "'This book is the property of Nolan Whitehouse. The contents are private and confidential. Any person who steals, shares, or publishes any portion herein will be prosecuted to the full extent of the law. Punishment will include jail time and severe fines.'"

"Dang," I said. "So much for my cunning plan to steal his bakery string."

"Is it just me," he asked, "or does this Nolan Whitehouse seem a tad unhinged?"

"This is the guy Amy mentioned the other night at Murray's. She said he died last month."

"That's right. She also said no one got along with him."

"No one except Scarlett, apparently," I said.

"What are you going to do with this?" he asked.

I sighed and closed the book. I ran my fingers over the shiny leatherette. "I'm finding so much stuff that I can't bear to throw away. I feel like I'm going to end up saving more than I toss."

Martin put his arm around my shoulders. "You want me to do it for you? Feed this thing to the dumpster?"

I considered his offer for about a nanosecond. "Scarlett

saved this for a reason. Not only that, but she kept it in kind of a hidden spot. I'd like to know why."

"Well, you don't have time to go through it now." He grabbed it and retraced his steps into the living room. "Take it home. You can toss it later."

I followed him. "I feel like I should ask Carolyn."

"Ask her what?" He shoved the scrapbook into my duffel.

"You know," I said. "Whether she minds my taking some of this stuff home. Scarlett's drawings. Nolan's book. She hired me to get rid of it all, one way or another."

"Well, this is the 'or another' option," he said. "Salvaging certain items that can't be sold and aren't valuable enough to interest Carolyn. Just promise me you won't cart too much of her stuff to our place. Your place," he quickly corrected himself.

I closed the distance between us and wrapped my arms around him. I loved the way he felt under the thin T-shirt, the shifting landscape of hard muscle as he returned the embrace and kissed me.

I smiled up at him. "It's not *my* place, Padre. It's our place now. Your home as much as mine."

"To be accurate, we're both mooching off that little troublemaker over there." He nodded toward Sexy Beast, snoozing on the sofa. "What was Irene thinking?"

The late Irene McAuliffe, who'd bequeathed her mini mansion to her beloved poodle, happened to be Martin's step-grandmother, but trust me when I say there was no love lost between the two.

Reluctantly I stepped away from Martin. "Any luck locating an address book?"

His raised finger said, *Wait for it.* He crossed to Scarlett's desk and wagged a battered-looking black-and-white composition notebook, the kind I practiced penmanship in way back in elementary school. "Ta-da!"

I took the book from him and flipped through it. It was filled with names and contact information written in various shades of ink as well as pencil. Clearly the entries went back several years. "I can't believe Carolyn didn't even bother to look for this."

"I can," he said. "After everything you told me about her?"

"Is that her calendar?" I nodded toward a green, spiral-bound notebook sitting on the desk.

He shook his head. "There's no calendar that I can find. Looks like Scarlett relied on sticky notes on her fridge. No idea what this thing is." He handed the notebook to me. "If you can figure it out, more power to you. It was in the same drawer as the address book."

I turned it over in my hands. It appeared to be your basic school notebook, about six by nine inches, but quite old by the looks of it. The words *Winner's Circle* had been written in large letters in permanent marker on the battered green cover. I opened it to the first page and saw that someone had drawn in several columns, which were filled for the most part with indecipherable combinations of letters, numbers, and made-up symbols. Flipping through the pages, I saw they all showed the same mysterious columns.

"No name," he said.

"I noticed. No date, either. But this thing's old, probably older than Scarlett. I wouldn't be surprised if it belonged to Nolan. It's certainly weird enough."

"Judging by his scrapbook," the padre said, "I wouldn't put it past the guy to spend decades scribbling secret messages in this notebook, communicating with aliens, maybe. Come to think of it, the Zodiac Killer used to send coded letters that looked like this. They never caught the guy, did they? Wonder what Nolan was up to back then."

I said, "The Zodiac was active in, what, the late sixties? Nolan was too young. Amy said he was about sixty." I knew Martin was kidding, but the very idea of Scarlett getting friendly with a notorious serial killer creeped me out. I turned my attention to the words on the notebook's cover. "'Winner's Circle.' Maybe he used to play the ponies, and this all has to do with horse racing. Like he wanted to make sure no one could steal his winning formula, so he wrote it in code. Well, whatever it is, you know I can't send this thing to the dump." I shoved it into my duffel. "It's just too darn intriguing."

I went into the kitchen and took a closer look at the multicolored squares of paper stuck to Scarlett's refrigerator, her version of a calendar. There was a reminder of the meeting she and I were supposed to have had five days earlier (I was still hoping to find out what that was about), a note regarding an upcoming videoconference with someone at the online magazine that bought her cartoons, and a short grocery list. She'd planned to buy tuna, apples, chicken, mango sorbet—

The doorbell rang, startling me. I reentered the living room in time to see Martin check the peephole and open the door.

5

Lifelong Friends

THE MAN WHO stood on the threshold appeared to be in his early sixties, of slim build and just under medium height. He had hazel eyes and a horseshoe of graying hair circling a shiny dome. To his credit, he'd made no attempt at a comb-over, nor had he opted to shave it all off or glue on some silly hairpiece. He *owned* that tonsure, and I couldn't help but admire what that said about him.

He wore well-tailored black pants, an expensive-looking brown leather jacket, and a cashmere scarf in a refined houndstooth check. If the term *understated elegance* hadn't already been coined, someone would've had to invent it to describe this guy.

"Can I help you?" Martin asked.

The man's calm smile was barely there, yet his entire face managed to get into the act. "Please forgive the intrusion. My name is Robert Jernigan. I'm a friend of the Proctors."

We shook his hand and introduced ourselves. Carolyn had mentioned this man. Their families had been close at one time, she'd said, and Jernigan had taken an interest in the sisters' welfare after their father's suicide.

"I know you're busy," he said. "Carolyn told me you've

been here since around nine-thirty, is that right?" The wristwatch he consulted wasn't flashy, but I'd bet it was worth more than… well, I was going to say more than my car, but we were probably talking my pre-owned Mazda, Martin's Harley, and his vintage Mustang combined.

"So you've been at it for over two hours," he added. "I was hoping you'd be ready for a break so we could have a brief chat. If not, we can talk later. I live just downstairs in Three-N."

"No problem." I moved some cartons out of the way and gestured toward the pink sofa. "Have a seat, Mr. Jernigan."

"Tell you what. Let's skate right past the formalities. I'm Bob." His default facial expression seemed to be that affable half smile.

"It's a deal," Martin said. "And to make the introductions complete, this little brat is Sexy Beast."

"Sexy Beast, huh?" Bob laughed as SB roused himself from his nap, stretched luxuriantly, and padded across the pink leather to investigate the stranger who was settling in next to him. "Did you name him after the movie?" He scratched the little poodle behind his ears.

"His original owner did," I said, as Martin and I sank down into the pair of retro butterfly chairs covered in dark-green leather, worn to a glossy patina. "She was a serious film buff."

Martin said, "Looks like you have SB's seal of approval." The little poodle was avidly sniffing the newcomer.

"He smells Boss Lady, my King Charles spaniel," Bob said. "And before you ask, yes, Boss Lady absolutely rules the household."

I watched Bob closely as he looked around, taking in his

surroundings. Far from being appalled as Carolyn had been, he appeared fascinated by this little museum of the weird.

"Is this the first time you're seeing Scarlett's apartment?" I asked.

"It is." The smile slipped a notch. "I'm afraid the two of us didn't quite get along recently. I will always regret not making more of an effort to repair that rift."

I avoided looking at Martin, knowing the question would be plain on my face. Perhaps it was anyway, because Bob said, "It's okay, I don't mind telling you. Scarlett resented me for the same reason Ed did."

"Ed?" Martin said.

"Their father, Edward Proctor. Ed and I met at Columbia University when we were both freshmen. We lived in the same dorm, took some classes together, hung with the same crowd. Hard to believe we graduated forty years ago."

"And remained lifelong friends, it seems," I said.

"Yes. Well, until last winter." He met my gaze directly. "Do you know about all that?"

"I know about his suicide," I said, "and the embezzlment charge that led up to it."

He stroked SB as the little dog snuggled closer to him. "After Ed was arrested, he asked me to represent him."

Martin said, "Which I assume means you're a lawyer."

Bob nodded. "At Abbott, Sandham and Jernigan."

The padre's eyebrows rose. "You're *that* Jernigan."

I'd heard of Abbot, Sandham. It was one of those stuffy Wall Street outfits. "Does your firm handle criminal cases?" I asked.

"Very rarely," he said. "We're a corporate litigation firm. Occasionally one of our more prominent clients will have a special need—the guy's facing a DUI charge, say, or his kid was picked up for shoplifting, something like that. And we'll handle it as an accommodation."

"And to keep the client's business," Martin said.

Bob dipped his head to indicate the padre wasn't off base. "But to bring in a brand-new client who's been arrested for stealing from his employer? That's not what we do. It's not what *I* do. I specialize in contract law."

I wondered if Ed Proctor could even have coughed up the fees Bob's white-shoe firm would have charged for defending him. I also wondered why Bob Jernigan had ended up living in this building. Surely he could afford ritzier postdivorce digs than a rented apartment at the Americana.

I chose to keep these thoughts to myself. Instead I said, "If what Carolyn told me is true, her dad was guilty."

Rather than comment on that, Bob said, "Everyone is entitled to effective assistance of counsel."

"Did Ed get what he was entitled to?" Martin asked. "Was his counsel effective?"

"I hope so." He appeared uncomfortable with the direction this conversation was taking. "I recommended a couple of people, experienced criminal defense attorneys, but he didn't want to hear it. He felt that I'd abandoned him in his time of need. He chose someone local. I don't know anything about the fellow."

"I take it Scarlett felt the same way," I said. "That you'd abandoned her father."

"She did, yes." He shook his head sadly. "Neither of them ever forgave me for not getting involved. And then after Ed died, Scarlett basically froze me out. Though she didn't come right out and say it, I know she blamed me for his suicide."

"Were they close?" I asked. "Scarlett and her dad?"

"Very. They say a parent's not supposed to have favorites, but…" He shrugged. "Ed shared a special bond with his younger daughter."

Martin said, "Maybe it was easier for Scarlett to blame you than to recognize that her dad was a human being with human flaws, and not the strong, morally upright man she'd always revered."

There was that genial smile again. "Are you a shrink?" Bob asked.

"Bartender."

"Close enough. You want to know what keeps me up nights, Doc? If Ed had just come to me sooner, I could've helped him negotiate restitution. He still would've lost his job, of course, but he might've avoided prison time and… the rest of it. He was with that company a long time, had a sterling record up until then. I think we could've worked something out."

"Did he really believe he could get away with it?" I asked.

"He really did," Bob said. "He thought he'd covered his tracks, but eventually someone noticed a hinky transaction, which naturally prompted them to take a closer look at all the invoices and receipts going back who knows how long. By the time they brought in the special auditor, Ed was beyond my help. I hadn't a clue about any of this, of course, until it was too late."

"When I spoke with Carolyn," I said, "she didn't seem angry with you."

"She has a more nuanced grasp of the situation than her father and sister did," he said. "She understands why my hands were tied."

"She told me you'll be representing her when she sues Joel and Joanie Devine for her sister's wrongful death. They own this building."

"I just came from Carolyn," he said. "I let her know that's not going to happen."

"Because it's not the kind of corporate case you handle?" Martin asked.

"No, it's not that. She's not eligible to file that lawsuit. In New York you need to be closely related to the deceased in order to bring a wrongful-death claim."

"More closely related than siblings?" I asked.

"Actually, yes," he said. "You need to be a child, parent, or spouse of the deceased. Or a representative of the estate—an executor. Since Carolyn was none of those, she's out of luck."

"Speaking of an executor," I said, "did Scarlett even have a will?"

"No, she did not. And with her parents gone and no spouse in the picture, there's no one in a position to sue the Devines. I know Carolyn is frustrated. When a tragedy like this occurs, it's natural to want to hold someone accountable. Sometimes it's just not meant to be."

Is that why Carolyn had tried to sue the building's owners? To hold the responsible parties accountable? At the risk of appearing cynical (who, me?), a successful wrongful-death suit would result in a monetary award to the individual who initiated it. Bob knew Carolyn far better than I did. He'd watched her grow up, after all. If he thought she was driven by nothing more materialistic than justice for her dead sister, then who was I to think otherwise?

Yeah, I know, but I was trying real hard to give her the benefit of the doubt.

"So Scarlett blamed you for her dad's death," I said. "Carolyn, on the other hand, blames Scarlett."

"I know." Bob sighed. "Scarlett's cartoons had nothing to do with what happened to Ed. She never referred to his crime in her art, certainly not in a way that would cause anyone to make the connection. His company discovered the embezzlement on their own, like I said, through a special audit."

"Carolyn also seems to believe Scarlett is responsible for the breakup of her marriage," I said.

Bob appeared dismayed. "She told you about that? I love Carolyn like a daughter, but that girl has no filter."

"So is it true?" I asked. "Did Scarlett's cartoons cause her sister's divorce?"

"No, it is not true. I had a front-row seat at Carolyn and Stefan's marriage. Without going into specifics, let me just say that Carolyn has always struck me as somewhat insecure. I believe that's why she can sometimes come off as negative, even abrasive. At a certain point, Stefan… well, I suppose he'd had enough. I suspect it was easier for Carolyn to blame Scarlett's cartoons than to take responsibility for the failure of her marriage."

"I just met Carolyn," I said, "but I sense she's not a very happy person."

"I would call that a fair assessment," Bob said. "And now the poor girl is left with no family at all. Parents, sister, husband, all gone. Going forward, I will endeavor to be there for her more."

I had nothing to say to that, and after a moment, Martin broke the silence. "We appear to have gotten sidetracked. I'm sure you had a reason for stopping by here, Bob."

"I did, and I apologize," he said. "I'm keeping you from your work. Carolyn mentioned that you brought up the subject of a memorial service, Jane."

"She told me she wasn't planning anything," I said, "and of course, it's up to her, but I just thought... well, I thought she might come to regret it someday."

Which was a big, fat lie. I doubted Carolyn would ever second-guess that particular decision.

"I understand you do this sort of thing for a living," Bob said. "Planning funerals and such."

And such, huh? If he only knew. I simply said, "That's right."

"I wonder if I could hire you to arrange a memorial service for Scarlett," he said. "I ran it past Carolyn, and she has no objections."

"I think that's a wonderful idea," I said.

He looked relieved. "It just didn't sit right with me, not doing anything. April will be happy to hear this. She's my fiancée. We're getting married next summer."

Martin and I offered congratulations, and I arranged for Bob to sit down with me on Wednesday evening to hammer out the details of the memorial service.

He gave Sexy Beast a few more scritches and a kiss on his furry topknot, then came to his feet, prompting the padre and me to haul ourselves out of the low-slung butterfly chairs. "I know you want to get back to it. This is a big job," he said, looking around. "I'm enthralled, I admit it. I had no idea all this was here. Based on what Carolyn told me, I'd expected something closer to a..."

"Hoarder's paradise?" I said, and he chuckled.

"Carolyn had initially told me she'd be getting one of those junk-removal companies to clear everything out," he said. "So I was a little surprised this morning when she mentioned hiring you to sift through everything first."

"I'm thinking she got nervous," I said, "picturing the Hope Diamond stuffed behind a sofa cushion."

"Do you mind very much if I give myself a little tour?" he asked. "I'll try to keep out of your way."

Martin swept his arm to indicate the whole apartment. "Look around all you want, Bob."

"And if you see anything you'd like to have," I said, "as a keepsake perhaps, just let me know. Most everything is up for grabs."

As Bob began to stroll around, closely inspecting Scarlett's myriad treasures, I casually crossed to my duffel bag and zipped it closed, concealing its contents. It's not that I thought Bob would object to my taking the bizarre scrapbook belonging to Nolan Whitehouse, or the mysterious old spiral-bound notebook. I simply wasn't prepared for him to ask why I wanted them.

Mostly because I didn't have an answer.

6

We Have a Winner!

"HI, COOKIE," I said, when the police detective answered her cell. "Do you have a minute?"

"I'm actually in your neighborhood," she said. "Put on some coffee."

With that, the line went dead. The coffeemaker had just finished dripping when the doorbell rang. I greeted Cookie with, "Brownie or bagel?"

"Ooh, a bagel sounds like heaven." She stepped into the foyer, shucked off her multicolored wool poncho, and tossed it onto the newel-post of the curving staircase. "I haven't had breakfast."

"Well, you're just in time for elevenses." Yeah, I was still on the elevenses kick. Don't judge.

I led the way through the two-story foyer with its Baccarat chandelier and macassar ebony floor (Irene had expensive tastes), down a couple of steps into the sunken family room, then up a couple of steps into the sun-washed breakfast room with its round, glass-top table and modern chairs upholstered in oatmeal-colored leather.

Cookie slumped onto one of them. "Give me coffee before I arrest you for interfering with an officer of the law."

"Yikes. Here you go." I set a steaming mug in front of her, along with the sugar bowl and a carton of milk. Detective Cookie Kaplan liked her joe sweet and light.

She'd been with the Crystal Harbor Police Department for a little under a year, and in all that time I hadn't seen the same pair of earrings twice. Today it was enameled palm trees, which somehow complemented her burgundy-framed eyeglasses. Her curly brown hair was, as usual, pulled back into a charmingly messy bun.

While she doctored her coffee, I cut a bagel and set out the cream cheese and smoked salmon.

"Lox!" She immediately perked up. "What do you want to know? I'll happily spill my guts as long as you keep the lox coming."

I sat across from her with my black coffee and brownie. "It's about Scarlett Proctor."

"Oh, that poor girl." Cookie looked up from her bagel, mid-schmear. "So young. What a horrible freak accident."

"Her sister, Carolyn Bailey, hired me to go through all her things and clean out the apartment."

"How's that going?" Cookie asked, as she very delicately arranged slices of pink smoked salmon on top of the cream cheese.

"We should be done in a few days. Martin's helping me." I was interrupted by a single deep bark from behind the back door, followed by a higher-pitched yip.

I excused myself to let Layla and Sexy Beast into the house. The dogs galloped through the laundry room and kitchen into the breakfast room. Well, Layla galloped. She was a large, black Great Dane – Labrador mix, recently adopted from the local animal shelter. Sexy Beast sprinted alongside his new sister, trying to keep up.

Layla was tall enough to take a good, long look at the food on the table—and big enough to scarf it all down in a single gulp. Instead, she sat and simply stared at our plates, licking her lips. Martin and I had been patiently training her, and she'd been making admirable progress.

When she started to scoot closer to the table, I said, "Stay," and she did so, apparently remembering that obedience has its rewards—which would come after the humans had eaten. "Good girl."

Sexy Beast watched this instructive tableau unfold, thought about it for a moment, then sat next to Layla on his little haunches. His training had been somewhat hit-or-miss while Irene was alive. His first owner had never internalized that she was supposed to be the boss. As SB's occasional pet sitter at the time, there'd been only so much I could do if Irene refused to reinforce the lessons. He'd made significant progress since I'd become his full-time guardian, however, in both basic doggie obedience and socialization with his fellow canines. Suffice it to say, visits to the local dog park were now much more enjoyable than they'd been in the past.

The (well-fed) dogs stared avidly as Cookie and I ate, but every time one of us looked in their direction, they turned their heads away. *Who, me? I wasn't coveting that delicious-smelling lox.*

"Why are you interested in Scarlett?" Cookie asked, between bites of her fully loaded bagel.

"Well, I've been going through her belongings, like I said, and it's made me real curious about her. And then there's this." I got up and retrieved Scarlett's dog-eared composition book from the granite kitchen island, opened it to a page I'd bookmarked, and set it in front of the detective.

"Ah," she said. "You want to know why she had my contact info."

"I've been going through her address book," I said, "looking for anyone she might've been close to. Close enough to want to go to her memorial service."

"Oh," Cookie said, "I was wondering about that. I hadn't heard anything about a funeral."

"It turns out Carolyn isn't interested in holding a funeral," I said, "but there's this old family friend, Bob Jernigan. I don't mean *Bob's* old. Well, not that old. Early sixties. But he's known the family forever and was close to the girls' parents. He'd gone to college with their dad. Anyway, he wants me to help him plan a memorial service. We're getting together this evening to hammer out the details, but I figured it made sense to go through Scarlett's contacts first, get an idea of how many people we can expect."

Cookie frowned and wiped a blob of cream cheese off her lip with her napkin. "The sister doesn't want a funeral? Why?"

"They seem to have had a rather fraught relationship. It's complicated." I did not add that the complications involved a certain handsome neighbor who just might have been cheating on one sister with the other. I couldn't say for certain whether it was true, and even if it was, that kind of mean-spirited gossipmongering left a bad taste in my mouth—regardless that it was the official Crystal Harbor pastime.

"So yeah," I said, "I guess I'm curious to know why Scarlett was in touch with you."

As Cookie sipped her coffee, I got the feeling she was deciding whether to answer.

Hastily I added, "Naturally, if it's some kind of official

police business, then I certainly don't intend to pry."

Judging by the sardonic look she gave me, the detective recognized this statement for the heaping helping of baloney it was. She said, "I can tell you that Scarlett had some concerns about another resident of the Americana."

"Oh." Was she talking about Carolyn? Probably not, since Cookie hadn't even known the sisters didn't get along.

Then I remembered what Amy had said about Hal. *More than once I got out of the elevator on Four and saw him talking to Scarlett through her closed door, trying to get her to open up, to give him another chance.*

"Was it Hal?" I asked. Perhaps he'd graduated from ex-boyfriend to stalker.

"Who's Hal?"

"They used to date. He lives in the building." Another thought whacked me in the noggin, in the form of a scrapbook Scarlett had shoved well out of sight under her bed. I said, "Nolan. Nolan Whitehouse."

Cookie paused with her bagel halfway to her mouth. "What do you know about Nolan?"

And we have a winner!

I made a snap decision not to tell Cookie about the scrapbook, at least not yet. "I know he was this grumpy old guy who didn't get along with anyone in the building except for Scarlett. I also know he used to go up to the roof with her and that he died about a month ago. That's about it."

The detective chewed in thoughtful silence. Finally she said, "I don't suppose there's any harm in telling you. After all, they're both gone now, and nothing came of her suspicions."

"What kind of suspicions? Did Scarlett have some trouble with Nolan?"

She waved away the notion. "No, nothing like that. They got along fine, like you said. She moved into the building about a year ago, and within a few months, around the beginning of February, she and Nolan had become friends. That girl must've had the patience of a saint, because by all accounts, the guy was a cranky old SOB."

"So then, what was the issue?"

"Well, Nolan died in early October," she said. "He was washing his kitchen floor and he slipped on the wet tiles and hit his head."

"Hard enough to kill him?"

"It's not unheard-of," she said. "Head injuries are often neglected until it's too late. Nolan must've hit the floor really hard, though, because he never got up."

"I assume he was alone when it happened," I said.

She nodded. "Scarlett found him later that day. She had a key to his apartment."

"Oh, that must've been terrible for her," I said.

"She went to check on him when he didn't answer his phone. It seems she'd taken it upon herself to see to his welfare. Make sure he was eating all right, going to the doctor, that sort of thing."

"I'm curious," I said.

"You?" she teased. "Curious?"

"How did Nolan support himself? He didn't have a job as far as I know."

"He relied on disability payments," she said. "I don't know the particulars."

"Any relatives?"

She shook her head. "No one claimed the body. Scarlett paid for his cremation. She told me she'd scattered his ashes at this park in New Jersey where he played as a child. Apparently his fondest memories were of that park."

Did I even want to know what Carolyn planned to do with Scarlett's ashes? She'd chosen cremation as the "cheap and efficient" option, after all, and considering how she felt about her sister…

I shook myself out of my dark musings, and said, "So to get back to why she called you…"

"It was the day before she died," Cookie said, "just after lunch, so around two in the afternoon. She called the precinct and they put her through to me. She'd convinced herself that Nolan had been murdered."

I failed to restrain a gasp. "What did she base that on?"

"She never knew Nolan to wash his floors," she said. "She used to do it for him."

"So, what, she thought someone killed him, then staged his death with a mop and bucket to make it look like an accident?"

"That's exactly what she thought," she said. "Mind you, he'd been dead for a full month before she called me. She'd already cleaned out his apartment by then, so forget about investigating the 'staged crime scene.' I ran it past Howie just to make sure I wasn't missing anything, and he agreed. There was nothing there. Nolan Whitehouse's death was an accident."

Detective Howie Werker was Cookie's partner. He'd been with the Crystal Harbor PD for years, as a patrol officer before being promoted to detective a little over a year ago. Howie was a great guy and a good friend, but he could be less than cooperative when I was on one of my frequent fishing expeditions. Cookie was more laid-back when it came to sharing information, so I'm glad she's the one Scarlett had ended up speaking with.

I felt a chill with the realization that Scarlett had recently performed the same service for her friend Nolan—cleaning out his home—that I was performing for her.

And I *was* doing it for her, not for her sister, though Carolyn was the one who'd hired me. Scarlett's many treasures, as I thought of them, had meant something to her, and no way were they going to end up in any darn landfill. Not on my watch.

I said, "You know, there are security cameras in the building's corridors."

"Right," she said, "and the footage is kept for thirty days before being overwritten. Nolan died on October third. Scarlett called me thirty-one days later. If someone else *was* in his apartment that day, we'll never know. And I'm not about to start questioning his neighbors to see if they recalled seeing anyone entering or leaving his place on a specific date a full month earlier."

"That's all she based her suspicions on?" I asked. "That the guy was too much of a slob to clean his own floor?"

"She did mention something else. Some sort of hint or clue that turned up while she was cleaning out his apartment. Which took her that whole month. Apparently Nolan was, well, he really was a slob. And no, I have no idea what this mysterious clue was."

"Well, did she say whether she had someone in mind?" I asked. "Someone who might've wanted to do him in?"

"Yes," she said, "but she clammed up. I wasn't taking the whole thing seriously enough, according to her. I thought I was being quite respectful under the circumstances."

I blew out a frustrated breath. "Well, I'm really curious

about who she thought did it."

"How to even narrow down a list of suspects?" Cookie said. "The guy was universally despised in that building. I'm sure most of his neighbors would've been happy to see him leave."

"One way or another," I muttered. "You know, Scarlett called me shortly after she spoke with you. Later that same day, in fact. The day before she died."

"To set up a meeting with you," Cookie said. When I nodded, she added, "You told us you didn't know what she wanted to discuss."

"Not at the time, but now I'm thinking it was the same thing she talked to you about. You told her you couldn't help her, so she called the Death Diva."

"Why you and not a private investigator?" she asked.

I thought about that. "A lot of PIs would probably be happy to take the case and 'investigate' until the money ran out. Maybe she wanted to get the perspective of someone who's seen her share of all kinds of deaths, accidental and homicidal included. Maybe she wanted to know whether I thought her suspicions were worth pursuing."

"Whether she could abandon them in good conscience, in other words," Cookie said, "and not feel like she was letting her friend down."

"Something like that."

I thought about how anxious Carolyn had been to find out what her sister had wanted to talk to me about—a "loose end" that had been nagging at her.

And I thought again about that scrapbook, the one Scarlett had taken such pains to hide. Was that the source of the mysterious clue she'd unearthed?

We'd finished eating. I rose and opened the canister of doggie treats, to the delight of my four-legged family members.

After they'd hoovered up the crumbs, I pointed toward the family room. "SB, Layla, go to your bed." Yes, I said *bed*, singular. Oh, sure, Sexy Beast still had his little bucket bed in the kitchen, plus a few others in various locations around the house, but nowadays he preferred to curl up with Layla in her ginormous, fluffy dog bed in the family room, surrounded by an assortment of toys.

After they ran out, I lifted the coffee carafe and asked Cookie if she'd like a refill.

"Thanks," she said, rising, "but my breakfast break is over. Bagel and lox, what a treat. You know, it occurs to me that you might like to know how Scarlett used to get onto that roof."

"I figure she must've gotten her hands on a key."

Cookie nodded. "They found it in her jacket pocket. It unlocks the door to that stairwell. What I think? I think Nolan had the key—probably swiped it from the office at some point, or from one of the staff—and he used to take her up there with him. Then after he died, she found it in his apartment and appropriated it."

After Cookie left, I retrieved Nolan's scrapbook from my duffel, cleared the table in the breakfast room, and sat down with another cup of coffee to see if the book contained anything more elucidating than bakery string and postage stamps.

Starting on the first page, I saw more canceled stamps and store receipts, haphazardly glued onto the sheets of kraft paper. Why he'd thought these items were worthy of preserving in this manner was anyone's guess.

The next page held a small metal mirror, about two by

three inches, the kind people go camping with when space is at a premium. As I stared into it, my own baffled expression gazed back at me.

"What's your story, Nolan?" I murmured.

The same page held a bird's feather, a dried leaf, and another Polaroid snapshot of the same four teenagers he'd photographed near the mailboxes, offering rude expressions and gestures as they hung out behind the building. Nolan seemed to have it in for those kids, who appeared none too pleased by the creepy old guy with the camera.

As I turned pages, I saw more everyday items—a cereal box top, a scrap of worn denim, and most perplexingly, a single piece of a jigsaw puzzle: blue sky with a bit of fluffy white cloud. I got myself irrationally worked up picturing a completed puzzle with a one-piece gap.

Another page held a scrap of shiny green wrapping paper, a crumpled wad of gold curling ribbon, and a gift tag that read *To Nolan with love from Scarlett.* A birthday card was affixed to the opposite page. The front of the card showed a close-up photo of one of those hairless cats wearing a pointed party hat. The cat's speech bubble said, *I made you a birthday present.* I tried to open the card, but Nolan had glued it shut. I'd never know what the cat's gift was, though I suspected it had been deposited in the litter box.

I turned the page and was stunned to see an exquisitely rendered pen-and-ink portrait. The subject was an older man with a buzz cut, short beard, and mesmerizing gaze. I knew instantly that I was looking at Nolan Whitehead. The name *S Proctor* was neatly written in the lower right corner.

I'd already known that Scarlett had talent, but her cartoons gave no hint that she was capable of something like this. The photographic detail, the dimensional shading, the way she'd coaxed Nolan's personality onto a flat sheet of drawing paper… I was in awe.

"Well," I said, "you're just full of surprises, aren't you, Scarlett?"

Then I smiled, remembering the unfinished cartoon on her drawing table. The old man on the park bench feeding pigeons. That old man was obviously Nolan. The similarities were unmistakable.

So she had indeed borrowed from real life for her cartoons, though probably not in the destructive way Carolyn seemed to believe. Bob Jernigan had claimed that Carolyn had read too much into her sister's cartoons, and I had no reason to doubt him.

As I made my way through the scrapbook, I saw more eclectic objects from the day-to-day life of Nolan Whitehouse. There were a few more photos of those four teens, hanging out in and around the building and getting on Nolan's nerves simply by, well, by being typical teenagers. One of those pictures was taken on the rooftop, which told me Nolan and Scarlett weren't the only tenants who found a way to get up there.

I turned a page and saw another photograph, but it wasn't of the teens this time. It showed Hal Kazarian standing in front of apartment 4K. Scarlett's apartment. His knuckles were making contact with the door and his mouth was open. He was leaning toward the peephole, his expression beseeching. This was the sight Amy said had greeted her more than once as she'd exited the elevator on the fourth floor.

This was not the cocky, overconfident man I'd met in Carolyn's apartment. This guy had the look of someone who'd messed up big-time and was desperate to undo the damage.

I stared at the picture for some time, pondering Nolan's reason for taking it. Up until that moment, it hadn't occurred to me to wonder how he'd felt about Scarlett's ex-boyfriend. Had he been motivated by a desire to protect his young friend? Or was it possible he'd felt something more than friendship for Scarlett, despite the age difference? Could he have been jealous?

Somehow I didn't think that was it. Nothing I'd learned about the man so far made that seem likely. As for what motivated Scarlett to befriend the irascible older man and become a kind of caregiver to him, I thought it was possible she viewed him almost as a surrogate dad. Ed Proctor had committed suicide a few months after Scarlett moved into the building.

The opposite page held a formal invitation to Nolan's forty-year college reunion dinner, along with the envelope it had arrived in. I was surprised to see he'd attended Columbia University. Talk about not making the most of an Ivy League education. I was just as surprised to learn he'd graduated the same year as Ed Proctor and Bob Jernigan.

Bob had mentioned that he and Ed had become friends during their freshman year at Columbia and that they'd graduated forty years ago. Had either of them known Nolan back then? Their paths must've crossed. The three of them were all in the same year, after all. I could only assume Bob had received the same invitation to the reunion dinner, which had been held at an elegant restaurant in Manhattan on October 4. The day after Nolan's sudden death.

Nolan had scribbled on the invitation in pencil. I squinted to make out the words: *RSVP'd yes.* So he'd been planning to go to the dinner. Which kind of surprised me. I mean, if I'd attended an elite university like that and ultimately ended up as he had—with no career or family, scraping by on disability payments, practically friendless and with obvious psychological issues—I wouldn't be so eager to rub elbows with my former classmates four decades later. I'd guess that many of his fellow alumni had, like Bob, become enormously successful in their chosen careers.

What would Nolan even wear to a fancy event like that? Had he even owned a suit?

I turned the page and was surprised to see a photo of Carolyn. It had been taken in the basement laundry room, and it looked like she'd been in the process of transferring clothes from a washing machine to a dryer. She must've taken exception to Nolan snapping her picture, because she was yelling at him and gesturing angrily. It was possible she'd been concerned for her safety. Heck, I'd be concerned, too, if some weird guy decided to photograph me while I was doing my wash.

Did she know he was a friend of her sister's?

The photo on the next page had been taken right in front of the building—precisely where Scarlett had fallen, as a matter of fact, though that tragic accident was still weeks or months away. It appeared to be summer, because Carolyn was wearing shorts and a sleeveless blouse. If anything, she appeared even angrier than in the previous picture, practically apoplectic, getting right in Nolan's face as he photographed her. Her own face was a snarling rictus, her finger outthrust in a stabbing gesture.

I flipped pages more quickly now, without stopping to linger over the stamps and store receipts, the odd little found items, or even the photos of the resident slackers, as I'd come to think of the four youths whom Nolan had been so obsessed with. I was hoping to come across another revealing picture of Hal or Carolyn. What I found instead was something even more intriguing: a typed, unsigned note on a scrap of white printer paper.

Leave Scarlett alone or you'll be sorry.

7

Suck It Up, for Cryin' Out Loud

I'D JUST EXITED the Americana apartment building and was trying to decide what to have for threeses (a bowl of Fruity Pebbles or a slice of leftover Buffalo chicken pizza?) when I heard rapid footfalls on the cement walk behind me. A breathless female voice called, "Miss… Miss… Miss, um, Death Diva!"

I turned and saw an older woman struggling to catch up to me. She was tall, with a neat cap of white hair and bloodred lipstick. I retraced my steps toward her, saying, "Please. Don't rush."

"I'm not used to running anymore." She pressed a palm to her chest. "Too old for all that."

I estimated her to be in her late seventies or early eighties. I held out my hand. "I'm Jane Delaney."

"Oh!" she said, as we shook. "Sorry for yelling 'Death Diva' Like that. That was rude of me, but I couldn't remember your name, dear."

"Not rude at all." I smiled. "I go by both names."

"I'm Joanie Devine," she said. "Me and my husband, Joel, we own the Americana. Would you have a few minutes to chat?"

"Of course."

"It's a lovely day." She gestured toward one of the wooden benches on the lawn in front of the building, near the crepe myrtle Sexy Beast had watered eleven days earlier, just before Scarlett took her fatal fall. "Is this okay?"

"It's perfect." I myself wouldn't have described the day as lovely, but it wasn't bad for an afternoon in the middle of November. The sky was more gray than blue, but the temperature was mild. I figured we were in for some rain, and I hoped it would hold off until I was home. I buttoned up my suede jacket and snugged my pink wool scarf around my throat.

As we settled ourselves on the bench, Joanie said, "I saw the cops talking to you and Amy Collingwood that day."

She didn't need to specify which day. I said, "We were the only witnesses."

Joanie gave a sad shake of her head. "The sister, Carolyn, she told me she hired you to clean out the apartment."

"You'll be glad to know I'm nearly done," I said. "I was in there just now, taking care of some last-minute sorting. I'll be having some of her belongings removed in the next couple of days, then a clean-out company will come in for whatever's left. After that, I'll bring in a regular cleaning service to get it ready for renting. The whole process shouldn't take more than another week, ten days tops. You'll be able to show the apartment before the end of the month."

"Oh my goodness," she said, "you're so efficient. If you need more time, don't worry about it, dear. I know these things don't get done in a day."

Carolyn had told me the Devines wanted the place cleaned out ASAP so they could rent it again right away. She knew this because she was so good at "reading between the lines."

Maybe not so much, I now realized. I suspected it was more a case of Carolyn projecting her own impatience onto the building's owners. *Her apartment is just this huge chore hanging over my head,* she'd said. *I don't need the pressure.*

"I appreciate that," I said, "but I know it does you no good to have an apartment standing empty."

Joanie suddenly looked even older. "It probably doesn't make much difference at this point, anyway."

When she didn't elaborate, I looked around to make sure no one was within earshot. Since it was a Saturday afternoon, there was a little more foot traffic than usual, but we were far enough from the building's entrance to ensure a private conversation. Finally I said, "I heard you might be selling the building."

"I suppose everyone knows about that now. We hate to do it. It's just that, well, me and Joel, we're not getting any younger, and it's just become too much for us. We were never blessed with children, so there's no one to take over for us."

"I also heard you have a buyer," I said. "A developer who plans to demolish the building and put up a mansion."

"We wanted the Americana to remain intact," she said, "to continue with a new owner, but the only offers we got were for a fraction of what the building is worth, and me and Joel, we can't retire on that. This place is fifty-one years old, but it's in excellent shape. We've worked hard all these years to make sure of that."

"And this developer," I said, "the one you're selling to. He offered a good price, I take it."

Joanie nodded. "He offered an excellent price, better than we were hoping for. His client has deep pockets, and they really wanted this location." After a moment, she added, "The tenants, they think we're betraying them. Some of them do, anyway. Scarlett, she was more upset than anyone."

"She felt betrayed?" I asked.

"Not really. I mean, she understood the bind we're in, me and Joel, but she was real worried about some of the tenants, especially the ones that aren't that well off." Joanie sighed unhappily. "They'll be getting a relocation allowance to help them find somewhere else to live."

But some of the tenants had been there for decades, according to Amy. The look on Joanie's face told me she was well aware of the hardship they'd be facing.

"But that's *my* problem, dear. No need to burden you with it." Joanie looked genuinely pained as she said, "I wanted to talk to you about something else. Carolyn Bailey, she's planning to sue me and Joel. She says we caused her sister's death by not keeping up the railing on the roof. That's a terrible accusation to make, for cryin' out loud, and it's just not true."

"Mrs. Devine, you don't need to—"

"Carolyn hired you," she said. "I know she respects you. Would you talk to her for us? Try to get her to back down? We're not rolling in dough, but we can offer some kind of settlement if that'll help smooth things over. And of course we'll pay you for being a, whatchamacallit, go-between. Joel, he has a bad heart, and he doesn't need the stress of this lawsuit."

I gave her arm a reassuring squeeze. "Mrs. Devine, there will be no lawsuit. Carolyn is not legally eligible to bring a wrongful-death suit, and neither is anyone else in this case. I've been told that by two separate attorneys." In addition to Bob Jernigan, I also ran it past my lawyer friend Sten Jakobsen, who concurred.

Joanie looked like she could hardly believe it. She and her husband had clearly been fretting over this since Scarlett's death. "Did anyone tell Carolyn? Because as far as we know, she's still planning to sue."

"Her lawyer told her a week ago that it can't happen," I said. "She should've shared that news with you so you could stop worrying."

Joanie sat back on the bench and took a deep breath, probably her first one in days. "Joel will be so relieved. It was terrible enough, what happened to that poor girl. But to pile a lawsuit on top of it…" She turned to me with shiny eyes. "Thank you, dear."

"So about that railing," I said.

"Well, there was just nothing wrong with it," she said. "It's as simple as that. It's actually pretty new. We replaced it… four years ago? No, five. And we hire an inspector to go up there several times a year to make sure everything's okay. The railing most of all, but he also looks for water damage, anything loose, checks the drains, flashing, masonry, all that stuff. He was here just last month. And of course, our super, he takes a look around the roof every day. If he finds a problem, no matter how small, we take care of it right away."

"I understand tenants aren't allowed up there," I said.

Joanie made a rude noise. "They haven't been allowed up there for the past half century, but has that ever stopped anyone? Why do you think we bend over backward to make sure it's safe?"

I recalled the photograph in Nolan's scrapbook of the resident slackers horsing around on the roof—near the railing, as a matter of fact. The accident that had taken Scarlett's life, as horrific as it was, would have been so much worse if it had involved those four teens.

"So, what do you think happened, Mrs. Devine?" I asked.

"I know you won't believe me, but someone must've gone up there and messed with that railing. Loosened the bolts and anchors so it'd fail if someone put their weight on it. It's the only thing that makes sense." Her flinty expression told me she expected her words to be met with derision.

Instead I said, "I've been waiting for someone to bring up that possibility."

Her eyes widened. "I figured you'd take me for some ditzy old lady just trying to cover up her mistakes."

I was quick to add, "I'm not saying I think that's what happened. I just think we shouldn't ignore the possibility. Did you mention this to the cops who were here that day?"

She wagged her hand dismissively. "They didn't want to hear about it. They thought I was just some old crackpot. All I got was this condescending BS about how the railing must've been faulty and good luck if her family decides to sue."

"Well, at least you don't have to worry about that anymore," I said.

"We replaced the missing piece of railing immediately, of course. The part that fell." Joanie turned and gazed up at the top of the building, where the new section blended in seamlessly. "The workmen, they couldn't tell whether it was tampered with, and the piece that came down was carted away that day. We made sure they inspected the rest of it, every inch. It was fine."

"Listen," I said, "would you do me a favor? I'd really like to go up there myself, have a look around."

Joanie didn't hesitate. "Sure, we can do that." She dug in the pocket of her plaid wool jacket for her phone. "Let me just call Joel first and give him the good news. About that lawsuit."

Three minutes later, following an elevator ride to Four, the unlocking of a door, a trek up a flight of stairs, and another heavy door, we were on the huge, flat roof. It was breezier up here, the sky a soggy, gray blanket just waiting to be wrung out.

Depending on which direction I turned, the views ranged from the pedestrian (suburban roads, an elementary school, a strip mall) to the serene (a swath of autumn-bare woods threaded with hiking trails and a creek). Not exactly the ideal location, in my opinion, to erect some ostentatious mansion, but what did I know? I'd never owned a home in my life, and my landlord was a neurotic, seven-pound poodle. I was not in a position to judge.

I shoved my hands into my pockets and took in my immediate surroundings. "I don't see any security cameras up here, Mrs. Devine."

"We never felt the need. Now I wish…" Joanie shrugged unhappily.

She didn't have to finish the sentence. If there'd been cameras on the roof, they would have recorded someone sabotaging the railing.

Correction: They *might* have recorded someone sabotaging the railing. It was pure speculation at this point.

The Americana's roof was a long rectangle covered in gravel and bookended by a pair of four-foot-high redbrick walls that wrapped around the corners. Two more short parapet walls were centered over the building's front and back entrances. The black metal railing bridged the gaps, bolted at its ends to these walls. More bolts secured the post anchors to the roof.

I approached the nearest section of railing and grabbed the cold metal with both hands, trying with all my might to shake it. Nothing. Not a hint of wobble. I strolled the perimeter, running my fingers over the bolts and connection points, until I came to the spot at the front of the building where Scarlett had fallen. It was easy to tell where the new section of railing had been installed a week and a half earlier, bolted to the brick parapet wall on one side and the existing railing on the other.

Holding tight to the wall (oh please, like you wouldn't have done the same thing), I leaned over the railing to peer at the concrete frontage four stories below where Scarlett had landed. An involuntary shudder ripped through me, and it had nothing to do with the damp chill in the air. The drop looked twice as long from up there. I couldn't help imagining Scarlett's terror as the metal support she was leaning on gave way and she plummeted to her death. No visual trace remained of her terrible accident.

Accident? Joanie seemed to think someone had deliberately weakened this stretch of railing. But then, it was probably easier to believe that than to acknowledge that she and her husband had caused the fatal accident through negligence.

I hadn't been lying when I'd told Joanie I'd considered the possibility of foul play. The thought had gnawed at the back of my mind for days, but I'd resolutely pushed it away. After all, what would be worse than a vibrant, talented young woman dying in a freak accident?

Answer: someone intentionally setting up the vibrant, talented young woman to die in a "freak accident."

I'd see her up there quite often, Amy had said, *always in that same spot.*

Amy couldn't have been the only person who knew this

was Scarlett's favorite hangout spot. Anyone entering the building would've noticed the slim figure leaning against this particular section of the railing, smoking her cigars or sketching ideas for her next cartoon.

For sure I was now clearly visible to those on the ground. Several people looked up and noticed me standing precisely where their neighbor Scarlett had stood immediately before her accident. No one waved. They probably assumed I was there on official business, a lawyer or insurance inspector or whatever.

This got me thinking. Wouldn't people have noticed someone up here fiddling with the railing? It would've been impossible to commit such a dark deed without being noticed.

Unless, of course, the dark deed had been done *in* the dark. I pictured someone slipping up to this roof in the middle of the night with a few tools. Scanning the immediate area, I saw no light fixtures. A quick search on my phone reminded me that the moon that night had been nearly full. Which made me think there might've been enough light to sabotage the railing but not enough for anyone on the ground to see it happening. And I mean, how many people would be wandering around outside the Americana at that hour on a weeknight, anyway?

When Joanie had unlocked the door to the stairwell, I'd noticed scratch marks on the door and jamb next to the knob. Those who weren't in possession of a purloined key had obviously figured out how to jimmy it. She'd acknowledged that the locked door had never kept determined tenants off the roof. I thought of the resident slackers. I wouldn't have been surprised if those kids had possessed a set of lock picks.

"She was a nice girl."

Joanie's voice behind me made me jump.

No, not *jump* jump. I'm still here, aren't I?

I turned to see her eyes welling. I said, "That's what they tell me."

She took a deep breath and let it out. "She was very kind to that crabby old so-and-so that lived in Two-K, kinder than he deserved."

"Nolan Whitehouse," I said.

"You heard about him? Folks used to complain, but Mr. Whitehouse, he never attacked anyone or did anything awful like that. Mainly he was just real suspicious, always accusing folks of all kinds of crazy things. But basically harmless as far as I could tell. You can't evict a guy 'cause he's got no social skills."

Should I go there? I wondered. *Oh, what the heck.* "Speaking of accidents that might not be so accidental," I said, "has anyone, to your knowledge, ever questioned how Mr. Whitehouse died?"

She frowned. "He slipped in his kitchen. The floor was wet."

"I know, but I just thought—"

"Is someone saying he was killed?" Her eyes widened in alarm, and I suddenly regretted mentioning it. This woman didn't need anything else to worry about.

"No, no one's saying that. It's just… it's this business with Scarlett. It's sending my imagination into overdrive."

"Okay. Jeez." She pressed a hand to her chest again. "You had me going there."

I suddenly realized something. Joanie said Nolan lived in apartment 2K. Carolyn is in 2J. They were next-door neighbors. Which meant the sisters must've run into each other fairly regularly since Scarlett was friendly with Nolan. And still, according to Amy, they basically ignored each other.

"Did Scarlett ever have any trouble that you know of?" I asked. "I mean with other tenants?"

She gazed into the distance while giving that some thought. "If she did, she didn't tell *me* about it. But that girl, she was kind of quiet, you know? Kept to herself. Nice, but quiet."

"She lived here for a year, right?" I said. "Did anything unusual happen to her during that time?"

Yeah, I was grasping at straws. So sue me.

"No." She thought some more. "Except her dad, he killed himself last winter, poor thing. Scarlett, I mean, she's the poor thing, not her dad, who you'd think would have more consideration seeing as his girls didn't have a mom anymore and he was making them orphans. I mean, I know the guy was facing prison time, but suck it up, for cryin' out loud."

Wow. Okay. "So if you can't think of anyth—"

"And then that sister of hers, she goes and gets divorced," she said, "and moves here, two floors down from Scarlett, and, well, it was no secret those two didn't get along. No idea why."

Um, maybe it was because Carolyn was doing the nasty with her sister's boyfriend? Just a thought.

I was about to suggest we head back downstairs (I'd decided on the Buffalo chicken pizza, and I wanted it *now*) when Joanie added, "But I figure that's why Scarlett had us rekey her lock."

"Excuse me, what?" I said. "Scarlett wanted her lock changed?"

"Yeah. About six weeks ago. End of September. Scarlett said she lost her key, but you ask me, that was a fib." Joanie wore a knowing smile. "That girl, she was too smart, too *organized*, to lose the key to her apartment. I mean, she paid her rent on the first of every month, like clockwork. She made doctor appointments for that old so-and-so and drove him to them, helped him pay his bills, picked up his medicine and groceries, all of that. Course, she had her cartoons, too, and she ran that like a business. Well, I guess it was a kind of business, wasn't it? I mean, she made money at it, right? Have you seen those cute cartoons of hers?"

"I have," I said. "So cute. So what's this about Carolyn and the key?"

"My point," she said, "is I don't think Scarlett lost her key. What I think happened? After her divorce, Carolyn moves into her sister's building. Scarlett gives her a copy of the key to her own place. For emergencies, you know? Time passes and now the two aren't getting along so great. So Scarlett, she thinks, I don't want that nasty so-and-so having a key to my apartment. Only she's too embarrassed to tell the super that's the reason she wants the lock changed, so she pretends like she lost her key."

"You think?" I wondered if Joanie knew that Scarlett and Hal had broken up around that time.

"Trust me, dear, this place is a real-life soap opera." Joanie gave me a knowing smirk. "The stories I could tell."

8

First Prize in the Dating Sweepstakes

I WAS STILL THINKING about that slice of leftover Buffalo chicken pizza as I made my way to the covered parking lot, which had assigned slots for residents plus additional spaces for guests. As I unlocked my red Mazda with the key fob, I noticed in my peripheral vision that someone was just pulling into a resident slot several cars away from mine—a male someone, I realized as he emerged from his black Tesla. Automatically I glanced around, noting that there was no one else in the vicinity.

Most females can identify with my gut reaction in that instant: the enhanced alertness, the self-protective impulse to get into my vehicle ASAP and engage the door locks. Yes, it was daytime, and no, this stranger had done nothing to warrant suspicion. Besides being, you know, a guy. My instinctive response might appear unwarranted on its face, but half the human population needs no explanation.

I heard rapid footfalls coming toward me and yanked the car door open while shooting the stranger a warning look, the kind of look one hopes will be interpreted as *I have a gun in my purse.*

And for the record, no, I did not have a gun in my purse.

"It's Jane, right?" the man said, with an engaging smile.

Not a stranger after all, though it took me a moment to place him.

"That's right," I said. "How are you, Hal?"

"I'm great. Terrific, actually." He leaned casually against the side of my car, exuding a cooler-than-thou vibe that set my teeth on edge.

With his height and his dark, wavy hair and the fact he was just so annoyingly handsome, Hal reminded me of a younger version of my ex-husband, Dominic Faso. Except Dom's eyes were dark brown, while Hal's were sapphire-blue.

Also, I'd never known Dom to be a slave to the preppy look. Today Hal wore a varsity jacket in brown and rust over an ivory button-down oxford shirt. What's that? You want to know about the lower half? Chinos and loafers, duh. I mean, seriously, did you really have to ask?

"Still going through Scarlett's stuff?" he asked.

"I'm almost done."

"Pretty trippy, that place, huh?"

I couldn't tell whether he meant good trippy or bad trippy. It was impossible to tell from his self-assured smile, which never faltered.

"Her apartment is amazing," I said, admiringly. "Or it was. I hated dismantling it all, but we really had no choice."

"'We'? Don't tell me Caro rolled up her sleeves."

"No, a friend is helping me," I said.

Hal looked at me steadily. "A close friend?"

Whoa. Was this happening? "Why do you ask?"

"Because I want to take you to dinner tonight," he said. Just like that.

This is where I was supposed to tell him that indeed, the friend was a close friend and in fact he was my boyfriend and in fact we lived together and in fact we were very much in love.

If I were playing by the rules, I would've told him all that, or at least the first part, and declined the invitation with thanks, I'm flattered but blah blah blah.

But here's the thing. I really wanted to get to know Scarlett's former boyfriend a little better. By which I mean I wanted to see how much info I could squeeze out of him. And if that required going on a kinda sorta date, then no one else needed to know about it, did they? It wasn't as if we were going to end up at his place or mine, after all.

"I have dinner plans," I lied. In my book, dinner is a Date with a capital *D*. I was prepared to go as far as small *d*, take it or leave it. "I'm free right now, though. What is it, about three-thirty, four? I could use a cup of coffee and a, um—" *slice of leftover Buffalo chicken pizza* "—pastry or something."

He straightened off the car and got in my personal space, never breaking eye contact. This close, I detected his spicy, masculine cologne. "Dinner plans can be canceled, Jane. Tell him something came up. There's this incredible new steak restaurant in Port Washington. They do a ribeye that's out of this world."

"How do you know I'm not vegan?" I asked.

"You would've mentioned it in the first thirty seconds. Where do you live? I'll pick you up at eight."

"You know what? Forget it." I tossed my purse onto my car's passenger seat and slid behind the wheel. "You're not listening to me. Life's too short to put up with that kind of disrespect."

A disbelieving chuckle erupted from him. Was this man

seriously so unaccustomed to rejection? I wasn't even rejecting him, I was simply placing my own perfectly reasonable limits on our first (and only) kinda sorta date.

"All right, all right." He caught the car door before I could slam it. "Luckily for you, I'm intrigued by women who give me a run for my money."

Oh yes, lucky me. I felt like I'd just won first prize in the small-*d* dating sweepstakes. I was pretty sure Hal was planning on getting lucky himself before this day was over. *Sorry, buddy. You and your small* d *will be going home alone.*

"Okay, pay attention, Hal. We're going for coffee. The place is called Juniper's Bakery Café." I'd been there a couple of times and knew it would be just the thing for this outing.

He entered it into the GPS app on his phone. His eyebrows jerked up. "It'll take us a half hour to get to Northport. Why'd you choose a place so far away?"

"For the same reason you picked a steak restaurant out in Port Washington," I said. "Less chance of us being recognized by someone who knows your girlfriend or my boyfriend."

While he groped for a slick comeback, I started my car. "I'll meet you there."

"I figured we'd both go in my car."

"I know you did, but that's not happening." I mean, please, that's Dating Safety 101. I reached out and jerked the door out of his grasp, slamming it shut. And yeah, I punched the lock button. I lost no time backing out of the spot, forcing Hal to scramble out of the way or risk getting tire tracks on those nice, shiny loafers.

"See you there!" I gave him a big smile and a merry wave, then gunned it out of the lot.

The worst that could happen was that Hal and his

overblown ego wouldn't show up at the café and I'd be forced to enjoy my coffee and pastry all by my lonesome while watching funny animal videos on my phone.

Which sounded kind of divine, but when I got there, his black Tesla was already in the small parking lot that served several businesses, including Juniper's Bakery Café. He was leaning against the car, ostentatiously waiting for me. The guy must've broken every speed limit to beat me there. Was I supposed to be impressed?

As for the Tesla, I saw now that it was the base model and nowhere near new. He'd probably bought his ride used, just as I had. I suspected he'd been after something with more pizzazz than your basic sedan or SUV but had been constrained by the size of his bank account.

I headed straight for the entrance to Juniper's, calling over my shoulder, "You can stay out here posing for a car ad, but I'm going inside before the skies open up." Which appeared imminent. I felt a drop as I pulled open the door and entered the warm, sweet-smelling interior of the café: an intoxicating blend of sugar, butter, and good, strong coffee.

Hal followed me inside, looking around with a smug expression as if trying to decide whether Juniper's, and by extension our so-called date, had been worth the drive. The interior of the café was a study in old-fashioned charm, from the tin ceiling medallions to the white subway tiles and wide plank flooring.

"So, what's good here?" he asked.

I didn't bother with the obvious answer—which was, of course, *everything*. I simply marched up to the glass case and gave my order to the young man standing behind it: a chocolate croissant and double espresso. Hal ordered a slice of

Death by Chocolate cake and cappuccino. He paid, and we carried our goodies to a table in an out-of-the-way corner.

Hal said, "Well, I guess this is better than nothing."

"Gee, thanks," I said, deliberately misinterpreting his words.

"I didn't mean you," he quickly added. "I just really wanted to take you somewhere special for our first date."

"Learn when to give it up, Hal." I lifted my espresso cup. "You're being tedious."

And yeah, I was giving my snark free rein for a reason. My gut told me the best way to deal with Scarlett's self-important ex was to keep him off-balance. Being sweet and accommodating would get me nowhere with him, which is too bad because you know how I love being sweet and accommodating.

Also, I intended to keep a close eye on my espresso. Not that I thought Hal was planning to roofie me, but I didn't *not* think he was planning to roofie me, if you know what I mean. What little I knew about the guy did not exactly inspire trust.

Which made me wonder what Scarlett had seen in him, aside from his good looks and sparkling wit. Okay then, aside from his good looks. Could she really have been that shallow? I preferred to think she'd chosen to give him the benefit of the doubt, at least until his true character became impossible to ignore.

Before he could get his hackles up, I smiled and asked, "So, what do you do, Hal?"

"What, you mean for a living?"

"That's usually what that question means."

"I'm the assistant manager of Vargas Sporting Goods." He shoveled a forkful of chocolate cake into his mouth.

"I know Porter and Lacey Vargas," I said. "Nice people. Porter gives you Saturdays off?"

He blotted his lips, and said, "Yeah, but I have to work Sundays. What about you? Caro told me about your weird little business. Can you really make a living working with stiffs?"

"You tell *me*. My 'weird little business' lets me live in a four-thousand-square-foot house on five acres in one of Long Island's most affluent communities." And okay, so I was omitting a few pertinent details, but this guy really needed to be taken down a notch.

He tried hard not to look impressed. "Well, I'm glad you get something out of it, 'cause your work sounds kind of disgusting if you don't mind my saying so."

Well, I thought, *I think cheating on your girlfriend with her sister sounds kind of disgusting, so we're even.*

I swallowed a bite of Juniper's buttery, flaky chocolate croissant, and said, "So you think sending invitations to a memorial service is disgusting?"

"Well, maybe not that," he said. "And by the way, I'll be there."

"Did you reply to the online invitation?" I asked, knowing he hadn't.

He shrugged. "I'm telling you now."

I said, "The invitation clearly states that only those who respond through official channels will be admitted to the venue. There'll be someone at the door crossing names off a list. So I suggest you respond properly like everyone else if you don't want to be turned away."

In fact, I wasn't going to be *that* strict, but I knew through experience that a bizarre, well-publicized death like this was catnip for curiosity seekers. Scarlett's memorial service was certain to attract individuals who had no connection to her and for whom the whole thing was nothing more than a grisly spectator sport. Martin would be the one manning the door with the list, and anyone not on it would need to be approved by either me or Bob.

We'd decided to hold the service on the Saturday before Thanksgiving, which gave me just one more week to finalize the details. Since we expected thirty-five guests at most, I'd suggested we book the Crystal Harbor Historical Society, an elegant venue of just the right size.

After poring over Scarlett's black-and-white composition notebook, I'd compiled a list of forty-three names, people in her life who I was pretty sure would be interested in knowing about the event. We didn't expect them all to attend. Some lived in other states or even, in a few instances, in other countries. I'd sent the invites by email through an online invitation service. Anyone whose email address wasn't listed received a phone call.

"All right, all right," he said. "I'll 'respond properly.' Are you always so bossy?"

"Always."

"Always?" He drew the word out with a suggestive smirk.

I sipped my espresso and set the cup down. "How old are you, Hal?"

He frowned. "Where'd that come from?"

"Just answer the question."

He offered a mocking, "Yes, ma'am," then, "I don't know why it should matter, but I turned twenty-eight last month."

"I'm forty."

"Really?" he said. "Because you don't look—"

"Save it. Yes I do. I look forty because I am forty. You will be shocked to learn I'm perfectly fine with that."

After a moment, he asked, "How old is your boyfriend?"

"Martin is forty-three," I said.

"Forty-three!" There was that smarmy smile again. "Has it occurred to you that a lover in his twenties might have certain advantages over some middle-aged schlub?"

My snort of laughter caught us both off guard. I nearly choked on my croissant. "I can see you haven't met my middle-aged schlub."

"Don't get the wrong idea," Hal said. "I have no desire to replace him in your life. I'm just talking about a little extracurricular fun. Grampy never has to know about it."

"Funny you should call him that," I said. "Martin recently became a grandfather."

"For real?" Hal's superior chuckle told me he anticipated an easy conquest.

The padre's daughter, Lexie, and her husband, Dillon, had welcomed their first child two months earlier. They'd named the infant Martin after his grandfather.

I leaned back in my chair and lifted my espresso cup. "So what you're proposing is that I cheat on Martin with you, just like you cheated on Scarlett with Carolyn. Is that an accurate summation?"

His smile faltered. I could almost hear him mentally debating whether to admit it. Finally he said, "She cheated on me first."

"Scarlett cheated? With who?"

He cast a sour look around the café, as if regretting the impulse that had made him ask me out. "You seem to know everything. Why don't you tell me."

I had a pretty good idea where this was going, but I decided a little torture was in order.

Oh, please. Like he didn't have it coming?

"Well, gee," I said, "for a woman to step out on a paragon like you, she must've been tempted beyond endurance. I mean, this other guy has got be an absolute stone hunk, am I right? Give me a clue. Does this Adonis live in the building?"

Hal slammed his cappuccino cup down so hard, I half expected the saucer to crack. "It doesn't matter who the guy was, all right? It just matters that she cheated first."

"What makes you think the two of them were romantically involved?" I asked. "Maybe she was just looking after someone who needed a little help with the day-to-day stuff. Making sure he had plenty to eat, helping to keep his place clean, that sort of thing."

His eyes narrowed. So I was right. The "Adonis" in question was poor old Nolan Whitehouse. "What else do you know that's none of your damn business?" he asked.

"Well, I know that Scarlett and Nolan weren't having any affair," I said. "She was just being a good neighbor. And a good friend."

"You're wrong about that," he said. "Don't ask me what kind of kinky impulse made her want to do it with an old freak like Whitehouse, but that's what they were up to, all right."

"How do you know?"

"Caro told me," he said.

"Well, what made her think they were having an affair?" I asked.

"Nolan lived right next door to Caro. She has eyes, she could see what was going on. Plus, sisters talk about stuff like that. Do you know Scarlett used to cut the guy's hair?"

"What does that prove?"

He leaned forward. "She used to cut *my* hair. That's the kind of thing you do for a boyfriend, not for some old nutjob that lives in a pigsty."

"Says who? She cut her own hair, too," I said. "She was good at cutting hair. So what?"

He shook his head. "You're twisting things around."

I was twisting things around? "You do know that Carolyn and Scarlett didn't get along, right?" I said. "From what I understand, they weren't even on speaking terms."

"It doesn't matter," he said. "Sisters know things about each other. Caro had no doubts about what Scarlett was doing with Whitehouse."

"Did you confront Scarlett about it?" I asked.

"What do you think? She denied it, of course."

I said, "Did she confront you about Carolyn? And if so, did you deny it?"

His mulish expression was eloquent. Of course he did. But unlike Scarlett's denial, his was a bald-faced lie. "Scarlett had no one to blame but herself," he insisted. "If she hadn't slept with that old freak, I never would've looked twice at her sister. Scarlett belonged to me. She had no business slipping around."

There was a lot to unpack in that self-serving statement, not the least of which was Hal's possessive attitude toward Scarlett. She belonged to him. End of story.

I thought about what Joanie Devine had told me, about Scarlett asking for her lock to be rekeyed. Joanie had assumed it was to keep her estranged sister out of her apartment. But Carolyn had told me she'd never seen Scarlett's apartment until after she'd died.

I said, "So when Scarlett discovered you were messing

around with her sister, she dumped you. Do I have that right?"

Hal's gaze swept the busy café. I got the feeling he was trying to decide whether to claim that Scarlett hadn't dumped him, that it had been the other way around.

Finally he said, "She acted all betrayed, like she didn't cheat first and then lie about it. Like she didn't practically push me into her sister's arms. The bitch had it coming."

I shivered, wondering what else he'd thought his cheating, lying former girlfriend had coming to her.

"Yet you begged her to take you back," I said.

He looked at me sharply. "Who told you that? That's a lie."

More than once Amy Collingwood had seen him standing outside Scarlett's door, pleading with her to give him another chance. Nolan Whitehouse had captured at least one of those encounters with his Polaroid camera.

I wasn't about to tell him that. Instead I said, "You refused to return the spare key to her apartment."

"How do you know about the key?" His icy glare made me glad we were in a public place, surrounded by Juniper's Saturday afternoon crowd. "Yeah, I hung on to it. So what? I knew she'd change her mind. It was only a matter of time."

"Only, she didn't, did she?"

"Her loss," he said. "And anyway, she changed the lock."

Which he would know only if he'd attempted to get into her place after she broke up with him. I pictured Hal trying to sneak into his former girlfriend's apartment in the middle of the night.

I said, "Now, what would make her go and do a thing like that?"

"After Scarlett died," he said, "I asked Caro to let me into her sister's apartment one last time. I wanted to look for a few things I left there. She said no. Can you believe it?"

"Gee," I said, "it's almost like she didn't trust you or something. What I can tell you, having sorted through all of Scarlett's stuff, is that if you did leave anything there, she must've tossed it long ago. I didn't find anything that looked like it belonged to someone else."

Apart from a certain hidden scrapbook and, oh yeah, a mysterious old notebook filled with coded entries, neither of which bore mentioning.

"It had nothing to do with trust," Hal said. "Caro's still jealous of Scarlett, of this imaginary hold she thinks her sister had over me. Jealous of a dead girl. How pathetic is that?" He leaned back in his chair, a speculative look in his eyes. "Caro not letting me into Scarlett's place, it makes me wonder if she was trying to hide something. Like maybe she was afraid of what I'd find there."

When, instead of taking the bait, I took another bite of my chocolate croissant, he added, "You say you went through all of Scarlett's stuff. Did you come across anything out of the ordinary?"

"You'll have to be more specific," I said. "When it comes to Scarlett's apartment, the words 'out of the ordinary' don't really narrow it down."

"Well, did you find anything that was kind of, you know, intriguing? Maybe about this Whitehouse character?"

"Intriguing?" I frowned in phony-baloney perplexity. "Like in what way?"

I could see him beginning to lose patience. "I saw you leaving her apartment with a box a few days ago," he said. "Looks like you're holding on to some of her stuff. Maybe I should take a look through it all, see if I can find my things."

"No need to go to all that bother," I said. "Give me a list of the items you're missing and I'll check."

He started to say something before flopping back in his seat, frustrated. "Forget it. You're useless."

Which brings us to the real reason (in case you haven't figured it out by now) that Hal came on to me. It was not, you will be shocked to learn, because I am so drop-dead sexy. Well, maybe that was a little of it. He was more interested in Nolan Whitehouse. But why?

Could it be he wasn't entirely convinced Scarlett had been cheating on him? Perhaps he was beginning to suspect Carolyn had concocted the whole story, and hoping to find definitive proof one way or the other.

Then again, what could be more "intriguing" than an anonymous, threatening note? Like, for example, the one I'd found pasted in Nolan's scrapbook: *Leave Scarlett alone or you'll be sorry.*

It occurred to me that Hal might be more concerned about being connected to an incriminating note—a note that could cause the authorities to reconsider the finding of accidental death in Nolan's case—than whether his dead ex-girlfriend had been stepping out on him.

I said, "So Carolyn was jealous of Scarlett? Of the bond she shared with you?"

"What can I tell you?" he said. "The girl's insecure."

I'd have questioned his armchair analysis if Bob Jernigan hadn't said the same thing about Carolyn. Bob had also mentioned that Scarlett had been their father's favorite.

"Did you ever meet Ed Proctor?" I asked. "Scarlett and Carolyn's dad?"

Hal shook his head. "He offed himself a few weeks before I moved into the building."

"From what I understand," I said, "he and Scarlett were particularly close."

"So?"

"So maybe Carolyn was jealous not just of what you and Scarlett had," I said, "but also of Scarlett's relationship with their dad."

"Well, Caro found herself another father figure," he said. "Course, she's known the guy forever."

"You mean Bob," I said.

"He lives on my floor. Only, *his* apartment is this big three-bedroom corner unit. Custom paint job, brand-new wall-to-wall. Furnished with high-end furniture and light fixtures. A maid comes in a couple of times a week. You'd never guess anyone lives like that at the Americana."

"All that space just for him?" I asked.

"Are you kidding?" he said. "He leased the place a year and a half ago when he first hooked up with his girlfriend. April Urban."

"While he was still married, you mean."

Hal wore a lopsided grin. "Now you're getting it. It's his secret love nest. Well, not so secret since the divorce."

"Which was when?" I asked.

"Last January. He gave April a ring before the ink was dry."

I was beginning to think of the Americana as Infidelity Central. Joanie Devine hadn't been wrong when she'd called the goings-on there a real-life soap opera. Carolyn had told me Bob moved into the apartment house *after* his divorce. Perhaps, as a newcomer to the building, she didn't know how long he'd actually been there. Either that or she'd deliberately fudged the timeline to conceal that her old family friend had been cheating on his wife.

"But why rent an apartment?" I asked. "Doesn't April have a place of her own they could go to?"

"Nope. She still lives with Mommy and Daddy in one of those big, fancy houses in the really rich part of town. *Your* neighborhood."

I ignored his smirk. "How old is she?"

"About thirty," he said. "Bob traded in the old broad for a newer model. I've gotta hand it to the guy, he knew what he was doing. Not only is April seriously hot arm candy, but she's rolling in dough—a win-win."

"I'm still trying to figure out the love-nest thing," I said. "I mean, why can't a thirty-year-old bring her boyfriend to the house she shares with her parents?"

"Oh, he's over there all the time," Hal said. "From what I hear, her folks like Bob and have given the marriage their blessing."

"Despite the fact he's twice as old as their daughter?" I asked. "He must be about their age."

He shrugged. "Doesn't seem to bother them. An old-money thing, I guess. They know she's crazy about him, and she's their little princess, so she gets what she wants. It helps that he's loaded, though nowhere near as rich as they are. They were actually relieved when she took up with Bob. Seems her last boyfriend was 'inappropriate.' Probably someone like me," he laughed.

"How do you know this?" I asked.

"Her friend Margaret told me."

I didn't ask why one of April's friends chose to share

personal information with him. I assumed it all came down to that patented Hal Kazarian charm.

"Let me guess," I said. "Bob is welcome to visit her at her parents' home, but they don't let him stay overnight."

Hal's disdainful chortle told me I'd guessed right. "Mommy and Daddy are super straitlaced. I mean, they have to know the princess is getting it on with her geriatric fiancé, considering she spends most nights at his apartment, but as long as it's not happening under their roof, they can pretend it's not happening, period."

"I assume Bob's ex-wife got the house," I said, "which would explain why he's now living at the Americana full-time."

Hal nodded. "After the wedding, April and him are gonna move into this huge house they found right near her parents."

"I'm curious," I said. "What did Scarlett think about Bob's little love nest?"

"She was disgusted," he said. "She moves into the building about a year ago and who does she run into on day one? Her dad's old, *married* pal Bob Jernigan, playing house with his hot little piece on the side."

"Talk about an awkward encounter," I said.

Bob had told me Scarlett had resented him because he'd refused to help her father fight an embezzlement rap. He'd neglected to mention her distress at finding him shacked up with his young mistress. Must've slipped his mind.

I finished my chocolate croissant and washed it down with the last few drops of espresso. The dull roar of a sudden downpour caused every customer inside Juniper's to turn toward the café's picture windows, now grayed-out with wind-driven rain. I thought about the half dozen umbrellas that had gradually taken up residence in my car. Good thing I hadn't brought one of them into the café with me. You don't want to get those things wet.

I would've suggested waiting out the storm, but I'd had more than enough of this small-*d* date and suspected Hal felt the same.

"Just one more thing." I rose and slipped my purse off the back of my chair. "What do you think about the Americana being sold to put up a mansion?"

He was suddenly animated. "It's the best thing that could happen. I just hope it goes through, the sooner the better."

"Really? A lot of your fellow tenants disagree. Some of them will be left virtually homeless."

His negligent shrug told me that was their problem. "Everyone's situation is different. As for myself, I signed a three-year lease last spring. All that unused time will translate into a hefty relocation allowance when they kick us out. I'm thinking I could end up with something in the five-figure range. *Ka-ching, ka-ching*, baby! I see a new set of wheels in my future."

"Well, I'm glad you won't be leaving empty-handed," I said, as we weaved around tables toward the entrance, "but won't you have to put most of that relocation allowance toward, you know, relocating? I'm pretty sure any other rental in our area is going to run you a lot more than what you're paying now. And if you decide to buy, you'll need that money for a down payment."

"Oh, I have options," he said smoothly. "Trust me, I'm going to come out on top. As long as nothing happens to tank that sale."

9

The Thing in the Casket

"WHY DO I let you do things like this?" Lenny Ahearn produced a handkerchief from the pocket of his black suit coat and blotted the sweat beading on his forehead.

I pressed the button on my lapel mic and whispered, "Shh! Lenny, keep your voice down. And you know darn well why you let me do things like this. It's because my clients know what they want and—now, here comes the important part—are willing to pay for it."

The padre pressed the button on his own lapel mic and muttered, "If you two don't stop bickering, this wingding will be over before it's even started. We're drawing attention."

We certainly were doing that, and not just because Lenny was being his usual whiny self. The instant Martin and I had stepped into the crowded visitation room at the Leonard T. Ahearn and Sons Funeral Home, all eyes were upon us. It's not that we were inappropriately dressed. Quite the contrary. We both wore black suits, white shirts, and conservative neckties. Yes, I wore a necktie, too.

And okay, so the impenetrable dark sunglasses that completely concealed our eyes might have seemed a tad unusual for an indoor wake. I'd tucked my red-blonde hair under a black, shoulder-length wig. Martin's wig was gray with a coordinated mustache.

Lenny was Leonard T. Ahearn, and this funeral home was his family business. He was in his late sixties, with thinning hair and a bit of a paunch. You might have deduced that Martin and I were communicating with Lenny, and each other, via those cute little lapel mics, but alas, our surveillance headsets (which included transparent earpieces and behind-the-ear coils) were strictly for show. There were no two-way radios clipped to our belts.

Martin and I had taken up position against a wall, shoulder to shoulder, staring straight ahead, occasionally murmuring into our dummy mics in response to some mysterious message from the higher-ups at whatever shadowy agency was directing our mission. CIA? NSA? U.N.C.L.E.? Take your pick.

Lenny, meanwhile, wouldn't stop hovering and fretting, fretting and hovering. "This is the last time you do one of your crazy jobs here, Jane, I swear. My heart can't take the stress."

Martin pressed his mic button. "Get lost, Lenny. You're blowing our cover."

"And if that happens," I told him, "you can kiss that big, juicy fee goodbye." Of course, I was due a significant percentage of that big, juicy fee, so I really needed Lenny to stop kvetching and let us get on with it.

Martin said, "Why don't you go back to your office, Lenny. Pour yourself a shot. Chris and Kev have things well in hand here." He punctuated his words with a none-too-gentle shove, sending Lenny stumbling toward the nearest exit.

The padre hadn't been lying. The two young men who represented the *and Sons* portion of the Leonard T. Ahearn and

Sons Funeral Home were playing their parts to the hilt, thoroughly enjoying themselves, by all appearances. I watched as mourners approached them to ask about the startling thing on display in the open casket. As instructed, Christopher and Kevin Ahearn responded with scripted responses that included such intriguing phrases as *Top secret* and *Need-to-know basis* and my personal favorite, *Pretend you don't see it.*

I know you're dying (yeah, I said it) to find out what the aforementioned *thing* was. You know, the thing in the casket? All will become clear. But first, a little background.

The deceased was one Barney Markusson, an eighty-seven-year-old retired dentist who'd lived in Crystal Harbor with his wife of sixty-three years. Her name was Irma. They'd raised three daughters, who now had families of their own.

What's that? No, Dr. Markusson wasn't the *thing.* How can you even suggest that? Be patient and pay attention. We're just getting to the good part.

It seems that decades earlier, whenever Dr. M wasn't filling cavities and fitting crowns, he was stealing vital secrets from America's enemies and passing them on to some unnamed, supersecret US intelligence agency. He was never too specific about which agency, except to say he'd been recruited while still in his twenties by a handler he knew only by the man's code name: Blue Scorpion.

Dr. M was, however, your basic blabbermouth about the rest of it. He just loved regaling his fishing buddies, great-grandkids, and the UPS guy with tales of his thrilling life in the espionage game. And yes, everyone knew it was all just a bunch of hooey, but he was such a nice guy and his stories were so wonderfully imaginative, no one had the heart to challenge the old guy about his rich fantasy life.

After Dr. M died peacefully in his sleep a few days ago, his granddaughter Heather, a stockbroker in her late thirties, decided she owed her beloved grandpa Barney a memorable sendoff, something to repay him for all the joy he'd brought her. That's when a plan began to take shape.

Barney's tall tales about being a spy had been believed by precisely no one, and with good reason. But what if his family and friends were suddenly confronted with startling evidence that he hadn't been making it up after all?

A lifelong practitioner of the art of the practical joke, Heather devised a simple yet ingenious little one-act play that would cement Grandpa Barney's reputation for generations to come. To pull it off, however, she needed backup: someone who would do (almost) anything for money and keep her yap shut about it afterward.

Cue the Death Diva.

The only other person Heather let in on her plan was her grandma Irma. Not only did she want to avoid giving the old lady a heart attack during her husband's wake, but she correctly predicted that Barney's feisty widow would appreciate the joke.

Now, about the *thing*. (I hear you: *Finally!*) Barney Markusson's mortal remains were indeed lying in that open casket, but the poor guy was dealing with some baggage.

No, I mean he literally had a piece of baggage in there with him, in the form of a securely locked aluminum briefcase. Well, of course it was handcuffed to Barney's wrist. What kind of rinky-dink spy operation do you think we were running?

The room was packed. Barney had been a much-loved friend and relative, as well as a popular local dentist. None of these folks had the nerve (get it? nerve? the guy was a dentist? okay, I'll stop now) to approach Martin and me directly, but judging by the startled stares bouncing between us and that briefcase, it was clear people were beginning to rethink Barney's fanciful stories. The constant hum of whispered conversation provided a piquant backdrop to our enigmatic presence.

Is it possible?

Was it all true?

Heather played her part to perfection, circulating among the attendees and deflecting their queries in much the same manner as Chris and Kev. I watched her shake her head in bafflement for what seemed like the hundredth time. *Grandpa Barney had his secrets. All I know is that it's highly classified.*

After a good hour of this, she finally caught my eye and gave an almost imperceptible nod.

I pressed the button on my dummy mic. "Show time."

The padre murmured into his lapel. "Copy that."

Anyone watching us would have assumed we'd just received orders from the director of the agency. Heck, maybe it was U.N.C.L.E.'s adorable Illya Kuryakin with his adorable fake Russian accent.

Martin and I abandoned our positions by the wall and started across the room toward the casket. The throng of mourners parted before us like the Red Sea, their mingled perfumes competing with the myriad floral tributes. Our dark glasses made it possible for us to gauge people's reactions without being obvious about it. I watched Heather and Grandma Irma exchange subtle winks, and then we were at the casket.

Lenny and his boys had done a good job with Barney. To answer the question I know you're wondering, yeah, he looked "natural," as natural as a dead guy can look with a few subtle cosmetic enhancements. I could swear he wore a sly little smile as I extracted a key from my jacket pocket, unlocked the handcuff, and lifted the briefcase out of the casket.

Martin's head pivoted slowly as he scanned the attendees, many of whom stumbled backward in alarm. They didn't have to see his eyes to feel his penetrating gaze. "You never saw a thing," he announced, his tone vaguely threatening. "There was no briefcase."

Most of them bobbed their heads up and down in agreement. *Nothing going on here. Just an ordinary viewing and nothing at all of interest in the casket.*

As we turned to leave, Heather shrieked, "What are you doing with my grandfather's briefcase?"

She charged me, and we commenced a tug-of-war with the briefcase as Martin muttered into his dummy mic. As far as our audience was concerned, he might've been asking Illya for permission to produce his Glock and blow the obstreperous granddaughter away.

"Ma'am," I said, "you're interfering with official government business."

"I don't know who you people think you are," Heather snarled as she fought for possession of the briefcase, "but whatever's in this thing, Grandpa Barney obviously wanted it buried with him."

Grandma Irma hollered, "For the love of God, Heather, let them have the darn thing! It's the government. They could kidnap you. Make you disappear. Make your *family* disappear."

Okay, a little dark, but it was nice to see Barney's widow getting into the spirit of the thing.

I wonder how many in that crowd knew that Heather had been a theater major in college. She'd become a stockbroker only because she was fond of, you know, eating. But she continued to hone her skills with roles in local community theater, and it showed. The lady was convincing.

There were quite a few very old individuals in attendance, as you can imagine, given Barney's age. While all this was going on, I saw one of them, a dapper gentleman who appeared to be in his nineties, approach the casket to say his personal goodbye to his old friend. His eyes glistened as he patted Barney's chest, then turned and headed for the exit.

As Heather and I continued to struggle over the briefcase, a man in the back shouted, "This is outrageous. I'm calling the cops!"

You might assume this was where it got sticky. Oh, come now. Do you really think I'd leave something like that to chance? My friends on the force had been forewarned about a possible kerfuffle at the funeral home. They'd been assured it was all part of one of those theatrical productions with audience participation. Sometimes audience members get carried away and do silly things like call the cops on the performers.

I might also note that the Death Diva never forgets the Crystal Harbor Police Department at Christmas. Or Easter. Or Thanksgiving. Or Veterans Day, President's Day, Mother's Day, Father's Day, Groundhog Day, Cinco de Mayo, you name it. It might be a five-pound box of chocolates. Maybe a case of wine or a shipment of gourmet sausages and cheese—in gratitude for the officers' service and in anticipation of the continuation of our warm working relationship, natch.

No, it's not a bribe for them to look the other way. Do you think so little of me?

I would remind you that not every question requires an answer.

You will be happy to learn I finally won our little tug-of-war. And yes, it was scripted that way, but I like to think I would've emerged victorious in any event.

Heather shook her fist. "This isn't over! I'm going to find who out who you work for and sue the whole lot of you. I'll take it all the way to the Supreme Court if I have to."

Martin and I enacted the final scene by standing at attention on either side of the casket and offering Barney a snappy salute.

No, I have no idea whether spies salute one another. There are military spies, right? Maybe Barney was one of those.

As I gazed down at his body, I noticed a tiny triangle of white against the dark blue of his suit. There was something tucked into Barney's chest pocket. By this time the assembled crowd had receded as far away from us as they could manage, so none of them saw me slide my fingers into the pocket and withdraw a small card. It was about the size of a business card, but there was no printing on it, just a handwritten note that read, *Adieu, old friend.*

Martin took the card from me and flipped it over. No words were printed on the front either, just a single image beautifully executed in raised ink.

A blue scorpion.

10

Unstoppable Force, Meet Immovable Object

"CHEYENNE, PUT YOUR phone away," I said. "You're here to work, not to text."

"But it's Neal," the nineteen-year-old said, as if chatting with her boyfriend took precedence over doing the job she'd been hired to do.

How, you ask, did I know Neal was her boyfriend? It might have something to do with the tattoo prominently displayed on the front of her neck: the name *Neal,* sloppily executed and surrounded by an even sloppier heart. This particular piece of body art (and I use the term loosely) had materialized the previous May, the names *Brian* and *Sean* on the sides of her neck having been crossed out in turn with tattooed *X*'s. Apparently she'd had no trouble affording amateurish tattoos, but laser removal was beyond her budget.

We were in the kitchen of the venerable stone manse that housed the Crystal Harbor Historical Society. Scarlett Proctor's memorial service had just wrapped in the large front parlor, which was right off the entrance hall. Thirty-two of Scarlett's friends, relatives, and work colleagues had turned up. I'd supplemented the existing seating with upholstered giltwood chairs from the well-stocked storeroom in the basement.

The service had been moving, marked by a dignified informality I like to think would have pleased Scarlett. She hadn't been religious, so Bob and I had agreed to dispense with clergy. Instead, we'd invited the guests to share their memories. Her California cousins had flown clear across the country to be there, belying Carolyn's statement that their out-of-state relatives considered her sister a virtual stranger. They shared wonderful stories about childhood visits with Scarlett, stories that had the rest of us both laughing and tearing up, sometimes simultaneously.

It turned out Scarlett had indeed been in touch with a handful of school chums. One of them honored her old friend by reciting an exquisite poem about love and mortality. Another, who'd brought his guitar, sang a song he'd written for her. The owner of the online magazine that published her cartoons broke down as he praised her talent and her insight into the human condition.

I kept my eye on Carolyn, hoping she'd decide to say a few words about her sister. Instead she simply sat and took it all in—but not, I was surprised to see, with her usual stony countenance. Her eyes welled and her chin quivered as she made a conspicuous effort to keep from breaking down. Bob, sitting next to her, had put his arm around her shoulders and murmured something soothing in her ear.

After the service, the guests had been ushered into the adjacent drawing room for the reception. I'd engaged my friend Maia Armstrong, a popular local caterer, to provide the luncheon vittles, which she and her helpers had set out buffet-style in the dining room, located between the drawing room and kitchen. Nothing overly elaborate: a selection of gourmet sandwiches and salads, plus a dessert table offering a variety of pastries and fruit as well as the requisite coffee and assorted teas. A self-serve bar provided wine, beer, soda, and sangria.

I was still in the kitchen, trying to get Cheyenne to put away her phone and assist with the food setup, when Maia entered from the dining room. The caterer was a pretty Black woman in her mid-thirties with catlike eyes and a gorgeous mass of natural curls, which she'd tamed that day with a twisted silk headband in dark teal. Her silk wrap dress was the same blue-green shade, patterned with large beige-and-ivory leaves.

Maia advanced on the shiftless teen. "That's it, Cheyenne. Go home. You're just in the way here."

The girl rolled her eyes. "All right, all right. I didn't know there was a *law* against texting." She took her sweet time finishing her message, no doubt telling Neal what a hard-ass her boss was being, before ostentatiously shoving the phone into the pocket of her black pants.

To be accurate, they weren't *her* black pants. Maia had instructed her three teenage helpers to wear a white, collared shirt and black pants. True to form, Cheyenne had arrived—twenty minutes late—in her customary skintight leggings and midriff-baring T-shirt. Her employer had not been impressed that she'd gotten the colors right.

By the time the girl had gone home and returned in her mother's baggy pants and blouse, another hour had passed and the initial work had already been done by Maia's other two teenage helpers for this event: Karina Faso, who was my ex-husband Dom's daughter, and Nate Robbins, who happened to be Martin's nephew.

Kari had worked for Maia before, but Nate was a new hire. I'd first met him two months earlier, and gotten to know him better during a couple of family get-togethers. I'd felt confident recommending him to the caterer.

And by the way, Kari and Nate had not needed to be told twice what they were expected to wear, or when to arrive for work. The kids continued to work nonstop, prepping food, all the while pretending not to hear their coworker getting chewed out by their boss.

Cheyenne gave the kitchen a lazy perusal. "Looks like everything's under control, and anyway, it's time for my break. I'm supposed to get a fifteen-minute break every, um, hour. It's the law."

Maia asked Kari and Nate to go collect dirty dishes. Once the kids had left, she turned to her other so-called helper. "You think I'm playing? You're fired, Cheyenne. Go."

The girl's slack-jawed outrage quickly morphed into sly opportunism. "You gotta pay me for the whole day 'cause I, like, showed up. It's the law."

Maia calmly turned to me. "Jane, would you please ask the head of security to come here and escort Ms. O'Rourke out of the building?"

"Sure thing," I said, and went to find him.

Guess who the head of security was that day. Oh, come on, guess.

"Hey, I know you!" Cheyenne said, when I reentered the kitchen with Martin, looking impossibly handsome in a charcoal suit, snow-white shirt, and burgundy tie.

"You ought to," he said. "I kick you out of Murray's Pub approximately once a week. How much money have you wasted on those fake IDs, Cheyenne?"

"None of your business. I mean, they're not fake."

"Come on, let's go." He offered his arm, like the gentleman he is. Cheyenne reflexively backed away, clearly thinking he meant to grab her. When he simply stood there expectantly with a bent elbow, she pondered the gallant gesture for a few moments before finally linking her arm through his.

Maia handed the girl her purse, a tacky, furry thing crafted to look like a pink kitten with huge, humanlike eyes and a sparkly crown. As the padre escorted her out of the kitchen, Cheyenne said, "You gotta serve me at Murray's if I show you ID. It's the law."

"Tell you what," he said. "When you turn twenty-one in a couple of years, I'll buy you your first drink to celebrate. How's that?"

When the door had closed behind them, I turned to Maia with a look that asked what the heck she'd been thinking, hiring a lazy good-for-nothing like Cheyenne O'Rourke.

She wore a long-suffering expression. "Dom vouched for her."

I groaned. "I should've known."

My ex, being the Nicest Guy in the World, believes in giving everyone, no matter how undeserving, a second chance. Or, as in the case of Cheyenne, a twentieth or hundredth or thousandth chance. Today's memorial service had been a onetime side gig for the girl. Most days she could be found behind the food counter of Janey's Place, the health-food café Dom had founded two decades ago when he'd been the same age Cheyenne was now.

The difference, of course, being that Dom had been a hardworking, ambitious nineteen year-old, with a hardworking, supportive girlfriend (yours truly if you haven't been paying attention) who could often be found behind the wheel of the very first Janey's Place location, which happened to be a food truck.

Over the years, Dom had managed to turn that modest little truck into a veritable health-food empire encompassing, at last count, thirty-seven locations in the Northeast, with plans in the works to expand into California.

If you're thinking my ex must now be quite wealthy, you would not be wrong.

Kari opened the kitchen door and held it for Nate, who entered carrying a tray laden with plates and glasses, which he deposited near the dishwasher. Kari pulled on a pair of disposable gloves, opened the big commercial fridge, and pulled out a tray of sandwiches covered in plastic wrap. The sandwiches had been constructed with a variety of yummy fillings stuffed between slices of multigrain, ciabatta, baguettes, and croissants, plus a gluten-free option.

Kari had inherited her father's height (or close enough for a girl, five-ten to his six-two) and dark brown eyes. Today her golden-brown hair (courtesy of her mother, Svetlana) was pulled back into a neat chignon.

As you've no doubt surmised by now, Dom and I never had kids. My wanting them and his adamantly *not* wanting them had spelled the end of our short marriage eighteen years ago, despite the fact we'd still loved each other. After our divorce, he'd tied the knot with, and subsequently divorced, two other women.

Those other wives had lost no time presenting Dom with three children, the oldest of whom was Kari. Mrs. Faso Number Two and Mrs. Faso Number Three had simply chosen not to consult their husband about the decision to reproduce, and whaddaya know, Dom discovered he absolutely loved being a dad. I mean, he *loved loved loved* it. Was looking forward to having a bunch more someday.

Funny the way things work out sometimes, huh? My biological clock and I are still laughing about it. What a knee-slapper.

Nate opened the fridge. "We're running out of shepherd salad out there."

"Bottom shelf," Kari said. "Behind the German potato salad."

It might've been my imagination, but I could swear I detected a frisson of awareness zinging between the two teens, of the *boy likes girl, girl likes boy* variety. Nate had turned seventeen last month, which made Kari a few months older than he, though I doubted the slight age difference mattered to either of them. Both were seniors in high school.

The son of Martin's half sister Claudia, Nate was tall (he had a good two inches on Kari), with brown eyes and wavy blond hair. He enjoyed sports, did reasonably well in school, and had a surprising hobby: baking. Once Maia had sampled his triple-chocolate brownies (his own original recipe), she'd asked him to bring a couple of dozen for the dessert table. It was his first sale, and he couldn't have been prouder.

"Hey, Nate," Maia said, "I know it's a half year away, but do you have any summer employment plans?"

"Not yet," he said, as he peeled plastic wrap off the bowl of shepherd salad, "so if you need help, I'm around."

"I'm sure I will, on occasion, but I was thinking you might be interested in something a little more regular. Are you familiar with Patisserie Susanne?" she asked, naming a French bakery café on Crystal Harbor's busy Main Street.

"Of course," he said. "I love that place."

"Well, Susanne Travert is always looking for extra help during the summer," she said, "and she likes hiring young people who are serious about the business. Think you could get there every day before dawn? I know you live out in Sea Cliff."

"No problem." His eyes shone with excitement. "I just got my license, and Mom gave me her old Prius when she got a new one. You really think Ms. Travert would consider hiring me?"

"I'll put in a good word," Maia said.

Kari was grinning almost as widely as Nate. She gave him a thumbs-up. "Sounds like a sweet gig."

The kids headed for the door with the sandwiches and salad. I held it open for them, and told Maia, "I'd better get out there, make sure everything's going smoothly."

As I passed through the dining room, greeting guests along the way, I noticed Carolyn at the drinks station, draining a glass of red wine and refilling it. In the drawing room, I saw Amy Collingwood sitting with her landlords, Joanie and Joel Devine. I wasn't close enough to hear what they were discussing, but they all looked calm enough. I knew how Amy felt about the impending sale of the Americana and trusted her not to make an issue of it during the reception.

Joanie scanned the room, clearly on the lookout for someone. Her gaze locked on a small woman who appeared to be around ninety years old. The woman's perky brown wig only served to draw attention to the advanced age of the face under it.

"Clover!" Joanie called. "Here, sit." She scooted over on the sofa to make room for Clover, who was struggling to balance the plate she'd just filled. The other three helped get her settled.

Amy noticed me then and waved me over. "Jane, have you met Clover Eklund? She lives in One-D."

"Oh!" I said. "You're the lady who sold that exquisite antique sewing machine to Scarlett." I perched on the arm of the sofa and took her hand very gently, cognizant of the swollen, arthritic knuckles. "I'm Jane Delaney. It's so good to meet you, Mrs. Eklund."

"It's 'Miss,' but call me Clover." She chuckled. "And I never thought of that old machine as exquisite. It was my mother's. I learned to sew on it."

"So did Scarlett," I reminded her.

She squeezed my hand with surprising strength. "You're the lady that sent out the invites. Thank you for including me today, Jane. That girl was something special. That she should go before me? And in such an awful way? I'm just heartbroken."

Joanie's husband, Joel, patted her shoulder. "We all are, Clover. So senseless." Joel was rotund, with iron-gray hair and a brushy mustache. Turning to me, he said, "Clover taught honors math at Crystal Harbor High for… how many years was it?"

"Forty-three," she said, with obvious pride. "I still hear from some of my former students, especially the ones whose careers involve math."

"Accountants?" I asked. "Financial planners?"

"A few of those," she said, "and of course, math teachers like me. There are a couple of data scientists. A meteorologist with the National Oceanic and Atmospheric Administration. Oh, and one girl is a big shot with the US Government Accountability Office. She sends me a box of Godiva chocolates every Christmas."

Amy said, "Clover's still got it. She's the go-to lady for anything math-related."

Joanie jerked her thumb at the former teacher. "This one, she solves mathematical puzzles and advanced equations *for fun*. Just looking at those problems makes my ears bleed."

"It keeps my mind active." Clover shrugged. "I've had a love affair with numbers my whole life."

I recalled Amy mentioning how concerned she was for Clover and other residents of the Americana who were just scraping by and couldn't afford to move. I thought this lady could use some good news.

"Clover," I said, "you'll be glad to know your sewing machine has found a new home. It was donated to a nonprofit theatrical company in Brooklyn for a play they're putting on about several generations of a Swedish immigrant family. The machine will actually be used onstage by the actors during every performance."

Clover grinned in astonished delight. "Well, isn't that something. And it's about a Swedish family? My people were from Sweden."

Amy said, "It's kismet."

"I can't remember when I last went to the theater," Clover said. "I think it was *Yentl* on Broadway in 1975. Live theater just became too expensive."

"Well, I'll bet I can snag us a couple of tickets to this play," I said. "It premieres next month. Will you be my date?"

The old woman giggled like a teenager. "Why, I'd be delighted. Imagine my old Singer up onstage. In a real play!"

Before taking my leave of the small group, I gave Clover my card and took her phone number.

The parlor, drawing room, and dining room all had big

bay windows, complete with cushioned window seats adorned with decorative pillows and throws. Each piece of furniture was either an authentic nineteenth-century antique or a convincing reproduction, such as the mahogany sofa the Devines and Clover were sitting on, upholstered in silver-gray and taupe striped silk jacquard.

Wireless speakers throughout the first floor emitted low-key jazz, a favorite of Scarlett's, according to Amy. The rooms had been decorated with live flowering plants along with about a dozen of Scarlett's most popular cartoons, blown up to twelve by sixteen inches and framed. In addition, there were photographs of Scarlett herself, plus a few with her whole family, including their two collies, taken when the girls were little. My favorite was a picture of the two sisters playing on a swing set and laughing. Scarlett and Carolyn looked to be about five and ten years old.

I thought about the tragedies that awaited these happy children: first the loss of their mother when they were quite young, followed by their father's disgrace and suicide nine months ago. And now Carolyn had lost her one remaining family member in a bizarre accident.

Yeah, I know. I kept telling myself it was an accident, but there was still the issue of that railing, the one that never should've failed. I believed Joanie Devine when she insisted she and her husband never cut corners when it came to safety. Even so, we all know things happen. Unexpected things. Things with no logical explanation.

And then there were Scarlett's suspicions regarding Nolan Whitehouse's death. How did that fit into the bigger picture? *Was* there a bigger picture or was I letting my imagination run away with me? Which you know has never, ahem, happened, but there's always a first time, right?

The padre had taken up position just inside the drawing room, where he had a clear line of sight through the parlor and entrance hall to the front door. Any uninvited latecomers would have to get through him.

Speaking of which, Hal Kazarian had not, despite my pointed warning and his reluctant promise, responded to the emailed invitation he'd received. Martin had been manning the building's front door a couple of hours earlier when the guests had arrived before the service, and yes, he'd been crossing names off an actual list attached to an actual clipboard. If any invitee besides Hal had casually mentioned to me, *Oh, by the way, Jane, I'll be there*, I'd have added that person's name to the list, no problem.

But this was Scarlett's arrogant cheater of an ex, and I had zero incentive to make it easy for him. Plus I was pretty sure his flouting the rules was some kind of test on his part—whether of his animal magnetism or my resolve, I couldn't say.

The padre knew darn well who Hal was. I'd told him all about our small-*d* date and the tidbits of knowledge I'd gleaned from it. I'd been busy in the parlor helping to seat guests for the service when I heard a familiar voice, raised in anger. I peeked past the folks milling around in the entrance hall and saw Hal attempting to bluster his way in. You can imagine how well that worked. He kept arguing as Martin admitted a group of Scarlett's neighbors from the Americana, chatting amiably with them and welcoming them to the memorial service.

Finally, in frustration, Hal tried to physically shove past the padre, only to land hard on his keister on the building's wide veranda. No doubt he'd considered himself an Unstoppable Force, only to come up against the Immovable Object that was the padre.

During this entire encounter, Martin never once raised his voice or dropped his clipboard. Did I mention? My man had another career in addition to bartending. He was also a bodyguard and occasional private investigator. For him, putting a self-important creep like Hal Kazarian in his place was child's play.

Hal struggled to his feet in eye-bulging outrage, slapping imaginary dirt off his steel-blue suit. Watching him size up his adversary, I saw the instant he realized he was no match for the older man.

That's when Hal started bellowing my name, but by then I was already moving toward the front door. It had been a fun show, one I think Scarlett would've enjoyed (and which was certain to fuel the Crystal Harbor gossip mill for days), but this was, after all, a memorial service. A certain level of decorum was in order.

"Jane!" Hal screeched when he spied me. "Tell this gentleman to let me in!"

Okay, you got me. He didn't say, "gentleman." He employed a somewhat earthier term. Use your imagination.

I cuddled up to Martin and gave him a quick kiss. "Hey, babe. What's going on here?"

Hal's gaze flicked between the two of us, and I watched him get it. This particular Immovable Object was the boyfriend he'd so blithely dismissed as a decrepit, sexually underperforming schlub during our so-called date a week earlier.

"I thought you decided you weren't coming, Hal," I said. "You never responded to the invitation."

"Why wouldn't I be here?" he said. "Scarlett was the love of my life."

I heard a whimper and turned to see Carolyn, her expression stricken. "So what does that make me, huh?" she demanded, before turning on her heel and pushing her way through the gawking onlookers.

I caught Bob Jernigan's eye and sent him a wordless plea, which he had no trouble deciphering. He addressed the crowd that had filled the entrance hall. "Ladies and gentlemen, it's time to return to the parlor and find our seats. The service will begin momentarily."

When it was just the three of us, I said, "You can go in, Hal, but if you even think about making another scene, Martin will immediately eject you, and he won't be nearly so gentle next time. Am I clear?"

Hal started to push past us. You will be unsurprised to learn he did not get far. He avoided making eye contact as he huffed, "Sure, fine. Just get the hell out of my way."

I'd nodded to Martin and we'd watched Hal follow the others into the parlor.

Just so you know, it had never been my intention to deny Scarlett's ex admittance to her memorial service, just to make him work for it—to turn it into a teachable moment, if you will.

Now, as the guests gathered in small groups to enjoy the refreshments and chat about how lovely and meaningful the service had been, I noticed that Hal seemed to be keeping his distance from Carolyn, for which I was grateful. For her part, Carolyn was clearly avoiding the Devines, having been frustrated in her attempt to sue them for wrongful death. As for whether she'd done the gracious thing and apologized for causing them needless worry... that would be too much to hope for.

Dom approached me in the drawing room, looking dapper as always in a bespoke Italian suit in deep navy-blue. His eyes and thick, curly hair were the same dark brown, a shade I'd always thought of as espresso. He gave me a peck on the cheek.

I asked, "Have you had something to eat?"

He nodded. "Everything's delicious, including the sangria. Maia never disappoints."

"As long as she has decent helpers." I gave him a pointed look.

He made a funny noise deep in his throat. "Okay, what happened to Cheyenne? I haven't seen her."

"What do you *think* happened, Dom? Maia had to send her home." I wasn't going to ask why he'd vouched for his young employee. It all came back to that Nicest Guy in the World thing. He hated to acknowledge that anyone was beyond redemption.

"Spare me the grisly details," he said. "I get it. Do you know who that boy is who's working with Kari?"

"His name is Nate Robbins. He's Martin's nephew."

Dom failed to repress a flicker of distaste at the mention of my significant other. He'd never trusted Martin, who admittedly had a sketchy past, the operative word being *past*. He'd long ago cleaned up his act.

That said, Dom's dislike of Martin had more to do with me than with the padre himself. My ex had decided that Mrs. Faso the First needed to become Mrs. Faso the Fourth. And while it was true there'd been a time I would've jumped at the opportunity to remarry Dom, that time was firmly in the rearview.

I wondered how he'd react if I told him I'd detected an attraction between his daughter and Martin's nephew. I wasn't going to do it, I was just, you know, curious.

Instead I said, "What did you think of the service?"

"It was perfect, Janey. Scarlett would've approved."

"I have to admit," I said, "I was surprised to find your name in her address book. How did you know her?"

"I assume you're aware the owners of the Americana are trying to sell the property," he said, and I nodded. "Scarlett was desperately trying to keep that from happening. She was worried about some of the tenants, but she also felt there's a need for affordable rental housing in an upscale community like Crystal Harbor."

"The Town Council does not agree," I said. "Well, except for Sophie, of course. They'd be happy to see the building razed to the ground and replaced with some big, gaudy mansion. Which seems to be the plan."

"Only because the Devines can't find a buyer who *doesn't* want to demolish it," he said.

"Oh, they've had offers for the building," I said, "just none that are anywhere near what it's worth. This developer, the one who plans to build a mansion, is willing to cough up a bundle."

"Which brings us to why Scarlett got in touch with me," Dom said. "She asked for a meeting just a few days before she died. She had this idea that if a group of Crystal Harbor business leaders could get together and form a kind of real estate investing consortium, we could buy the Americana and save it."

"Wow. Ambitious," I said. "But is it realistic?"

"I thought so at first, but I've spent the past couple of weeks pitching the idea until I'm hoarse. No interest. Zilch."

I felt deflated, after a momentary surge of hope. "So you

kept working on it, even after Scarlett was gone?"

He seemed surprised by the question. "Of course. I gave her my word. I couldn't have lived with myself if I hadn't followed through."

I sighed. "Well, it was a good idea."

I knew one person who wouldn't be sad that Scarlett's plan had fizzled. Hal was looking forward to spending the hefty relocation allowance he had coming to him when the tenants were evicted. He anticipated a payday somewhere in the tens of thousands, a significant chunk of change for the assistant manager of a sporting goods store.

Dom, no doubt sensing my mood, decided to change the subject. He looked around the room, admiring the period décor. "This place was a good choice."

"Thanks," I said. "I think Scarlett would have approved. She had a soft spot for vintage everything."

The two-story stone edifice that housed the Crystal Harbor Historical Society had an intriguing history. It had been built in the early nineteenth century by a wealthy local farmer to house his growing family. Within a decade, however, personal and financial tragedies had taken their toll, causing the property to pass through a succession of owners. During the late nineteenth and early twentieth centuries, it was a boardinghouse and brothel catering to a diverse clientele that included more than a few prominent movers and shakers.

The building's basement was turned into a speakeasy during the twenties when booze was outlawed, and was currently serving as a Prohibition-era museum, housing an assortment of artifacts from the town's rum-running past when it was a major conduit for smuggled hooch, thanks to its location on the North Shore of Long Island. Picket ships crammed with said hooch hung out three miles away, just outside U.S. waters, an irresistible invitation to Crystal Harbor's fishermen and lobstermen, many of whom supplemented their legitimate incomes by ferrying the illicit cargo to shore.

The Historical Society had purchased the derelict property in the 1960s and set about reversing the neglect and ill-advised renovations it had been subjected to. Yeah, I'm not the only one who suffers from It Seemed Like a Good Idea at the Time syndrome. Eventually the house had been restored to its original grandeur, complete with ornate carved mantels, giltwood chandeliers, leaded-glass windows, and herringbone parquet floors.

Dom scanned our immediate area for eavesdroppers before saying, sotto voce, "The sister. Carolyn, right?"

I nodded. "What about her?"

"Don't know whether you've noticed, but she kind of parked herself at the bar. She's working her way through a bottle of wine."

"Oh, goody," I muttered. For someone Carolyn's size, that was a lot of alcohol.

He looked past me. "Speak of the devil."

I turned and saw Scarlett's sister enter from the dining room and wobble her way past the guests who'd congregated in the drawing room. She was carrying an open bottle of pinot noir but no glass. A couple of people tried to snag her attention, to express their condolences, I assumed, but she ignored them.

As she passed Martin, he gently waylaid her and asked if he could get her anything, or if she'd like a quiet place to rest. She shrugged him off and toddled into the parlor.

"Oh, brother." I looked around the room. "Have you seen Bob Jernigan? He's the—"

"I know Bob," Dom said. "He went outside a little while ago. Said he wanted to show his fiancée the grounds."

The building sat on seven acres, which included gardens (less than showy this time of year), a pond, and a thatch-roofed children's cottage as old as the house.

"I was hoping he'd deal with Carolyn," I said. "He's kind of a father figure to her." That's how Hal had put it.

"I could go out there and find him," Dom offered.

"No, leave him be. I'll take care of it." Bob was, after all, paying me to run this event. I should be able to handle one inebriated woman. Heaven knew I'd dealt with worse.

As I entered the parlor, I saw that a handful of people had drifted back in there, but Carolyn was nowhere in sight. I proceeded into the entrance hall, which was vacant, then opened the front door and checked the veranda. She wasn't out there either.

Martin had followed me. "I saw her go upstairs."

I sighed.

"I'll go get her." He started to move past me.

I grabbed his arm. "I've got this, Padre. You're the head of security. You've got to stay down here and make sure everything's, you know…"

"Secure?" There was that sexy smile I couldn't get enough of.

I gave him a quick kiss and climbed the stairs to the second floor.

11

How Could His Love Be Anything but Pure?

THE LONG UPSTAIRS hallway was deserted. I checked the open anteroom at the front of the house, which was just big enough to hold a pair of antique chairs and a scallop-edged piecrust table. She wasn't there or on the adjoining balcony.

There were five rooms off the hallway, plus a bathroom. Four of the rooms were reserved for Historical Society business. The last one on the right was a small library filled with books and maps about Crystal Harbor, and decorated with framed articles and photos about the town's long history.

Across the hall from the library was a locked door that, if opened by someone proficient in the use of lock picks (oh, you know who I mean), would reveal a second staircase, this one leading to the attic. I'd been in that attic, and let me just say, that one visit had provided nightmare fuel for weeks.

"Carolyn?" I called. I listened intently, but heard nothing.

I made my way down the carpeted hallway, peering inside the offices as I went. A woman's shoe—left foot, black, two-inch heel—lay abandoned in front of the second room on the left. I picked it up and continued my search.

I strove for a reassuring tone as I announced my presence. "Carolyn? It's Jane. I just want to make sure you're okay."

The bathroom was the next-to-last room on the right. I poked my head in there. No Carolyn.

That's when I heard it: soft sobs coming from behind the closed door of the last room on the right. The library.

I grasped the knob, took a deep breath, and opened the door. The four chairs surrounding the round table in the center of the cozy room were vacant. Ditto for the upholstered settee. Most of the wall space was occupied by floor-to-ceiling bookcases.

Looking around, I finally spied her sitting on the floor, leaning against bookshelves. She wore a conservative dark-green dress. Her legs, clad in black tights, were splayed on the antique carpet. Did she even realize she'd lost a shoe?

Carolyn raised the wine bottle and took a long swig. Some of it ran down her neck. Rivulets of black mascara streaked her face. Scarlett's sister had apparently never gotten the memo about waterproof mascara and funerals.

I wore my usual gray skirt suit, along with a white blouse, black pumps, and faux pearls—what I thought of as my Death Diva uniform. I set aside Carolyn's shoe, reached into a jacket pocket, and produced a packet of tissues. In my line of work, I'd long ago learned never to leave home without them.

I sat on the carpet, pulled a couple of tissues out of the pack, and offered them to her.

She ignored them. "Leave me alone." At least, that's what I think she said. It was kind of garbled.

She lifted the bottle again but was suddenly sobbing too hard to drink. She didn't resist when I confiscated it and moved it out of her reach. It was practically empty.

"It's my fault," she blubbered. "It's all my fault."

I went still, staring at her. Finally I said, "What's your fault, Carolyn?"

She took a deep breath and blurted, "Dad. I—I made him do it."

Careful, I told myself. "I thought you said his suicide was Scarlett's fault?"

Carolyn appeared to be having difficulty corralling her thoughts. She looked around, blinking. "Where's my wine? I had wine."

I shoved the tissues into her hand. She stared at them in confusion for a moment before wiping her eyes and blowing her nose.

I couldn't let it go. "What did you make your father do, Carolyn?"

She drew in a shaky breath. "He never would've thought of it on his own. Never would've done it if—if I hadn't given him the idea. If I hadn't shown him how it could be done."

"What do you mean?" I prayed we weren't talking about, well, what it sounded like we were talking about. I pulled more tissues out of the pack to replace the soggy ones she'd tossed onto the carpet. "How *what* could be done, Carolyn?"

"You know. All that money." She gestured broadly and honked into the tissues. "The money his company made. Millions and millions. He gave them so many years, worked so hard for them. They *owed* him."

"So you, um, you suggested that he—"

"Millions and millions. And he only took…" Carolyn squinted at her thumb and index finger, the two digits nearly touching as if she held something infinitesimally small. "I told him they wouldn't even miss it. They *shouldn't* have missed it."

"Did Scarlett know," I asked, "that you encouraged your father to, you know, take what was owed him?"

She said nothing for long moments while conflicting emotions duked it out behind her eyes. Resentment. Jealousy. Guilt.

"She was his favorite," Carolyn said. "Everyone knew it. I thought… I thought things would be different after…"

After her father took her advice and stole a couple of hundred grand from his employer. It sounded like Carolyn had planted the idea in his head, given him pointers, encouraged him to go through with it.

She must've reasoned that once she'd helped her father procure "what was owed him," then she would naturally become the favored daughter. Only, she hadn't counted on him getting caught.

A fierce look came into her eyes. "But the rest of it… the rest of it was Scarlett's fault. Dad never would've killed himself if she hadn't told the whole world about it—about what he did. In those stupid cartoons of hers."

Bob Jernigan had already assured me Scarlett's cartoons had had nothing to do with either her father's suicide or her sister's divorce. Clearly, Carolyn was unable to acknowledge the responsibility she bore for both of those sad events.

I said, "I think you misplaced this," and worked her left foot back into her shoe. "Come on, Carolyn. Let's get you cleaned up."

With effort, I helped her stand. She took one step and groaned, clamping a hand over her mouth. Then it was a mad dash next door to the bathroom, where that lovely pinot noir she'd guzzled made its encore. Thankfully, it all ended up where it was meant to while I did the classic buddy move and held her hair back.

I found some mouthwash and an actual terry washcloth in a cupboard, and within minutes she was cleaned up and looking fairly presentable. She followed me back into the library, where she discarded her used tissues while I got rid of the wine bottle.

"Do you feel up to going back downstairs?" I asked.

"You go." She sat heavily on the settee. "I need a few minutes."

Clearly it had done her good to get the alcohol out of her system, though she was still pale and woozy.

I pulled out my phone and texted the padre, asking if everything was under control and could they spare me for a little longer. No problem, he answered, and promised to let me know if that changed.

I took a seat next to Carolyn, and said, "I've been meaning to ask what you intend to do with Scarlett's ashes."

It seemed an effort for her even to shrug. "They're on a shelf in my coat closet."

"Well, if you're uncertain, I can give you some ideas," I said. "When you're ready."

She looked at me then, as if really noticing me for the first time. Her brown eyes were bloodshot, and she looked younger after crying off her eye makeup. Her chin wobbled. In a small voice, she said, "I should've done it."

"Should've done what, Carolyn?"

"I should've given her a green burial," she said, "like she wanted. It was… It was important to her. She mentioned it last winter after Dad died. She told me she didn't want to be buried next to our parents when her time came, she wanted this other thing, this 'green' thing. And I just—" her breath caught on a sob "—couldn't be bothered. After everything… I owed her that at least."

I squeezed her hand and hauled out the tissues again. "It's not too late to give Scarlett what she wanted."

"It *is* too late," she insisted. "I had her cremated."

"You can still give her a green burial, in a natural burial ground using a biodegradable urn for the ashes."

I watched her mull that over. "It's not what she—"

"I know," I said, "it's not exactly what she wanted, and I admit I didn't know Scarlett personally, but from what I've learned about her, I have a feeling she'd be fine with it."

These were not empty words. The Scarlett I'd come to know during the past two and a half weeks since her death would not have wanted her sister, whatever their differences, to suffer pangs of guilt over an impulsive decision made in the immediate aftermath of a sudden tragedy.

Carolyn nodded listlessly. "Okay." She took a deep breath and let it out. "Okay, let's do that."

"Good," I said. "Maybe we can get together tomorrow to go over your options."

She ran her hands over her hair, frowning when she realized how tangled it had gotten. "God, I'm a wreck," she said. "Is Hal still downstairs?"

"He was when I came up here."

She said, "He's going to take one look at me and run in the opposite direction."

That was the best thing that could happen to her. I wanted to tell her that. I wanted to tell her the creep wasn't worth it. She'd just heard him describe Scarlett as the love of his life, for heaven's sake. How could she still be hung up on him?

That's what I wanted to say, for all the good it would do.

Instead I dug into my pocket for a hair tie and gently turned Carolyn's head so I could finger-comb the long, dark-blonde strands. I smoothed the top and sides into a half-up ponytail. "There. Good as new."

She patted her head. "Thank you." She looked at me, then away. "For everything."

"No problem. How are you feeling?"

"I've been better." She stood, and I was relieved to see she she was steady on her feet, though still somewhat tipsy.

"Did you eat anything?" I asked. When she shook her head, I said, "We'll remedy that. Come on."

Back on the first floor, I noticed the gathering had thinned out as guests had begun to leave. Those who remained had all settled in the drawing room. Carolyn avoided meeting anyone's gaze as we passed through it. No doubt she was excruciatingly aware that all these people had witnessed her drunkenly staggering around a short while ago.

I nodded to Martin, who was sitting with Joel Devine, the two of them deep in conversation. Hal was leaning on the fireplace mantel and chatting up one of Scarlett's pretty young California cousins. Thankfully, Carolyn didn't notice him.

As we entered the dining room, she murmured, "I'm gonna go home."

"Have a bite to eat first. But not out here." Firmly I steered her past the buffet table. Nate had just finished refreshing the ice bucket. Seeing us heading for the door to the kitchen, he beat us there and held it open for us.

"Thanks, Nate," I said. "Would you bring a chair for Ms. Bailey?"

Maia looked up from the big steel kitchen island where she was uncorking a bottle of rioja for another batch of sangria.

She had a firm rule: Underage workers were forbidden from handling alcoholic beverages.

The caterer greeted Carolyn with a warm smile and a bottle of cold water from the fridge. "You know, I've been so busy, I haven't had a bite to eat. Thought I'd slap some turkey on a baguette. Will you two join me?"

I could've kissed her. It was precisely what Carolyn needed in her current state, something simple and bland to replace the wine she'd just jettisoned. A better choice than the fancy sandwiches we were serving the guests, which were slathered with a variety of strongly flavored spreads. Think horseradish mustard and garlic aioli, for starters.

Carolyn looked like she still wanted to run home (perhaps to open another bottle of wine), so I said, "That sounds perfect, Maia. I haven't eaten either. You're busy with the sangria. Just point me toward the baguettes."

Nate came in with one of the giltwood chairs, which he set in an out-of-the-way corner. Carolyn gratefully sank into it. Seeing me slap a baguette onto a cutting board, he said, "Can I do that for you?"

"Thanks, Nate, I've got this. Do you happen to know where Mr. Jernigan is?"

"I saw him having a smoke out on the veranda. Would you like me to, uh…?" His gaze flicked to Carolyn.

I nodded. "If you could ask him to join us."

Two minutes later, Bob entered the kitchen and made a beeline for Carolyn. "Hey," he said gently, stroking her back. "How are you feeling, hon?"

She raised sad, damp eyes to him. "I made a complete ass of myself, Bob. I can never face those people again."

"Nonsense." His signature calm smile was firmly in place.

"You had a little wine, that's all. You're allowed, under the circumstances. And if anyone thinks differently, to hell with them."

I could see she found his words reassuring, though a worried frown still marred her brow.

He said, "Of course, if you tear off your clothes and dance naked on the dining table—again—people might start to talk."

She gave a surprised little chuckle and playfully slapped his arm. "I'll try to control myself."

I caught Bob's eye and sent him a silent thank-you.

"When you're done eating," he told Carolyn, "come out and find April and me. She hasn't had a chance to talk with you all day." I suspected he'd be sticking close to Scarlett's sister for the duration of the reception.

Carolyn managed to put down—and keep down—a good part of her sandwich. She was still eating when I left the kitchen. I found Bob and his fiancée, April, in the parlor, perched on the window seat abutting the bay window at the front of the house. They both held glasses of white wine. There was no one else in the room at the moment.

"Do you mind if I join you for a bit?" I asked.

"Please." Bob started to rise and offer me his seat.

"No, stay there." I moved a chair closer and sat facing them.

He said, "I wish I'd known Carolyn was… Shall we be polite and call it self-medicating?"

April said, "I feel so bad for her. I didn't realize until today how hard she's taking her sister's passing. She must've been keeping it all inside."

April Urban was a strikingly beautiful woman, around thirty, with large, gray-green eyes and glossy auburn hair, pulled back now in a simple, sophisticated updo. She wore an elegant dress in slate-blue wool with an asymmetrical neckline. Her jewelry was understated with the exception of the pear-shaped sparkler on her left ring finger. That thing must've weighed at least five carats.

I'd met April earlier when we were setting up for the memorial service, and had been surprised when she'd rolled up her sleeves to give us a hand moving chairs and decorating.

She said, "This place is so lovely, Jane. And it's an important piece of Crystal Harbor's history, which I think Scarlett would have appreciated."

"I hope so," I said. "I've always loved this old building. My friends know that, which is why they held my surprise fortieth birthday party here last spring."

The real birthday surprise had come when Martin and I had retreated to the attic for a quiet conversation. I won't tell you what we found up there, because you might be, you know, eating.

"My parents are looking for a venue for our engagement party," April said. "I'd suggest they hold it right here, but I'm afraid there's not enough room. They're anticipating about two hundred guests."

"You're right," I said. "No way could this place hold that many. There's always the Crystal Harbor Country Club. Are they members?"

April nodded. "I have a feeling that's what they'll choose. Less character, but it's the practical solution."

"We bought a house," Bob told me. "A beautiful six-bedroom Georgian a few doors down from April's parents on Bristol Road."

"Really!" I pasted on a surprised smile, as if Hal hadn't

already mentioned it to me. "That's wonderful."

"Well," April said, "we haven't actually *bought* it yet, but we should close well before the wedding."

I turned to Bob. "Which I think you mentioned is planned for next summer?"

"July eighteenth," he said. "In Galway."

It took me a moment. "Oh! You're getting married in Ireland."

April squeezed her fiancé's hand. "In an eight-hundred-year-old castle. Can you imagine anything more romantic?"

"No," I said. "No, I cannot."

This was not the first time I'd been smacked upside the head by the fact that, well, that the rich are different. The very concept of a destination wedding was exotic enough to me, but *Ireland?* In a damn *castle* that was built when the damn *Crusades* were still in full swing?

I mean, *damn!*

My expression did not reveal my thoughts, at least I hoped it didn't. I groped for something to say, and settled for, "It sounds incredible."

Bob said, "Our wedding planner has her work cut out for her, coordinating it all."

"She has a good team," April said. "I have faith it'll all come off without a hitch."

Faith was all well and good, but it could only take you so far without Mommy and Daddy's money to back it up.

"So, April," I said, "what do you do when you're not planning the perfect fairy-tale wedding?"

"I'm the associate curator of American Painting and Sculpture at the Met," she said.

My eyebrows shot up. "Well! I'm impressed." I'd spent

countless hours wandering around The Metropolitan Museum of Art in Manhattan, one of the finest art museums on the planet. "So since you're the expert, I have to ask, what do you think of Scarlett's artwork?"

April was suddenly animated. "Her cartoons are absolutely wonderful. Not just the artistic execution, but how she used that talent to tell a story, to comment on modern society. It makes you wonder what she could've accomplished if..." She shook her head sadly.

I said, "Her work wasn't restricted to cartoons. She was proficient with various media." Which I'd discovered once I'd had time to go through some of the art portfolios the padre and I had hauled back to my house. "For example," I continued, "there's this exquisite pen-and-ink drawing she did of one of her neighbors, this older gentleman she was friendly with."

This seemed to surprise Bob. "I don't recall seeing anything like that when I was looking through her artwork."

He was referring to that day when he'd shown up just as Martin and I started going through Scarlett's possessions. He'd asked if he could give himself a little tour, a stroll through what I would always think of as her cabinet of curiosities. I'd assumed he'd give the place a quick and casual perusal and be on his way.

Instead, Bob had lingered over every quirky item, clearly charmed and intrigued by it all. His curiosity had him exploring every shelf and closet, opening every drawer and cabinet. I'd had no problem with it since Martin had already packed up anything sensitive, such as bank statements and medical records.

"I thought I saw everything," he said. "How did I miss this portrait?"

"We'd already packed up some stuff before you got there," I said offhandedly. "It must've been in one of those boxes."

His brow started to crease into a frown—for the briefest moment, before his normal pleasant expression reasserted itself. "That must be it," he said.

As you know, the portrait had not been in any of the boxes. It had been pasted in Nolan's scrapbook, which I concealed in my duffel along with the Winner's Circle notebook, simply to avoid awkward questions. I hadn't even known that particular drawing existed until I looked through the scrapbook several days later. And why did Bob even care?

To distract him, I said, "You know, you actually knew this man—the subject of the portrait. I mean, besides the fact he was your neighbor. Nolan Whitehouse. He lived one floor down in Two-K, right next to Carolyn. You must've run into him at some point."

"Yes, of course," he said. "We saw each other in passing, but we never spoke. Carolyn told me Scarlett used to be a sort of caregiver to him. Admirable, though I don't know where she found the patience."

"Why do you say that?" I asked.

"The man was difficult to get along with," Bob said. "Everyone in the building seemed in agreement about that. And about the fact that he was almost certainly faking whatever disability he'd claimed. Cheating the system."

April spoke up. "I know that's what Carolyn thinks, but how can any of us really know such a thing? There are all kinds of disabilities that would preclude someone from working, and they aren't all obvious to the casual observer. And as for cheating the system, isn't this the same system he was paying into while he was employed?"

"You have a good heart, darling," Bob said. "I know you hate to think ill of anyone, but just ask Carolyn about the man. She had a few run-ins with him. There's a reason she considered him a bad influence on Scarlett."

"Carolyn did say that, yes," April said flatly. "She also called him 'a waste of space' and threatened to report him to the authorities."

Bob said, "Well, if he *was* faking his disability—"

"The poor man is in his grave," she snapped, "and people are still gossiping about him."

A muscle twitched in Bob's cheek, his only outward response to being called a gossip. He patted her hand. "You're right, of course, darling. Poor Nolan deserves to rest in peace." He turned to me then. "I'm curious, Jane. What did you mean when you said I knew Nolan apart from us being neighbors?"

"Um, did I say that?"

"You said, 'You actually knew this man, besides the fact he was your neighbor.'"

It was easy to forget that genial Bob Jernigan was a high-octane lawyer until you found yourself squirming under his questioning. "Well, I just meant, you know, since the two of you went to Columbia at the same time. Graduated the same year."

His expression was one of pleasant curiosity, so why did my mouth go dry? He said, "I don't recall mentioning that."

"No, um... I came across his invitation to Columbia's forty-year reunion dinner," I said, and quickly added, "It was in one of those boxes."

"The boxes you packed before I got there." His eyebrows rose ever so slightly.

My head bobbed up and down. "Right."

Yeah, more lying. I know I'm lousy at it. You don't need to rub it in.

"Sadly," Bob said, "Nolan passed away the day before that dinner. He'd been planning to attend, though I don't doubt he'd have felt out of his element."

"How do you know that?" I asked.

"I just mean," Bob said, "since he'd had, shall we say, reversals and was no longer in the same socioeconomic—"

"No, I mean how did you know he was planning to attend?" I asked. "Since you just said the two of you never spoke."

Bob seemed to be groping for a response, until April said, "Well, they announced it at the dinner. His place card was the only one left unclaimed. The head of the planning committee said some lovely things about Nolan, about his time at Columbia and his years as a chemical engineer. It made me wish I'd made more of an effort to get to know him."

Bob shook his head, chortling at his own forgetfulness. "Yes, of course. That's how I knew he was planning to be there. They honored him at the dinner."

Something behind me snagged April's attention, turning her warm expression to ice.

I looked over my shoulder and saw Hal Kazarian saunter into the room, with a bottle of beer. "Who got honored at a dinner?" he asked. "What are we talking about? Something juicy, I hope."

Since neither of the others seemed inclined to answer, I said, "Nolan Whitehouse."

He gave a dismissive snort as he pulled up a chair next to mine. "Why are you wasting your breath on that old freak?"

April said, "I'd have thought you'd cease the childish

name-calling now that the man is dead."

"Since we're talking about the son of a bitch that stole my girlfriend," Hal said, "I get to call him whatever I like."

Oh, here we go, I thought.

"If you really believe Scarlett was sleeping with Nolan," she said, "then you're delusional."

"Is *Caro* delusional?" he said. "Because she's the one that clued me in to what was going on."

April stared Hal down. "So you're essentially admitting that Scarlett broke up with you because she derived more—how to put it delicately?—*satisfaction* from 'that old freak' than from you."

Bob feigned interest in the painting over the mantel as he chewed back a grin. I covered a fake cough with my hand.

"Yeah," Hal said, then, "What? No, that's not what I said. I never even inferred it."

"Well, that seems to be what you're *implying*," April said, correcting his word usage. "That the breakup had everything to do with Nolan Whitehouse and his role as Scarlett's lover, and nothing whatsoever to do with the individual who reported this supposed affair to you. Did you never question her motive?"

It took Hal a few moments to catch her drift. When it was well and truly caught, he turned an unbecoming shade of fuchsia. "You mean Caro? What are you infer—implying?" He glanced behind him to ensure our conversation was private. "You think Caro made it all up? About Scarlett and Nolan? Just to get with me?"

"Just to steal something of value to her sister," April clarified, "though I can see how you might prefer your interpretation over mine."

It would seem April was not Carolyn's biggest fan, despite

the fact that her fiancé was a kind of father figure to his late friend's daughter.

Bob said, "I don't think this is the appropriate setting to get into—"

"I know why you're doing this, April," Hal said. "You can't stand that Margaret and me are together."

Where had I heard that name recently? Ah yes. Hal had mentioned her during our so-called date.

Bob turned to me. "Margaret is April's best friend. They grew up together. She was visiting us a few weeks ago and we ran into Hal. I guess you could say the two of them hit it off."

I caught April's eye, and we shared a brief, silent convo that went something like this:

Jane: I assume you've informed your friend Margaret that her new boyfriend is a lying, cheating creep.

April: Oh, but he's so handsome. And charming. How could his love be anything but pure?

The hint of an eye-roll drove home her message. This Margaret was one of those dewy-eyed young women who was allergic to sensible advice, thus forcing her to learn important life lessons the hard way.

"We're going to live together," Hal said. "As soon as I cash my relocation check, I'm moving in with Margaret. She has this really nice house, right here in Crystal Harbor."

"Will you be paying her rent?" I asked, though I was certain I knew the answer.

"Nope," he said. "She won't hear of it."

"Splitting utility bills?" I persisted. "Real estate taxes? Anything?"

He shook his head. "Margaret loves me. She doesn't want me to worry about all that mundane stuff."

So he'd snagged himself a rich one. Rich and naïve.

"I know you're planning to pocket the relocation money," I said, "and use it for a new car or whatever, but what if the Americana *doesn't* get demolished? There goes your windfall."

"The only way that building could keep standing," he said, "is if someone outbids the developer that's planning to tear it down. At this point the Devines know that's never going to happen."

Some little devil made me say, "I wouldn't be so sure, Hal. Some white knight might appear and make a fair offer for the place. Or," I added, recalling what Dom had told me earlier, "a *group* of white knights. Some sort of consortium could band together to save the Americana."

April said, "That's a wonderful idea. Do you think it could work?"

"It's been tried." Hal's features hardened in anger. "Never made it past the idea phase."

So Hal had known about Scarlett's plan to save the Americana. As for why her ambitious consortium strategy "never made it past the idea phase," the answer was simple: The plan had died with her. At least that's what he no doubt assumed. I wondered how he'd react if he knew that Dom had spent the past couple of weeks trying, in vain, to drum up interest in it.

During our small-*d* date a week earlier, I'd suggested that Hal might want to put his relocation allowance toward housing. Crazy idea, I know. *I have options*, he'd said. *Trust me, I'm going to come out on top. As long as nothing happens to tank that sale.*

His "options" had turned out to be a gullible rich woman with a weakness for good-looking scoundrels. This guy obviously considered himself a world-class player.

I said to Hal, "I'm not even going to ask whether Carolyn knows about Margaret. But have you told Margaret about Carolyn?"

He gave a dismissive wave as Bob mumbled, "Uh, Jane—" April silenced her fiancé with a gentle touch, her gaze fixed on something behind me.

I turned and saw Carolyn halt in the middle of the room as Hal announced, "Caro's not important. Why muddy the waters? Anyway, Margaret's the real deal. We're in love."

The three of us remained mute for long, agonizing seconds, staring at Carolyn's pale, shocked face. Hal looked from Bob to April to me, his expression evolving from smug to alarmed as he began to figure it out. Abruptly he leapt up and faced Carolyn, overturning his chair in the process.

My muscles tensed as I unconsciously prepared to intercede. I could picture Carolyn launching herself at Hal, physically attacking him for being, well, a player.

Instead she simply stood there, her expression a mixture of pain, betrayal, and disgust as she stared at her lover.

Hal took a step toward her. His smile just then was so patently manipulative, I didn't know whether to hate him or pity him. "Caro, babe—"

"Don't." That single word was more of a growl, and it stopped Hal in his tracks.

He said, "I need to expl—"

"Shut up." She was trembling. "You used me."

He shoved his fingers through his hair. "We never made promises, Caro. We were both free to—"

"Liar. You told me I was the one. And I believed you. Even when you kept crawling back to Scarlett, the 'love of your life.' Begging her to take you back."

"I never—"

"He showed me," she said. "Nolan. Showed me picture after picture of you groveling at her door. Lurking in the fourth-floor hallway. Accosting her whenever she left her apartment. Making a fool of yourself over her. I shut him out. I didn't want to believe it. I made up stories in my mind to explain your pathetic actions."

Hal pulled himself up. "*I'm* pathetic? That's a laugh. Have you looked in the mirror lately?"

Bob stood. "Carolyn, honey, he's not worth what you're putting yourself through. Let me take you home."

Hal took a menacing step toward Carolyn, and suddenly we were all on our feet.

"You lied about Scarlett and Nolan," Hal accused, stabbing his finger toward her. "You knew damn well she wasn't sleeping with him. You made up all that crap just to pry me away from her. And you made sure she found out about us. I thought it was just coincidence when she caught us in the laundry room, but you knew she'd walk in on us, didn't you? *I* used *you*? Try again, babe. It was the other way around."

I'd already deduced that Carolyn had been jealous of her sister's bond with their late father. Now I wondered if that jealousy might've been what prompted her to steal Scarlett's boyfriend.

I gave Carolyn credit. She managed to hold the tears at bay, though the effort clearly cost her. She hugged herself, trembling harder, and appeared on the verge of collapse.

April rushed forward and wrapped her arms around the other woman. "We're done here," she announced, in a tone that brooked no argument. "Come on, Carolyn, we're taking you home."

12

Mopping the Floor with Nolan

THE NEXT AFTERNOON, Sexy Beast and I found ourselves headed for the stairwell in the Americana's second-floor hallway. We'd just left Carolyn's apartment, where I'd helped her make arrangements to inter Scarlett's ashes in a green cemetery. As you can probably guess, we'd both studiously avoided mentioning Hal or any of the drama that had transpired the day before.

As for SB, he'd been a welcome guest in Carolyn's home. She'd heard him bark in the background during our phone call that morning and had asked to meet him. It turned out she was thinking of getting a small dog and wanted to see if a poodle would be right for her. They'd taken to each other right away, and I wouldn't be surprised if she'd started researching poodle breeders as soon as we left. I did suggest she visit the local animal shelter first, but didn't have much hope that she'd heed my advice.

I figured we didn't need the elevator to go down just one flight, and taking the stairs meant I could pretend I was getting a little exercise. Sexy Beast peeked over of the top of his straw bucket tote as I pulled open the door to the stairwell. The sound of a buffalo stampede greeted us, and I watched as four teenagers, three boys and a girl, pounded past us up the stairs.

One of the boys, a tall, beefy fellow, glanced our way as he took the steps two at a time. His bored expression morphed into delight when he noticed SB. He said, "Hey there, little dude," without slowing down.

I waited long enough to hear them make it all the way to Four, the top floor. The stairwell door up there clanged shut, and something told me they had one more set of stairs to climb.

I debated with myself: Proceed to the ground floor and out of the building as I'd originally intended, or follow the teens up to the roof? The instant I'd seen them, I'd recognized the kids I'd come to think of as the resident slackers, the subject of so many of Nolan's photographs. I had to admit I was slightly apprehensive about confronting them.

Now, where did that *confronting* come from? I just wanted to chat, right? See if I could clear a few things up. Nothing to be apprehensive about.

"What do you say, SB? You want to go visit the roof again?" His enthusiastic yip settled the matter, though I suspected he was hoping "roof" was another word for Vienna sausage.

By the time we made it up two flights to the fourth floor, I was regretting not having taken the elevator. Yeah, I know, it wouldn't kill me to work a little cardio into my busy daily routine. I might be able to find a few minutes in between elevenses and shoveling Cherry Garcia into my maw during *Law & Order* marathons.

When I got to the locked door that led to the roof, I set down SB's tote, which he took as his cue to hop out. I clipped the leash onto his harness, instructed him to stay, and retrieved my wallet from a zippered compartment inside the tote.

Martin had taught me some useful tricks. Oh, there you go again, you and your dirty mind. It just so happens this particular trick involved a credit card and a run-of-the-mill doorknob lock. If the Devines were serious about keeping residents off the roof, they should've installed a deadbolt.

It took me a few tries, slipping the card between the door and jamb, and flexing it just so, but eventually my efforts were rewarded. It was a good news, bad news thing, because the instant the door swung open, Sexy Beast ran up the steps and past the open door at the top, which had been propped open with a brick.

So much for my precious pet obeying the most basic of canine commands. Clearly he needed a brush-up on his training, but in the meantime I pictured the balusters of the roof railing, which were spaced far enough apart for a seven-pound poodle to easily squeeze through. I raced after him, hollering, "SB! Come!"

Once on the roof, I looked frantically around and spied Sexy Beast sprinting across the gravel toward the teens, who'd taken up position near the four-foot-high brick parapet wall that wrapped around the far end.

The big guy said, "Where ya goin', little dude?" He grabbed the leash SB had been trailing, then squatted to give him scritches while the little dog adopted the canine play stance: chest down, rump high.

In contrast to the damp chill and gloomy gray cloud cover that had marked my first visit to that roof a week earlier, it was a brilliantly sunny afternoon, with a vividly blue sky punctuated by a few cottony clouds. The day was unseasonably mild for late November, and I was able to get away with a light fleece jacket.

I made my way across the roof to the kids, who greeted my cheerful smile with flat, suspicious stares. "Thanks," I said, as the boy rose and handed me the leash. "This little troublemaker has a mind of his own. I spend half my day running after him."

The boy shoved his hands into the pockets of his green, army-style jacket. He was about six foot three, broad-shouldered, with curly, light-brown hair.

Another boy, who looked Latino, avoided acknowledging me by playing with his phone. The third boy, pale with carroty red hair, was sitting on the gravel, leaning against the wall and smoking. Good guess, but it was an actual cigarette, the kind with tobacco and a filter. The only girl in the group appeared to be South Asian. As the breeze picked up her long, dark hair, she twisted the strands and tucked them into the collar of her pink, quilted jacket.

It was clear they were all waiting for me to leave.

"My name's Jane," I said. "Jane Delaney."

The kids looked at each other as if to say, *Is she still here?*

I pointed to my dog, now energetically sniffing their sneakers. "This is Sexy Beast."

All four kids stared at SB, as if trying to figure that one out.

My friendly, fluffy little poodle could usually be counted on to break the ice. This was one tough crowd. Time to get their attention.

I said, "Nolan Whitehouse sure took a lot of pictures of you guys."

That did the trick. They weren't bored now.

The girl said, "You know Nolan? Knew," she corrected herself. She had a faint Indian accent. I suspected she'd immigrated with her family when she was very young.

"No," I said, "but I'm in possession of some of his photos. It's a long story." Okay, not so long, but I wasn't prepared to share it at that juncture.

The redheaded boy ground out his cigarette on the brick wall. Sexy Beast watched the butt sail over the wall, then made himself comfortable on the boy's lap while I handed over the leash. The kid eyed me while stroking the little dog. "I've seen you around the building," he said. "They call you the Death Something."

"Death Diva," I said. "I didn't choose the nickname, but I can't deny it fits." I followed this up with a brief description of what I do, including a few examples of some of my more bizarre and gruesome assignments. I was rewarded with wide eyes and incredulous snickers.

I knew I was making progress when the Latino kid put away his phone. "People really pay you to do that stuff?" he asked.

"Well, I'm not running a charity." Okay, the truth is, I do a lot of work gratis for those in need and to support various charities, but my aim here was simply to get these kids talking, not to launch into a detailed discussion of the Death Diva business model.

"How'd you get started in it?" he asked.

"By pet-sitting if you can believe it," I said, "back when I was in high school. Which led to my best client hiring me to deliver floral arrangements to the local pet cemetery, and the rest is history. I built my business through referrals."

The big kid spoke up. "I do a little of that. Pet-sitting, I mean, not the cemetery thing. And dog walking. I mean, just for my neighbors across the street for now. They have these two huskies. Those guys are a riot, the way they kind of talk back to you." He emulated the huskies' comical vocalizations.

The girl said, "God, that sounds so much better than babysitting. I can't *stand* watching people's kids. Rich kids especially. Entitled little delinquents."

"I hated it, too, when I was your age." I turned back to the boy. "So you enjoy pet-sitting?"

"I love it. My family has three dogs, two cats, a guinea pig, and a cockatoo, and I'm the one that mainly takes care of them. I love animals."

"The reason I ask," I said, "is that we recently adopted a second dog—a big girl named Layla, part Great Dane—and at this point we could use someone reliable to take up the slack when my boyfriend and I are both away from home. You interested?"

Grinning, the girl slapped him on the back. "Go for it, Elliott."

"Hell yeah, I'm interested!" he said. "The thing is, I have school weekdays, plus there's always something after school—basketball practice and Mathletes and stuff."

"We can work around your schedule." I handed him one of my business cards with my contact info. "Why don't you give me your number. We can decide on a time for you to swing by and meet Layla. I'll pay you for that initial visit, of course." I took out my phone. "What's your last name, Elliott?"

"Epstein." He rattled off his phone number and email address, and I entered them in my contacts list.

"Do you know Kari Faso?" I asked. "She volunteers at the local animal shelter. That's something else you might consider."

The girl said, "I know Kari. She's in my AP psych class."

Basketball? Mathletes? College-level advanced-placement courses? Resident slackers indeed. More like the resident nerds, though scholar-athlete might be a more apt description of Elliott.

"I'm Jasmine Reddy," the girl said, and pointed to the Latino boy. "That's Richie Esparza." Richie offered a little nod.

The redheaded boy wagged one of SB's legs in lieu of a wave. "Liam Ormond. If you need an assistant for that gooey corpse stuff, I'm your man."

"It sounds more exciting than it is, but I'll keep you in mind, Liam. You all live in the building?" I asked, and they nodded.

Jasmine said, "So how'd you get ahold of Nolan's pictures of us? I know you didn't clean out his apartment. Scarlett did that."

Richie grimaced. "And my mom thinks *my* room's a mess. How can someone live like that?"

"Scarlett did her best with his place," Elliott said, "but it was a losing battle."

I said, "Looked like you guys did what you could for him, too."

I knew these four kids had been in Nolan's apartment because of some of the pictures he'd taken. Not the earlier ones where the teens were sneering at him and giving him the finger. Those had been taken in the building's public areas and right here on the roof.

The later pictures, the ones glued onto the final pages of the scrapbook, showed the interior of Nolan's apartment: Jasmine sitting at his kitchen table, saying something as she looked up at him from a laptop computer. Elliott and Richie moving a dilapidated sofa. Liam hauling a couple of bulging garbage bags out of the apartment. Richie and Scarlett standing at the stove, cooking up a big batch of something in a pot.

"How did all that come about?" I asked the group. "You helping Nolan. I assume Scarlett had something to do with it."

Jasmine nodded. "She mostly kept to herself. That's just the way she was. But then I find out she's the artist that does those amazing cartoons, and I'm, like, no way! She lives in my building? So then I go all fangirl on her, and there's no way she can shake me." She laughed.

"Jasmine introduced Scarlett to the rest of us," Richie said, "and she told us about Nolan, all about, you know, his whole life and how he ended up the way he was, and… I don't know, I guess we started to feel kind of bad for him."

"It began with her asking me to teach him how to do email and look stuff up online," Jasmine said. "He had this laptop Scarlett dug out of some rich fool's garbage bin, can you imagine? It wasn't even that old. Not enough juice for gaming, but adequate for helping him connect with the world."

"And then the rest of us got sucked into Project Nolan," Liam said, with a lopsided grin. "Still don't know how Scarlett managed that. I wrote an essay about him for English language and comp," he added, naming another advanced-placement course. "He was an interesting guy, once you got to know him. Had some really cool stories."

Richie smiled. "When Nolan found out I was in the chess club at school, he brought out his set and made me play every time I was over there. He was pretty good, too."

"Still," Jasmine said, "there's no denying the guy had issues. Not serious mental illness, at least I don't think so, but paranoid for sure. And by that I don't mean generally fearful, the way ignorant people use the term. I suspect Nolan suffered from clinical paranoia."

"As in everyone's out to get him?" I asked, recalling that Jasmine took advanced-placement psychology.

Liam said, "You should've seen his apartment. It was practically wallpapered in these notes to himself, warnings about—this is my favorite one—how the government is spying on him with a tiny drone that looks like a housefly. Sometimes he sees two or three of these drones at the same time."

"He thought the checkout girl at the supermarket was trying to steal his identity," Richie said. And when one of his lightbulbs died, he convinced himself that the super was sneaking in to steal his working bulbs and replace them with duds."

"It wasn't just notes to himself," Jasmine said. "He also tacked up stuff he got in the mail or picked up during his walks—clothing catalogs, menus from local restaurants, political tracts, whatever. He scrawled notes all over them, warnings to himself to be on the lookout. He was convinced everyone was up to no good."

I recalled Joanie Devine describing Nolan as suspicious and prone to baseless accusations.

"I know where you found those pictures Nolan took of us," Elliott said. "You're the one that cleaned out Scarlett's apartment. I saw you and your boyfriend carrying boxes out of it. She must've kept some of his stuff when she went through his place."

"That's right," I said. Let them imagine a shoebox filled with Polaroid snapshots. I wasn't ready to talk about the scrapbook. I looked at each of the kids in turn. "So I'm curious. What was your first reaction when you found out Nolan died?"

"I was real sad," Richie said. "The guy had such a hard life, and then to go like that, slipping on a wet floor. So pointless."

"Scarlett found him." Jasmine stared off toward the nearby woods with their bare trees. "That had to be rough."

"It didn't make sense to me," Liam said.

"Why not?" I asked.

"Nolan never washed his floors the whole time he lived there. Since way before we were born. Scarlett told me the first time she saw his kitchen floor, it was so black with grime, she spent hours on her hands and knees just getting down to the linoleum. After that, she made sure it stayed clean."

"I actually mopped it a couple of days before he died," Elliott said. "So yeah, it doesn't make sense, him suddenly deciding to clean his kitchen floor for, like, the first time ever."

I said, "Well, what if he, I don't know, spilled a whole pot of soup or something? Wouldn't he have gotten the mop out?"

The kids all wore knowing smiles. Jasmine said, "That soup would've stayed right where it was until the next time Scarlett came over."

"She was there just about every day," Richie said.

"Did Nolan have any other visitors that you know of?" I asked.

He shook his head. "No, no one. Scarlett said he didn't have any family, at least none that wanted anything to do with him."

Elliott and Liam exchanged a look. I waited, and finally Elliott said, "We heard something, Liam and me. We were passing Nolan's apartment and we heard all this yelling. I don't know if it means anything."

"Who was yelling?" I asked.

"Just Nolan," Liam said. "We didn't hear anyone else."

Elliott said, "We thought maybe he was alone and, you know, just kind of acting crazy like he sometimes did."

"What did you hear?" I asked. "What was he saying?"

"Stuff like 'You think you're so special,'" Liam said.

"Were those his exact words?"

The boys looked at each other as if to verify their recollection. They nodded.

Liam said, "And clear as anything, he says, 'You think *I'm* a waste of space? Wait till she finds out about you.'"

"Yeah, that's right," Elliott said. "I never heard him sound like that before. So angry, I mean."

"Is it possible he was talking to Scarlett?" I asked. "You said she was there almost every day."

They shook their heads in unison. "No way," Liam said. "He'd never talk to her like that. He adored Scarlett. She was like a daughter to him."

A waste of space. The words triggered a memory. Where did I recently hear that phrase?

Then I remembered. Yesterday when I was talking with Bob and April during the reception. She mentioned that Carolyn had called Nolan a bad influence on her sister and a waste of space.

"When did you hear this?" I asked.

Liam looked troubled. "The day Nolan died. We pass his door every morning on our way to school. Elliott and me, we both live on Two, and we walk to the bus stop together. What day of the week was that?"

I dragged out my phone and opened the calendar app. "Let's see. He died on October third, which was a Friday."

"Then we had concert choir practice before school that day," Liam said. "Practice starts at seven. We catch the early bus at twenty till, so it must've been about six twenty-five, six-thirty that we heard him shouting."

"It's been bothering me for weeks," Elliott said. "Like, really? He slipped while mopping the floor? *Nolan?*"

"Did you mention your concerns to anyone?" I asked.

"My folks," he said. "They thought I was overreacting, 'cause I never knew someone that died before. But that's not it."

"No, I get it," I said. "The facts don't add up."

The boys nodded, clearly relieved that an adult finally agreed with them.

Jasmine said, "You're the Death Diva, right? If you bring this to the cops, they have to listen to you. You have a, you know, a track record."

"Scarlett already discussed it with a detective," I said. "There was no interest."

"They *know* about this?" Angry color stained her cheeks. "And they're not *doing* anything? That's so typical. If it was one of those rich bastards that live in those mansions, they'd sure as hell look into it."

I wished I could disagree. I knew Detectives Howie Werker and Cookie Kaplan were pros who cared deeply about solving crimes, but they were constrained by their workloads and the capricious decisions of the powers that be.

Sexy Beast abandoned Liam's lap, stretched, and decided to explore his surroundings. Liam rose with him and kept hold of the leash. SB made a beeline for the stairway bulkhead, the shedlike structure that covered the stairs and provided access to the roof via the door that the kids had propped open with a brick. Sure enough, my dog lifted his leg on the bulkhead. No one else seemed to care, so I decided not to let it bother me.

My priorities lay elsewhere at that moment.

Richie turned to me. "That's why you asked how we felt when Nolan died. 'Cause you think it was no accident."

"I'm not jumping to any conclusions," I said. "I just think there are some unanswered questions that need to be addressed."

"What about Scarlett?" Jasmine asked.

I'd been waiting for one of them to make that leap. Um, so to speak. "What about her?" I said.

"Oh, come on," she said. "Two accidental deaths a month apart? In the same building? And one of them totally bizarre?"

I shrugged. "Coincidences happen. Bizarre accidents, too."

Elliott crossed to the section of railing that had been replaced, marking the spot where their friend Scarlett had fallen. I could tell it wasn't the first time he'd examined the connection points where the new piece had been installed. Joanie Devine had said the workmen couldn't tell whether the railing had been tampered with. It was too late for police forensics to get involved. The section that had given way under Scarlett's insubstantial weight was long gone.

He said, "We sometimes hang out right here. You can watch all the activity below, everyone coming and going." He shoved his hands into his pockets and strolled back to us.

Liam rejoined the group, and now it was Jasmine's turn to pick up Sexy Beast and cuddle him. The kids looked at one another, silently debating something. As curious as I was, I knew better than to try to hurry the process along.

Finally Richie said, "So anything we say to you is, like, confidential, right? Like client privilege or something."

Still cradling SB, Jasmine lightly slapped the back of Richie's head, causing the little dog to bark happily at this fun new game. "She's not a lawyer, idiot. And we're not her clients. Wait." She turned to me. "*Are* you a lawyer? I mean, in addition to the Death Diva thing?"

"Nope," I said. "I'm just a regular person with a ghoulish career."

"I saw this thing on TV," Elliott said, "where a lawyer asks someone for a dollar, and then it's like the guy is officially his client and anything he says is confidential. Think that'd work here?"

"She's not a lawyer!" Jasmine cried. "I thought you guys were supposed to be smart."

"All right," I said, "let's cut to the chase. Are we talking about a crime one of more of you might have committed?"

"Naw." Liam grinned. "Unless you count certain recreational activities."

These kids wouldn't be of legal age for either a beer or a bong for a few more years. "I don't care about that stuff," I said.

"But our folks might," Elliott said, "if it got back to them."

Jasmine said, "My parents would freak."

"I'm not going to narc you out, okay?" I said. "I get the feeling you're holding something back. Something about Scarlett. Now, what is it?"

Richie said, "Okay, so the thing is, we sometimes come up here in the middle of the night."

"It's really restful up here when it's so dark and quiet," Elliott said. "Especially when there's no moon and it's just, like, stars everywhere."

"We bring camp chairs." Liam's smile was impish. "Sometimes we'll share a, you know, lemonade."

"You do this on school nights?" I asked, and received

shrugs in response. *Yeah, so?*

"If my parents knew I snuck out after they're asleep," Jasmine fretted, "they'd lock me in my room till I'm thirty."

For what it's worth, I didn't sense any romantic entanglement between Jasmine and any of the boys. These four appeared to be nothing more than a tight group of friends.

"So that's what has you worried?" I asked. "That your folks will find out you sneak up here in the middle of the night to schmooze and—" yeah, I made air quotes "—'drink lemonade'?"

"Well, when you say it like that," Liam said, and laughed.

"No, seriously," Jasmine said, "my parents—"

"I get it," I said. "And I'd like to promise they'll never find out, but if you know something, if you *saw* something, then you might have to report it. Scarlett deserves to have the truth come out, whatever it is."

"Oh, man…" Ricky groaned, and that's when I knew it was serious.

Jasmine, the one who seemingly had the most to lose in terms of parental outrage, faced me squarely and said, "There was someone else up here. The night before Scarlett… before she fell."

My breath caught. "Okay. Tell me about it."

"It happened real fast," Elliott said. "It was around three a.m. that Monday—"

"Just to be clear," I said, "are we talking three a.m. on Monday the third or Tuesday the fourth?" Scarlett had fallen to her death on the afternoon of the fourth.

Liam answered. "It was three in the morning on *Tuesday* when we came up here. The fourth."

"Oh, right," Elliott tapped his noggin. "It was after

midnight, so Tuesday. We came up the stairs and, well, we always prop the door open like that 'cause it's a little sticky. Otherwise you have to wrestle with it."

"We came over here with our folding chairs." Richie pointed to the gravel at his feet. "This is where we always like to hang, next to the wall. No one can see you from below when you're sitting."

"But then we heard this noise," Jasmine said. "We turned around and saw someone dash out from behind the hut there and run into the stairwell." She pointed to the stairway bulkhead and its open door.

"Did you see who it was?" I asked. "Can you describe the person?"

"Not really," Elliott said. "It was real dark and he was dressed all in black, and I think he was wearing one of those ski masks that covers most of your head."

The others nodded.

"'Him'?" I said. "So it was a man?"

"Coulda been a woman," Liam said. "Hard to say, 'cause he—she, whatever—disappeared in about a split second."

"They were a blur," Richie said. "I thought it was an animal at first, it was that hard to see."

Liam smirked. "How would an animal that size get up here?"

"You can't even say whether it was a dude or a woman," Richie said, "so get off my case."

"What about body size?" I asked. "Height?"

They thought about that. "Not fat," Jasmine said, and the rest agreed. "But tall."

"No way," Elliott said. "Were we looking at the same dude? He was *short*."

Liam said, "I got the feeling the guy was running bent over, like to make himself less visible." He demonstrated. "And he had kind of a hunchback, but then I figured it was a knapsack or something."

Richie said, "Maybe that's why I thought it was an animal at first. But then I heard him running down the stairs on two feet, and that settled it."

13

Beware of Seven-Pound Poodle

WE WERE DRIVING westbound on the Long Island Expressway when I got the call. It was a clear, cold night, almost nine p.m. on Friday, the day after Thanksgiving, and Martin was behind the wheel of his 1966 candy-apple-red Mustang convertible. We were headed to Manhattan for a late dinner and show at a comedy club when my cell buzzed. I'd already silenced it so the entire audience wouldn't be treated to the Latin-flavored tune "Tequila," my custom ringtone, in the middle of the comic's routine.

The caller's name was displayed on the screen. I frowned. What could Elliott be calling about? We'd been on the road less than half an hour, having just left the teen with our dogs for his first pet-sitting gig with us.

Elliott had come by the house a few days earlier to meet the newest furry family member and for all of us to get better acquainted. By the end of the visit, the padre and I felt confident the boy was both capable and trustworthy. Since we'd be gone just a few hours and he had no school the next day (and was happy to have somewhere quiet to do his homework away from his three rowdy younger siblings), we all agreed he'd stay at our house the whole evening instead of doing a standard drop-in visit.

I answered the phone. "Elliott? What—"

"There's been a break-in." He sounded out of breath. "Someone pried open the window in the—the—that room in the corner, next to the laundry room."

He was referring to my home office, originally intended by the architect as the maid's room.

"Oh my God." I put the phone on speaker as I demanded, somewhat louder than necessary, "Are you okay?"

"I'm fine," Elliott said. "So are SB and Layla."

Martin's voice was tight. "Tell me."

I said, "Someone broke in."

The padre immediately switched lanes so he could get off at the next exit and turn around. He said, "Elliott, listen to me. Are you still in the house? You need to get out, *now*."

"The guy's gone," Elliott said.

"How can you be sure?"

"'Cause Layla and I chased him into the woods behind your place. But he got over the wall before we could catch—"

"You *chased* him?" I screeched. Yeah, I screeched. It's been known to happen.

"I didn't stop to *think* about it," Elliott said. "It was just, like, instinct."

The padre repeated my question. "And you definitely didn't get hurt? The truth. This is not the time to suck it up."

"Seriously, dude, I'm fine," he said. "We all are. I called nine-one-one right away. I think I hear the sirens."

Which explained why Layla and Sexy Beast had started howling in the background.

Martin said, "We'll call the cops and tell them who you are and why you're at the house. Be prepared to show ID."

"Oh. Right," Elliott said. "I didn't think of that."

Neither did I, I must admit. Of the three of us, Martin was the only one with, shall we say, hands-on experience when it came to breaking and entering. That experience had ended for good when he was around Elliott's age, and he'd gone on to earn a degree at John Jay College of Criminal Justice, so his youthful transgressions were ancient history as far as I was concerned.

"Lemme go get leashes on these guys," Elliott said.

"Better yet," Martin said, "why don't you shut them in the laundry room until we get there."

Good idea, I thought. No sense distracting the responding officers with a big, excitable, unpredictable dog. "We'll be there as soon as we can," I said.

By the time we got back to the house, the joint was hopping. As soon as Detective Howie Werker had learned Jane Delaney's home had been broken into, he'd jumped in his car, raced over, and taken immediate charge of the investigation, such as it was.

In B&E terms, we were talking about the breaching of one window and the entering of one room. My home office is located at a back corner of the house, which sits on five acres, far from its nearest neighbors and concealed by trees and a six-foot-high flagstone wall. The burglar had forced the locked window with a crowbar and done it so quietly that Elliott, in the family room at the opposite end of the house, had heard nothing. It helped—from the intruder's perspective at least—that the door between my office and the hallway was always kept closed, a precaution to keep curious canines out of my stuff.

As it happened, said stuff currently included the six cartons we'd brought home from Scarlett's apartment, which themselves included some of the items she'd held on to while cleaning out Nolan's place.

Whether the burglar somehow knew those cartons were being stored in that room, or whether that window was simply the easiest spot to break into, I couldn't say. But as Howie and I stood in my office, surveying the scene, one thing was crystal-clear.

Howie said it first. "He was looking for something in those boxes."

"No. Ya think?" I said, as I took in the mountain of papers, drawings, and assorted objects that had been unceremoniously dumped out of the cartons. "Not being a seasoned detective myself, I'll have to take your word for it."

That "seasoned detective" thing was a running gag between us, one I don't think this particular seasoned detective appreciated at the moment, judging by his longsuffering sigh.

Howie was a tall, well-built Black man in his early forties. I'd known him forever, since his days as a young patrolman. I'd watched his hair and neat beard begin to go gray, which somehow made him even more appealing (as if guys didn't already have too many unfair advantages). So yeah, Howie was one tasty specimen, but he was also devoted to his wife of two decades, Lucille, so our friendship had never been compromised by any of that awkward *Oh my gosh, does he like me?* business.

I nodded toward the crime-scene tech, framed by the window as she stood outside, dusting for prints. She'd already finished inside. "What do you think?" I asked Howie. "Is she going to find anything?"

"Doubtful. The perp probably wore gloves, but we'll take

elimination prints from you three just in case."

"That was pretty bold, no?" I said. "Breaking into a house where someone was home—not to mention a very large dog."

"There are no warning signs on your property about the dog," Howie said. "Is she loud? Does she bark a lot?"

"Not really, unless she has a reason."

"Then the burglar might not have known about her," he said.

I didn't mention Sexy Beast's ability to deter a break-in because really, who would I be kidding?

By the time the padre and I had arrived back home, the dogs had been released from their laundry-room prison. They were currently hanging in the living room with Martin, Elliott, and two uniformed officers.

Howie produced his little notebook and a pen. "When did Elliott arrive?"

"Martin picked him up around eight-fifteen or so."

"Did he park in front or did they come in through the garage?"

"The garage," I said.

"And it was fully dark by then," he said. "So if someone was watching the house, he'd have seen Martin's car enter the garage, but he might not have noticed there was someone in the passenger seat. And then when you and Martin left—"

"He thought no one was home." My pulse picked up speed. "You're telling me this guy was hiding in the trees or something, waiting for us to leave."

"Did you tell anyone you were going out tonight?"

"Um, let me think," I said. "I know I mentioned it to my family yesterday at Thanksgiving."

"Where was that? Roy and Gillian's place?" Howie had

met my parents several times. "They still in Sandy Cove?"

I nodded. "Every time one of their friends moves to Florida, they talk about joining them, but I'll believe it when I see it. My aunt and uncle came up from North Carolina, and a couple of cousins. Martin was there, plus Stevie and Ben," I said, naming the padre's mother and her significant other. "How we all managed to squeeze in around Mom and Dad's dining-room table is one of those unfathomable mysteries. Like D.B. Cooper or Stonehenge."

"Who else might've known you'd be out of the house?" he asked.

"No one. Oh, wait. I was at Carolyn Bailey's apartment last Sunday—we were discussing the disposition of Scarlett's ashes—and it came up in conversation. We were talking about our plans for Thanksgiving weekend."

"What was she planning?" He knew Carolyn, having spoken with her after Scarlett's fatal accident.

"I think she said something about getting together with a couple of her old sorority sisters for dinner. Don't recall which day."

He looked up from his notebook. "Anyone else?"

I thought about it. "I don't think so."

He nodded toward the mess heaped on the carpet. "I don't suppose you can tell if anything's missing."

I was about to say no, but decided to look around the room, just to make sure. The daybed and overstuffed chair appeared undisturbed, as did my laptop, which lay closed on my desk, precisely where I'd left it. It was a small, pretty, antique desk, the kind that at one time had been called a lady's desk. I guess the idea was that ladies didn't write anything more important than the occasional billet-doux, for which a dainty desk was sufficient.

But something was wrong. When I realized what it was, I groaned. I might've said a bad word.

"Okay, let's have it," Howie said.

I stood over the desk, as if by staring hard enough I could make the items reappear. "There were two books here," I said.

"Books?" He frowned. "The burglar stole books?"

"Not *book* books," I said. "One of them was an old spiral-bound notebook, and the other was a scrapbook."

"I assume there was something special about these books?" he said.

"Yes." Realizing he'd be expecting more detail, I said, "Carolyn hired me to clean out her sister's apartment, and they came from there."

"So these books belonged to Scarlett," he said.

"Actually, no. They belonged to Nolan Whitehouse. Well, the scrapbook did for sure. Jury's still out on the notebook, but my money's on Nolan."

"Whitehouse," Howie said. "He's the guy that slipped and fell in his kitchen last month. And Scarlett found him."

I nodded. "She cleaned out his apartment." I gestured toward the clutter at our feet. "Some of this is his."

"What's so special about these things?" he asked. "The scrapbook and the notebook."

"That's what I was trying to figure out, frankly. I'd set them aside to study more closely. The scrapbook was pretty weird for the most part. Nolan had issues." I made a snap decision: The police needed to be brought up to speed. "But there's this one thing in it that's kind of disturbing. A note— 'Leave Scarlett alone or you'll be sorry.' I'd left the scrapbook open to that very page."

"I take it this note wasn't signed."

"No. And it's printed out, like someone typed it on a computer, so there are no handwriting clues."

Howie scowled. "You make me nervous when you start talking about clues."

The detective never liked it when I did a little, you know, detecting.

"Well, wouldn't you like to know who sent him that note?" I asked.

"The man's death was an accident, Jane. I know Scarlett didn't think so. She spoke with my partner about it," he said, meaning Cookie Kaplan. "Something about Nolan never washing his floors. Apparently Scarlett also mentioned some kind of mysterious clue. I'm telling you right now, a vaguely threatening note aimed at a guy who was as popular as herpes is not what I call a legitimate clue."

"I'd say that note was more than *vaguely* threatening," I said.

"Maybe someone thought the old crank was taking advantage of her." He raised a palm before I could respond. "Not *that* way, necessarily, but by letting her do all that work for him. I understand she functioned as a kind of caregiver. Doing the kinds of things family does for one another."

"He didn't have any family," I said. "Scarlett seemed to be the only person who cared what happened to him." At least until she got the four teens involved, toward the end.

Howie said, "I'm willing to bet you have a theory about who wrote that note."

"A couple of possibilities did kind of leap out at me."

"Let me guess," he said. "The sister. Carolyn. She seems like the type that could find fault in anything."

"Including her sister helping out a neighbor in need. Yeah, I could see her threatening him." I told Howie about the photos Nolan had taken of an enraged-looking Carolyn. "She thought he was scamming the disability system and that he was a bad influence on Scarlett. They had a few set-tos, according to Hal."

"Hal?"

"Hal Kazarian," I said. "He lives in the Americana. Third floor. He and Scarlett were an item for a while. She dumped him two months ago because he was getting it on with Carolyn."

"Lovely," Howie said, deadpan, as he jotted the ex-boyfriend's name in his notebook. For an experienced cop who'd seen as much as he had, this salacious detail didn't warrant even a flicker of surprise. "The guy gets around."

"Carolyn intentionally sabotaged her sister's relationship by convincing Hal that Scarlett was sleeping with Nolan. Which she wasn't," I hastened to add. "Hal only found out Carolyn made the whole thing up last week, after the memorial service. Until then, he'd had it in for Nolan. Trash-talked the guy even after he was dead."

"So you think Hal might've been the one who wrote the note," he said.

I shrugged. "That'd be my guess, him or Carolyn."

Of course, Hal wasn't the only one who'd insulted poor dead Nolan. Bob had shared some less-than-flattering observations last week after the memorial service. Still, I could think of no reason he'd have warned Nolan to stay away from Scarlett. Bob and Scarlett hadn't even gotten along, though he'd had the grace to express regret at not having done more to repair the rift.

"What about the other book?" he said. "You mentioned a spiral-bound notebook."

"That's even weirder than the scrapbook," I said, "because it's filled with all these columns of coded entries."

Now I had his attention. "Coded?"

"Gobbledygook. Meaningless combinations of numbers, letters, and all kinds of weird, invented symbols. Well, meaningless to me, but someone must know the code. Or maybe not. That notebook is so old, whoever wrote in it might be long gone."

Howie didn't respond, and I knew we were both thinking of Nolan Whitehouse.

Finally he said, "Anything else missing that you can tell?"

I shook my head as I gave the place another once-over. "I mean, my laptop's right there, but does he take that? No. He grabs these two strange things, the scrapbook and notebook, which are sitting right next to the laptop. So that was a clear choice. You see where I'm going with this?"

He tapped his pen on his little detective's notebook. "I'd like to know what else is in that scrapbook."

"I'll make a list of what I can remember," I said. "There were some photos, like the ones of Carolyn I mentioned. But the rest of it was just a lot of junk, for the most part. As for why the burglar snatched those particular items, I figure there are two possible explanations. Either they're really valuable to someone—"

"Or they're really dangerous to someone," Howie finished.

I studied his intense expression. "You're thinking it's that second thing. I can tell."

"So if the guy wants what's in the books," he said, "and the books are right out there in plain sight, why empty the cartons?"

"Just to be sure he didn't miss anything else?" I suggested. "He must've thought he had more time here than he did."

Elliott appeared in the doorway. "Uh, Detective? The officers said if it's okay with you, I can get going."

Howie put his hand on the boy's shoulder. "Just a couple of more questions if you don't mind, Elliott. Let's find a place to sit."

I followed them down the hall and through the kitchen into the breakfast room, where we took seats at the glass-topped table.

Howie flipped back several pages in his notebook. "I know you gave a statement to the officers, Elliott, but just bear with me. You were in the family room when the break-in occurred?"

Elliott nodded. "I was doing homework."

"Watching TV at the same time? Listening to music?"

"No. I was studying for a history test. I concentrate better when it's quiet."

"Where were the dogs?" Howie asked.

"They were in there with me—just napping, playing with their toys. You know."

"Did they go outside after you got here?"

The boy shook his head. "I was gonna take them out around ten, like Martin told me to. Unless one of them needed to go out before then."

Howie nodded, and I read his mind. No TV or music coming from the house, no evidence of a canine presence. Like many people, we normally left a few room lights on when we went out, so that alone wouldn't indicate someone was home. The drapes were all drawn. Anyone observing the house, after watching Martin's car pull away, might reasonably assume the place was vacant.

Of course, the windows were connected to the alarm system, but that had been turned off while Elliott was there. I imagine that when the intruder had pried the window open, he'd figured that either we'd neglected to arm the system before we left the house or that it was the silent kind, in which case he'd need to work fast, before the cops responded.

"And the dogs were fairly quiet?" Howie asked. "No loud barking or anything?"

"No, nothing like that. They were pretty calm. Well, until they weren't."

"Tell me about that."

"Well, I'm studying, like I said, and suddenly both dogs jerk their heads up, like they hear something."

"You didn't, though?" Howie asked.

"No. I listened, but I didn't hear anything. Then after a couple of seconds both of them, Layla and SB, they just bolt out of the room, barking like crazy."

"Then what?"

"I ran after them," Elliott said. "They went right to Jane's office, and as I was reaching for the knob, I heard the lock turn. I tried it anyway, but it was no good. The dogs were jumping on the door, growling, going crazy. I heard this kind of scrabbling sound and I knew there was a window in there, which is how the guy must've gotten in. And now he was escaping the same way."

Howie didn't bother telling the boy what he *should* have done at that point, which was get to a safe location and call 911. He simply asked, "What did you do then, Elliott?"

"I wanted to kick the door in, but the dogs were in the way and I didn't want them to get hurt. And I knew there was no point anyway, 'cause by then the guy, the burglar, he had to be running like crazy for the woods. Then Layla suddenly reverses course and nearly knocks me over. She runs into the laundry room next door, and I think, duh, that's where the back door is. She's throwing herself against that door like she's gonna knock it down if it kills her."

"And then?" Howie asked.

Elliott shrugged. "Then I unlocked the back door and ran after the guy. Layla too."

I asked. "Where was SB?"

He grinned. "Oh, the little dude tried real hard, but he couldn't keep up."

Howie said, "You told the officers that the intruder ran into the woods and got over the wall before you could reach him."

"Yeah, he used one of Jane's deck chairs to give himself a boost," the boy said. "He must've placed it there before he broke in, so he could get away fast. Layla tried to follow him over the wall. I had a hell of a time holding her back."

"I think I know the answer to this one," Howie said, "but I'm going to ask anyway. Did you get a good look at him?"

Elliott shook his head dejectedly. "I wish. All I saw was this dark shape disappearing through the trees. I think the guy was carrying something, like some kind of bag."

"Any idea whether it was a man or woman?"

"No. And I'll tell you what I told the officers. I couldn't make out skin color or height or anything like that either. I wish I could." He faced me. "I'm sorry, Jane."

I said, "What on earth are you sorry for? I'm the one who should be apologizing. You should've been completely safe here, and instead you found yourself running after a burglar."

"Yeah, about that." Howie put on his no-nonsense cop

face. "You seem like a bright young man, Elliott. I don't have to tell you how dangerous that was, chasing down an intruder. What if he'd been armed?"

"Yeah, I know," Elliott said. "My parents are going to have a fit."

"When Martin takes you home," I said, "he can help explain the whole thing to them." Still, I wouldn't be surprised if they forbade their son from sitting for us again.

After the boy returned to the living room, I turned to Howie and said, "Elliott has this tight group of friends. You and Cookie need to talk to them."

14

The Rosetta Stone

"I BROUGHT AN ASSORTMENT," I said, after Clover Eklund ushered me into her apartment. "I saw you eating a brownie at the memorial service, so I figured sugar isn't an issue for you."

"Never has been. Ooh, you went to Patisserie Susanne!" She accepted the white box adorned with the bakery's distinctive gold-and-white label. "Now, *this* is a treat. Thank you, Jane."

I followed her into the kitchen of her neat little home and inhaled the heady aroma of fresh-brewed coffee. She lifted the lid of the box to reveal a Napoleon, a chocolate éclair, a piece of opera cake, and a pair of chocolate croissants. Yes, I got *two* chocolate croissants because it happens to be my favorite, and if it also turned out to be Clover's, I didn't want to have to wrestle a ninety-year-old for it.

"If you prefer tea," she said, reaching into a cabinet for a platter and dessert plates, "I can make some. Have no use for it myself."

"No, I'm a confirmed coffee addict," I assured her. "Black."

"Me, too. What do you have there?" She nodded toward

the manila folder I'd set on the counter to free my hands so I could pour coffee.

"It's something Scarlett wanted you to have."

"Well, doesn't that sound intriguing." Clover placed everything on a hammered-aluminum tray.

"I've got this." I lifted the tray and headed into the living room. "If you'll just bring the folder?"

It was midafternoon on Saturday, less than twenty-four hours after my home had been burgled. I'd spent the morning gathering up the items that had been dumped out of the cartons, and taking a closer look at them as I did so. That's when I'd discovered a large envelope containing several beautiful pen-and-ink drawings, similar to the one Scarlett had done of Nolan. I didn't recognize most of the subjects, but one jumped out at me.

It was clearly Clover, whom I'd met at Scarlett's memorial service, and who would be accompanying me to the premier of the play starring her old sewing machine. In this picture, Scarlett had depicted Clover sitting at a table with pencil in hand and with papers and books spread out around her. The expression on the old woman's face was one of intense concentration.

Seeing it, I'd been reminded of what the Devines and Amy had told me about her, that she'd taught honors-level math and still enjoyed solving tough equations and puzzles. A note on the back of the drawing made it clear Scarlett intended for Clover to have it. I'd called her to ask if I could drop by.

"Your home is lovely," I said, with absolute sincerity, as I set the tray on a long, elliptical coffee table that put me in mind of a blond-wood surfboard. I sat on a streamlined sofa with a pronounced space-age vibe, upholstered in burnt-orange velvet.

"Why, thank you." She chose the chocolate éclair before settling back on a lounge chair made of black leather and walnut with a matching footstool. The leather looked supple and burnished with age. When she noticed me admiring it, she said, "A genuine Eames chair. I bought it in the sixties. It took me almost three years of scrimping and saving—a few bucks out of each paycheck—but eventually I got my chair. I bought most of my furniture the same way, over time. I've been a fan of midcentury modern since... well, since the middle of the last century, I suppose."

Colorful pillows and throws made the sofa and Eames chair even cozier. The sleek sideboard, end tables, and bookcase were crafted of pale wood, devoid of embellishment yet somehow warm and inviting. I knew that the starburst light fixture over the table in the dining area was sometimes referred to as a Sputnik chandelier: a dozen thin arms tipped in small round lights. There were a few pieces of framed art on the walls, no doubt collected the same way the chair was, over time as Clover could afford them.

"So everything here is vintage," I said.

"Like me," she chortled. "Now, let's see what you brought me."

I watched Clover's face as she opened the folder. "Oh my..." She brought the drawing closer to her face to study it. "Oh my," she repeated. "Scarlett took my photo that day. She must've based this drawing on it. Good Lord, but that girl was talented."

"She wrote 'for Clover' on the back," I said, my voice hoarse with emotion. I cleared my throat. "She meant to give it to you."

Clover's eyes were shiny. "Thank you for bringing this to

me, Jane. This is just… well, what a wonderful surprise. Something truly special to remember her by. I'm going to frame it and give it a place of honor."

"You look like you're studying something really intently in that picture," I said, as I claimed a chocolate croissant.

"Well, I was. Scarlett needed help decrypting this strange notebook she'd gotten her hands on, and I was happy to oblige. Plus that sort of thing keeps my old mind from getting too rusty. Are you all right, Jane?"

I hadn't heard anything after the first sentence. I was too busy choking on my croissant. "Did you say—" I croaked, and took a sip of coffee. "Did you say you decrypted Scarlett's notebook?"

"Well, to be accurate," she said, "it wasn't *Scarlett's* notebook. I mean, none of the writing in it was hers. Someone gave it to her. She didn't want to tell me who, and I didn't pry. Especially when I realized what was in it. That's the sort of thing that can get a person in trouble, even all these years later. Oh, but I've said too much." She flapped her hand. "Scarlett wanted me to keep it all hush-hush and here I go running my mouth. What were we talking about? Oh, the picture. How do you think it would look over the sofa, next to the Lichtenstein?" She pointed to a spot on the wall behind me.

My thoughts were pinballing around my cranium. I raised my hand like a stop sign. "So, um, first things first, Clover. This notebook you mentioned—*Wait.*" I whipped my head around to stare at the painting she'd indicated, a cartoony pop-art close-up of a woman putting on lipstick. "Is that a *real* Roy Lichtenstein?"

"Well, of course, and isn't it just delightful? My friend gave me that painting fifty-one years ago as a housewarming gift when I moved into this apartment. She bought it very early on, of course, before Lichtenstein was well known. Goodness, who can afford him now?"

I said, "So your friend, she what, just *gave* you an original Lichtenstein?"

"Evelyn was my special friend," Clover said, as if that explained everything.

I said, "Oh."

Then I thought, *Oh!*

"She passed seventeen years ago. I still miss her every day." Clover gave a wistful sigh. "I'm grateful that I have a few things to remember my Evelyn by."

Such as a painting that was potentially worth millions. Amy was worried about what would become of Clover once the sale of the Americana caused a mass eviction. She could probably stop worrying.

That is, if Clover was willing to part with this gift from her special friend.

"Forgive me," I said, "but I have to ask. You do have that painting insured, right?"

"Well, of course. Why does everyone always ask me that? I might be a sentimental old dame, but I still have a few gray cells left. I never married or had children, so when I pass, the Lichtenstein will go to the Museum of Modern Art. It's all arranged." She took a bite of éclair and washed it down with a sip of coffee.

So much for living off the Lichtenstein for the rest of her days.

"What a generous bequest, Clover. I didn't know Evelyn, of course, but I imagine she'd have been thrilled to know her gift is going to be part of MOMA's collection." I struggled to mentally switch gears. "So what you were saying before about, you know, decrypting. We're talking about an old spiral-bound notebook, yes? Green, with 'Winners Circle' written on the cover?"

"Yes, that's the one. You've seen it?"

"I'm the one who cleaned out Scarlett's apartment," I said. "It was in her desk."

"Then I suppose her sister has it now. Carolyn."

"She… well, I guess she doesn't have enough space for all of Scarlett's belongings," I said, because it sounded better than *Carolyn's only interested in the big-ticket items.* "So I have the notebook. That is, I did have it. It was stolen from my house last night during a burglary."

"Oh, no! I hope no one was hurt."

"No, thank goodness," I said. "So to be clear, you actually managed to decode the contents of that thing?"

"Yes. Although it turned out to be more challenging than I'd anticipated, so I reached out to an expert. One of my former students, Brent Nguyen, is a cryptographer with the FBI. Of course, now the job is all about cybersecurity. Encryption this and algorithm that. But Brent grew up making and breaking codes for fun, the old-fashioned way, on paper. Well, so did I, for that matter. Anyway, he was happy to help me crack this one—on his own time, of course, and he knew better than to ask too many questions."

"Okay. Wow. A real FBI guy," I said. "But the thing is, I didn't find any notes about this among Scarlett's things— about, you know, the notebook getting decrypted."

"And you won't," Clover said. "She was afraid the wrong person might get their hands on it. She scanned the entire notebook and printed it out. That's what we worked from, that printout. And she left everything with me."

"Not everything," I said. "The notebook itself was right there in her desk."

"Scarlett picked it up from me the day before she passed. I knew she was worried about it all being kept together in one place—the original notebook along with all our paperwork. She told me not to worry, that the notebook would be kept where no one could get their hands on it. At one time we'd talked about putting it in a safe-deposit box in a bank, so that must've been what she meant."

"Unfortunately," I said, "she died before she could bring it to a bank. I'm curious. When did she first show it to you?"

"September first. She brought it over along with the printout, and we went to work on it that very day—which was kind of fitting, seeing as it was Labor Day. It took us a few weeks to hammer out the code, but by the end of September the decryption was completed. We celebrated with a bottle of bubbly."

I said, "Well, thank goodness the scanned printout still exists—along with the decoded translation, yes?"

"That depends on whether Scarlett's sister decided it was worth saving."

My stomach dropped. "You gave it to Carolyn?"

Clover nodded. "I felt that as Scarlett's next of kin, The Cabbage rightfully belonged to her."

"Excuse me, did you say, 'The Cabbage?'"

She grinned. "You have to understand, Jane, we were working with an ever-expanding collection of papers. There was Scarlett's scanned printout of the notebook, our voluminous working notes, and the decryption itself. One day Scarlett referred to the whole mess as The Cabbage—a reference to the color of the notebook, you see—and it stuck."

"And now Carolyn has it," I said. So that was it, then. There was no way she was going to share something like that with me. What reason could I even give for wanting to see it? I could almost hear Scarlett's sister informing me that the old Winner's Circle notebook was none of my business.

"When did you hand it over to her?" I asked.

"Last week after the memorial service," she said. "Seeing her there reminded me that I was still holding on to The Cabbage, keeping it safe for Scarlett, so I brought it over to Carolyn that evening."

"Well," I said, "can you at least tell me what the notebook was about? I know I don't have any right to ask, but I've been puzzling over that thing for the past three weeks."

"Nonsense, Jane," Clover said. "You have every right to ask. Didn't you just tell me someone broke into your home and made off with the thing? That puts you right in the middle of it. Did they take anything else?"

"Just one other item." I was going to dance around the specifics, then thought, the heck with that. Scarlett had obviously trusted this woman. I said, "He also took a scrapbook belonging to Nolan Whitehouse. Those two things, the scrapbook and the notebook, were lying out in plain view. I couldn't say whether the burglar specifically targeted them or whether he just snatched them on the fly. He was in the house for a couple of minutes at most before my dogs ran him off."

"What did the police say?" she asked.

"That it's possible someone considered those two items either very valuable or very dangerous."

"That makes sense." The old woman straightened and scooted to the edge of her lounge chair. "Are you ready for more coffee?"

"I think I could use a refill, but let me get it." I started to rise.

Clover waved me back down. "Sit. It does me good to keep active."

She disappeared into the kitchen and returned a minute later with the coffee carafe and an oversize clasp envelope, bulging with its contents, which she dropped onto my lap.

"What's this?" I asked.

"Hope you like cabbage," she said, as she filled my mug.

Hurriedly I unfastened the flap and pulled out a thick stack of papers. Then I could only gape in wonder as I flipped through the first few sheets. "I thought you said you gave all this to Carolyn."

"If there's one thing I've learned in my nine decades on this earth," she said, as she helped herself to the slice of opera cake, "it's that you never let an important piece of paper leave your hands until you've photocopied it. I don't have a safe, so I stashed that in my pantry behind the cereals. That other chocolate croissant is calling your name, Jane."

"Oh, I'll answer that call, don't worry." I looked at Clover as she settled back in the Eames chair. "Does Carolyn know you have this copy?"

"She didn't ask, and I didn't volunteer the information. I worked hard decrypting this thing. I figure I have as much right to it as anyone."

I leafed through the pile of papers that constituted The Cabbage, taking a quick inventory. The complete contents of the notebook had been copied onto a sheaf of pages held together with a binder clip. Then there were notes on the decryption process, which I found impenetrable for the most part. Several more pages contained the final result of all that cerebral exertion, the key to the code: the notebook's Rosetta Stone, if you will.

The last stack consisted of the decrypted results—a column-by-column translation, in plain English, of the entire notebook. I saw people's names, dozens of them, along with dates and some other words and letters that looked instantly familiar.

"Are these grades?" I asked. "And the names of college courses?"

"They are," Clover said. "You're looking at the detailed records of an academic cheating scheme."

"So this column here—" I pointed "—represents test scores. And these are the letter grades. It looks like everyone did very well in their midterms and finals."

"You would, too," she said, "if you'd been handed the correct answers ahead of time."

"So someone was, what, stealing tests and giving the answers to other students?"

She paused before shoveling a bite of cake into her mouth. "No one was *giving* anything to anyone, Jane. Take a look at the last few pages. They lay out the details of the scheme, including a month-by-month list showing how much money it was bringing in. I imagine there must've been a separate ledger specifying who paid what, but this notebook only gives general numbers. Whoever cooked up this little extracurricular project made a boatload of money from it."

I flipped to the pages she'd mentioned. The monthly haul started out in the hundreds and quickly grew into the thousands. "I see what you mean. Looks like the ringleader was raking it in."

"He might've had to share his ill-gotten gains," she said.

"If you keep reading, you'll see they didn't just swipe upcoming tests and answer sheets, they also hacked into the university's computer system and altered grades. Also, there were a couple of teaching assistants on the take. I was a teacher for a long time, and I know a little something about academic cheating. This was a very sophisticated scheme."

"And they weren't afraid someone would spill the beans?" I asked.

She lifted her coffee mug. "They must've been. If one of them got caught, they'd all go down. But it would appear they got away with it."

"'The Winner's Circle.' So cheating your way to academic success makes you a winner." I flipped through more pages. "I don't see any mention of which university this was."

"That was easy to track down, based on the course subjects, dates, and student names. It was Columbia. What?" she said, when my eyes went wide.

"Well, it's just that I know of three people who attended Columbia back then. All these dates are during a four-year period ending forty years ago. That's when they all graduated."

Clover continued to devour her opera cake as I flipped pages and ran my finger down the long list of names. Finally I sat back and released a stunned exhalation. "Oh brother."

"Let me guess." Clover pinned me with a hard stare, making me feel like one of her former math students being grilled on trigonometric functions. "You hesitate to name names."

"I don't think I *need* to name them, though, do I?" I said. "You must know who I was looking for. They're all connected with this building."

She ticked them off on her fingers. "Robert Jernigan, who

lives here. Nolan Whitehouse, who lived here before his death a few weeks ago. And Edward Proctor, Scarlett and Carolyn's father. I wonder what Carolyn thought when she saw his name included in the papers I gave her."

Knowing Carolyn, I could see her turning The Cabbage into coleslaw: shredding it and feeding it to a dumpster.

"So all three of them participated in this cheating scheme," I said, "but what I'd like to know is, who's the criminal mastermind that came up with the whole thing? I don't suppose he's identified anywhere in all this." I lifted the heavy stack of papers, aka The Cabbage, and let it drop back onto my lap.

"No, he isn't," Clover said. "Not a hint. But I think we can safely assume it was one of the men I just named."

I nodded. "Because the Winner's Circle notebook obviously belonged to the ringleader, so presumably that's who Scarlett got it from. And she personally knew all three of them—Ed, Bob, and Nolan."

"But here's what I don't get," she said. "Whoever this person is, he chose to hang on to that incriminating notebook for forty years. And suddenly he just hands it over to Scarlett Proctor? Why would he do such a thing?"

My mind was already working on that. I had a few ideas, but I wanted to give it more thought before I started speculating.

"Do you mind if I keep this for a while?" I asked. "I promise not to let it out of my—"

"I made two copies." She wagged her hand. "That one's yours."

An hour and another chocolate croissant later, I stood to leave.

"I'll walk you out," Clover said, reaching for her jacket and scarf on a coat tree by the door. "I like to take a stroll around the neighborhood every day, weather permitting. And all that sugar has given me energy to burn."

"That's funny," I said, "all it gives me is tighter jeans."

Stepping outside the building, we encountered Bob Jernigan coming toward us on the concrete walkway. He was leading an adorable black-and-tan King Charles spaniel on a leash.

"Good afternoon, ladies." He wore his usual genial smile.

We greeted him, and I leaned down to pet his dog, who was sniffing my legs. "This must be Boss Lady."

"The very same," he said. "She smells Sexy Beast on you."

"And Layla, too," I said, straightening.

His eyebrows rose. "I didn't know you had another dog. What kind is she?"

"She's a mix," I said. "Lab and Great Dane."

His smile broadened. "Layla and little Sexy Beast must make quite a pair. Are you two out for a walk today?"

"I am," Clover said. "Jane and I just had a nice visit."

I saw his gaze land on the large, bulky envelope I carried. I said the first thing that came to mind. "Clover needs this overnighted to her lawyer. I offered to take care of it for her since I have a FedEx account."

"Oh, those pesky lawyers," he said, "and their unreasonable demands."

We all chuckled at this dumb gag. I wouldn't describe the lawyer we were chatting with as pesky. Entitled, maybe. I'd read Bob's bio on his firm's website. He'd graduated summa cum laude from Columbia before being admitted to Yale Law School. Clearly the world owed him a privileged life, and he'd achieved it, at least in part, by cheating his way through his undergraduate career. I could only wonder if he'd had a similar advantage at Yale.

"Well, have a good evening, ladies," he said. "Come on, Boss Lady, let's go see what Mommy's up to."

15

Multitasking

"THIS THING," I said, "is big enough to do an autopsy on. Maybe even two autopsies simultaneously, side by side."

Sophie's impassive stare, from across the kidney-shaped continent of beige marble that was her desktop, told me she was unamused. Which I knew meant she was amused. That's the kind of friendship we have, that I can, you know, read her like that.

"That's the first thing that pops into your head?" she asked. "Autopsies? Think maybe you've been in the Death Diva racket a little too long?"

"Nonsense," I said, as I pulled the bundle of papers out of the oversize envelope I'd brought with me. "I'm just hitting my stride."

"In more ways than one," Martin said, as he wrapped his arms around me from behind and planted a soft kiss on the side of my neck. I shivered and bit back a goofy grin.

"No hanky-panky in the mayor's office," Sophie ordered. "This sacred space is for serious town business only."

"As I'm sure you know," the padre said, "a mere century ago this 'sacred space' was a speakeasy and gambling den. It was *the* place for hanky-panky."

Sophie's large office, which occupied the top floor of the four-story Town Hall building, offered no hint of its notorious past. We were surrounded by ultramodern furnishings in pale and soothing tones. The blue-gray sofa and matching stuffed armchairs were softly curved, made even more nestlike with a scattering of fringed throw pillows. The round coffee table was, like the desk, topped with beige marble. The fluffy area rug, with its abstract design in complementary muted tones, had an irregular, organic shape.

As soon as we'd arrived, Sexy Beast had hopped out of his straw tote bag and given that rug a good, thorough inspection, finally selecting a spot under the coffee table, turning in a few circles, and settling down for a snooze.

It was late afternoon on Monday, the first of December, a day that was both blindingly sunny and bitingly cold. I'd already brought Sophie up to speed on everything, including the decryption of the notebook. Once she'd found out I possessed a copy, she'd politely asked to see it in her usual soft-spoken, deferential way: "Bring that damn Cabbage over here, pronto!"

I'd secured Clover's permission to show it to the padre and the mayor, having assured her they could be trusted to keep it to themselves. She also knew I'd be sharing it with the detectives.

By the time we'd arrived at her office, Sophie had already transferred the piles of folders and assorted paraphernalia from her enormous desktop to the nearby maple credenza, giving us plenty of room to spread out the photocopied pages. My companions took their time poring over the columns of names, course titles, test dates, and grades.

Sophie yanked off her reading glasses and tapped them

angrily on the papers. "There are dozens of names here. A *schande*! Never once during my entire academic career did I cheat. I never even *considered* cheating. Am I supposed to feel like some kind of hopeless schlemiel because I actually *studied* and played by the rules? 'Winner's Circle'? *Feh!* The unmitigated chutzpah!"

When the mayor gets worked up, it pays to know a little Yiddish.

Martin pointed to the last column on the right. "This is interesting. 'Dodged payment, had to chase him.' He moved his finger down a few rows. 'Unhappy with an *A*, demands *A*-plus.' Looks like the guy in charge kept notes about some of his… What do we call the students who paid to cheat their way through college?"

Sophie had a suggestion. I shall refrain from repeating it. You're welcome.

She shoved her glasses back on and recited other entries from that column. "Let's see… 'Good repeat customer, trust-fund baby, keep her happy.' Oh, and how about this beaut? 'Too lazy to memorize answers, now wants *D* changed to *A*-plus, charged him another grand.'"

Wanting to join in the fun, I turned the page toward me and read, "'She offered to pay me with a—' *Whoa!*"

Sophie and the padre leaned in to find out what this particular student had offered in lieu of cash.

"So this one's not just a shameless cheat," Sophie said, "she's a shameless prostitute, as well."

Martin said, "I think we're supposed to call them sex workers now." One look at her scary raised eyebrow prompted a mumbled, "Never mind."

I continued reading. "It says here he declined her, um,

barter suggestion and demanded his usual fee."

"But who was 'he'? That's what I want to know." He lifted the page and waggled it. "Who masterminded this lucrative scheme? If we can figure that out, we're one step closer to finding out who broke into our home to steal the notebook."

I was happy to hear him refer to it as *our* home. Progress. "You're assuming the burglar was after the notebook," I said. "It could've been the scrapbook, or it could be those things were simply easy to grab on his way out the window once he realized he wasn't alone in the house. Your basic crime of opportunity."

"But he left your laptop."

"True," I said. "And he spent precious seconds dumping out the cartons I'd taken from Scarlett's place, yet he never bothered opening my desk drawers. Which is where a lot of people keep spare cash and credit cards, not to mention other stealable goodies, like handguns, watches, what have you."

"Which kind of does a number on your crime-of-opportunity theory," he said. "What does that reliable gut of yours tell you?"

I didn't hesitate. "That it's all about the notebook."

"Works for me," Sophie said. "First question. How did Scarlett get her hands on it?"

"Someone gave it to her," he said. "Someone who knew her well enough to trust her with it. Which means the ringleader of the cheating scheme is almost certainly one of these three." He tapped the names I'd helpfully highlighted in yellow: Ed Proctor, Bob Jernigan, and Nolan Whitehouse. Each name appeared many times in the pages.

"How can we be sure Scarlett didn't just come across it somewhere?" she asked. "You said she's the one who cleaned out Nolan's place."

"He died more than a month *after* Scarlett and Clover started decrypting the notebook," I said, "so she couldn't have found it during the clean-out. And Scarlett told Clover that someone—she didn't say who—gave it directly to her."

"Some names don't have anything written in the notes column." Martin flipped through the pages. "And that includes our three guys. Nada. No clue in here about which one of them was in charge."

"Only one of the three is still alive," Sophie pointed out.

"True," Martin said, "but Scarlett's dad could've given it to her before he died. Same goes for Nolan."

"Let's start with the father," she said. "If he had the notebook, why would he have given it to his daughter?" Before either of us could respond, she answered her own question. "For safekeeping. So no one else could get ahold of it. He trusted her. There are a lot of names in there, a lot of people who could get hurt if it came out they were part of this *farshtunken* cheating scheme, even at this late date. The thing's a ticking time bomb."

"Then why keep it around at all?" he asked. "Why wouldn't he have destroyed it decades ago?"

"Sentiment?" I suggested. "An ego boost? A souvenir from a time when the guy was the bad-boy brainiac behind a major cheating ring? Think about it. He got away with bamboozling an Ivy League university, for years. Maybe he just enjoyed looking at the notebook and reliving his glory days."

"And if someone else did stumble across it," Sophie said, "it wasn't as if they could just pick up the thing and find out all about the cheating scheme."

I nodded. "It took math whiz Clover Eklund and an

honest-to-God FBI cryptographer a full month to decipher it."

"Maybe her dad never had it," the padre said. "Maybe Nolan's the one who gave it to her."

"Hold that thought. Follow me, troops." Sophie led the way to the cozy seating area. She sank into one of the pair of stuffed armchairs, while Martin and I chose the cushy sofa. He draped his arm around my shoulders, drawing me close.

From his hidey-hole under the coffee table, Sexy Beast drowsily noted the location of each human pack member before tucking his nose back into his curled-up body, releasing a lusty sigh, and resuming his power nap.

Sophie turned to Martin. "You were saying? About Nolan?"

"I mean, Scarlett was over there all the time, doing things for him. He must've come to trust her."

I said, "But did he trust her enough to hand over a notebook detailing his… Was it a criminal enterprise? Does a college cheating scheme fall under that category?"

"If it doesn't, it should," Sophie muttered. She was really steamed about this *farshtunken* cheating scheme.

"Was Nolan even capable of devising something like that?" Martin asked. "It would've taken serious brain power not only to concoct and run the whole thing but also to lock down the notes with a hard-to-crack code."

"Well, it's pretty clear the ringleader had accomplices," I said, "but you have to remember, the Nolan we've been told about, the sad old guy with a questionable grip on reality, is decades removed from the bright young student who managed to get into one of the country's finest institutions of higher learning. Who's to say he couldn't have engineered a sophisticated scheme like the Winner's Circle back then? And speaking of engineering, did you know he used to be a chemical engineer? Bob's fiancée mentioned that. Whatever you may say about the guy, he was no dummy."

Sophie said, "And he would've given Scarlett the notebook why?"

"From what I know of the guy," Martin said, "he was troubled but not completely delusional. He must've known he wasn't firing on all cylinders. Maybe he was aware the notebook could be used to hurt people and wanted to make sure it didn't fall into the wrong hands."

"That's a good point," I said. "Scarlett was probably the *only* person he trusted. Someone I recently met knew Nolan pretty well, and in her opinion he was clinically paranoid." I was thinking of Jasmine Reddy, one of the resident nerds as I now thought of them, and our discussion on the rooftop eight days earlier.

"But again," he said, "if the notebook is potentially that dangerous, why not burn it right after graduation? Why would he have kept it around?"

Sophie said, "When we were discussing Ed, we speculated it might be an ego thing. Maybe that would apply to Nolan as well."

I wasn't sure I agreed with that, but before I could comment, Martin said, "What about Bob? If he was the ringleader, why would he have given the notebook to Scarlett?"

We all pondered that for a few moments. Finally I said, "He wouldn't have. He and Scarlett were no longer on speaking terms, and there's no reason to think he would've trusted her with something like that. If he'd been the brains behind the Winner's Circle, he would've either destroyed the notebook or locked it in a safe."

There was a knock on the door. It opened, and Sophie's young secretary, Amanda, popped her head in. "I just wanted to let you know I'm leaving for the day, Mayor."

"Oh, is it that time already?" She glanced at the clock on her credenza. "It's twenty past. You should've skedaddled by now."

"I was updating your Instagram and lost track of time. Can I order you folks some takeout before I go? That new Chinese place down the block delivers, and they're fast."

That earned a chorus of affirmative responses, including a tail-wagging yip from Sexy Beast, who didn't know what he was agreeing to but figured if the rest of us were that enthusiastic, it had to be about food. Amanda produced a paper menu, we circled our selections, and the three of us commenced our quick-draw battle of the credit cards. Sophie was victorious this time. The padre made the expected gentlemanly noises, which resulted in the mayor telling him to knock it off, and him promising to pay next time. Our usual Takeout Tarantella.

After Amanda left, we took a seventeen-minute break until the food came (yes, it was that fast), at which point we cleared the papers off the desk, pulled the chairs up to it, and spread out our Szechuan feast.

Sophie gesticulated with her chopsticks. "So now we know the mastermind behind the Winner's Circle was either Ed Proctor or Nolan Whitehouse."

I felt compelled to add, "Probably."

"Call it ninety percent," she said. "Which brings us to the burglary. Your young friend who was at your place that night. The pet sitter. What's his name again?"

"Elliott," Martin said.

"Elliott said he didn't get a clear look at the perp, right?"

"Right," he said. "It could've been a man or a woman. All we know is that he, or she, is fit enough to scramble through a window, run from a big, scary dog, and get over a six-foot-high stone wall."

"With the aid of a deck chair," I reminded him. "He's not Superman, leaping tall buildings in a single bound." I lifted a piece of twice-cooked pork, only to watch it leap from my chopsticks onto the rug. SB was more than happy to snap it up. At least it wasn't one of the spicy dishes.

"And we know the burglar was after the notebook." Sophie raised her palm as I started to respond. "Call it ninety percent. Who are our suspects?"

"What, just like that?" I said. "There are so many variables—"

"Stop," she commanded, around a mouthful of kung pao chicken. "You're wasting my time, and I'm the damn mayor of this burg. Whose face popped into your head when I asked about suspects?"

Automatically I glanced at the closed door to the outer office, though I knew we were alone. "Just between us three?"

"Oh, for the love of—" She made an ostentatious show of checking an invisible wristwatch. "Tick tock, Jane."

"Okay, Hal Kazarian, for starters," I said.

"Now, was that so hard? Why Hal?"

"Besides the fact that he's a lying, cheating narcissist with stalker tendencies?"

"Those traits don't place him in your home office," she said, "swiping a notebook written all in code."

"Okay then, try this," I said. "When Hal and I went on our date—"

Sophie's palm came up again. "Back up. Your *what?*" She looked at the padre, who appeared maddeningly unruffled as he helped himself to more stir-fried green beans.

"Oh, didn't I mention that?" I managed to scoop up a wad of rice with my chopsticks and felt ridiculously proud of myself for about a half second until the inevitable occurred. Fortunately, Sexy Beast possessed (you should excuse the expression) catlike reflexes. "Purely a fact-finding mission, I assure you. Anyway, as it turned out, *he* kept trying to pump *me* for information."

"About what?"

"About anything intriguing I might've found in Scarlett's apartment."

"As I understand it," she said, "just about everything in that girl's apartment was intriguing."

"He was specifically interested in anything that had to do with Nolan."

"Really. Did he say why?"

"No, but I told you about the threatening note, right?" I asked. "The one I found in Nolan's scrapbook?"

"Oh, right. 'Stay away from Scarlett or I'll shoot you, stab you, poison you, chop you up into fifty little bitty pieces, and bury each piece in a different state.' Something like that."

"Close. It says, 'Leave Scarlett alone or you'll be sorry.' The scrapbook was lying open to that page when the break-in occurred. The burglar would've seen it."

"And you think Hal sent that note to Nolan," she said.

"I think if he *did* send the note, he might be getting nervous about it being traced back to him, now that people are beginning to question whether Nolan's death really was accidental."

"And by 'people,' you mean you."

"Not just me. The day before she died, Scarlett spoke with the police—specifically Cookie Kaplan—about the possibility that Nolan was murdered." I gave Sophie a brief rundown of the mop-and-bucket brainteaser. "Hal saw me taking a carton out of Scarlett's apartment. He knows I brought some stuff home."

"So if he *was* the burglar," Sophie said, "it might mean he was the one who sent the threatening note, and that's what he was after. But why would he assume Nolan had kept it?"

"Because Nolan kept everything," I said. "I've been told his whole apartment was basically plastered in every scrap of paper he came across, with paranoid notes scrawled all over them."

Martin said, "So Hal would've grabbed the scrapbook because it was lying open, with the note plainly visible. Bingo. He got what he came for."

"Then why take the Winner's Circle notebook, too?" I asked.

His exaggerated shrug said the answer was obvious. "Because you left it out on your desk, right next to the scrapbook. He has to assume it's just as important, or valuable in some way. If I were him, I'd have done the same thing. In a situation like that, you don't have the luxury of time. You have to be prepared to make snap decisions."

It still made me a little uncomfortable hearing the padre speak so knowledgeably about breaking and entering. I told myself that chapter of his life was in the deep, dark past and to get over it. I loved this man, and that wasn't who he was now.

"Who else is on your burglary suspect list?" Sophie asked.

"I don't have a li—"

"Yes you do," she said, "so just knock it off or I'll sic this vicious animal on you."

At that moment the vicious animal in question was avidly tracking every bite of spicy chicken that entered her mouth, and emitting the occasional pitiful whimper in case she failed to comprehend the magnitude of his suffering. I rose, retrieved a couple of doggie treats from my tote bag, and settled him on the sofa. His grumpy response sounded like Yiddish.

"Okay, another suspect might be Bob Jernigan," I said, as I resumed my seat. "He stopped by Scarlett's apartment when we'd just started cleaning it out. He seemed real eager to look around. I couldn't blame him, the place was like a fascinating little museum."

"He spent a long time inspecting everything thoroughly," Martin said. "I mean *really* thoroughly. I didn't think anything of it at the time."

"But then later," I said, "when he found out he hadn't gotten to see everything and that we'd taken some things home, he seemed a bit perturbed."

"Did you get the feeling he was looking for anything in particular?" she asked.

"Hard to say. For what it's worth, I can't see Bob writing that threatening note. It's true he was no fan of Nolan's, but he and Scarlett were on the outs, like I said, so why would he tell Nolan to leave her alone?"

"Okay," she said, "so if Bob's the one who burgled your house, he wasn't after the scrapbook. He would've just grabbed it up along with the notebook."

"And he definitely would've wanted to get his hands on that notebook," Martin said. "We're thinking Ed or Nolan was the ringleader, but Bob took full advantage of the cheating scheme. His name appears in that Winner's Circle book at least a dozen times. That thing is a threat to him, even all these years later."

"Enough of a threat," Sophie asked, "to risk breaking into someone's house? A man in his position?"

"But that's precisely why he'd do it," I said, as I lifted my can of orange soda. "Think of all he has to lose."

Sophie ate in silence for a few moments before saying, "Bob was estranged from Scarlett's father, Ed, at the time of Ed's death, right?"

"Right."

"So if Ed was the Winner's Circle ringleader," she said, "he might've given the notebook to his daughter so she could use it against Bob. Maybe he did it knowing he was going to end it all. Bob is a high-powered lawyer. Just participating in a cheating scheme back in his undergrad years, even if he wasn't the head honcho, could put him in hot water with his fancy law firm. It might even be an issue with the New York bar."

"Not to mention," I said, "his fiancée's family is extremely wealthy and very conservative. April herself strikes me as principled, verging on self-righteous."

"Principled?" she said. "Are we talking about the woman who was sleeping with Bob while he was still married?"

Martin said, "Self-righteous people tend to be pros at justifying their own bad behavior."

"Be that as it may," I said, "I think a revelation like a college cheating scandal, and the professional fallout that would result, might very well prompt her to give Bob the old heave-ho."

"There's no doubt he lucked out with April," Martin said. "She's young, beautiful, and smart. She has an impressive career even though she doesn't need to work. Bob's twice her age and nowhere near as rich."

"I was chatting with the two of them after the memorial service," I said, "and at one point April chided Bob for badmouthing Nolan. He backtracked immediately, like he was anxious to placate her. I got the feeling he has a lot riding on this marriage and is wary of jeopardizing it." Something told me Bob's conciliatory attitude would be undergoing a one-eighty after the wedding.

"So Bob has a lot to lose," Sophie said, "if that notebook comes to light."

"He has to know who the Winner's Circle ringleader was," Martin said, "since he participated."

I said, "That scheme helped Bob graduate summa cum laude. Don't start," I added, when the mayor began grumbling.

"So if that notebook is such a threat to Bob," he said, "why would he wait until now to do something about it?"

"Maybe he didn't know it still existed," she said. "I'm sure everyone involved was sworn to secrecy. Maybe it was just assumed that the ringleader destroyed the evidence."

"Or maybe the ringleader *claimed* he destroyed it," I said, "but secretly kept it, either to massage his ego or as a kind of insurance policy."

"Something he could hold over the cheaters' heads, in other words," Martin said.

He tried to pass me the twice-cooked pork, but I waved it off. "Thanks, Padre. I'm stuffed."

"So let's say Bob is our burglar," she said. "How would he even know Scarlett had the notebook?"

We all thought that one over. I said, "She was close to both Ed and Nolan, one of whom was the presumptive ringleader. Ninety percent," I added, before Sophie could beat me to it.

"I'm thinking this guy, the ringleader, might've taunted Bob with the fact that he still had the Winner's Circle notebook with its detailed records. After the guy died, Bob would've reasonably assumed it was in Scarlett's possession."

Martin said, "Bob's how old? Sixty-one, sixty-two? Could he really outrun a big dog and a high-school basketball star?"

"Well, don't forget, the burglar had a head start," I said. "And Carolyn once mentioned that she and Bob go to the same gym, so chances are he's not a total weakling. Do you think *you'd* be able to outrun Layla and a teenage athlete when you're Bob's age?"

"Well, yeah, but—" He broke off when Sophie and I laughed. "Okay, I'm optimistic. But it stands to reason that someone younger would have a better chance of getting away."

"Someone like Carolyn?" I asked. "She knew Martin and I were going out that night. I'd mentioned it to her a few days earlier."

"And she had a copy of the notebook, yes?" Sophie said.

I nodded. "Clover gave it to her. Before that, I doubt she even knew about it."

"She couldn't have been happy," she said, "learning that her dad had aced his college career by cheating."

Martin said, "She'd already had to deal with the scandal surrounding his embezzling."

"Carolyn feels responsible for that," I said. "She urged him to do it, gave him pointers. She let that one slip when she was…" I made a drinking gesture.

"Then she might also feel responsible for how he handled his shame afterward," Sophie said. "By throwing a rope over a beam in the attic."

"I believe she does," I said, "though she's trying to

convince herself it was Scarlett's fault. She must be worried that if this cheating thing becomes public knowledge, it'll be one more humiliation heaped on her father's memory."

"And by extension," she said, "on her family and herself."

"I can tell you she feels compelled to clean up anything she considers a 'loose end.'"

The padre said, "Like finding out your father participated in, and possibly masterminded, an extensive college cheating scheme? There's a loose end for you."

"I told Carolyn I'd brought some of her sister's things back to my place," I said. "She had no problem with it. I even mentioned where in my house I'd stashed the cartons—just making small talk, you know?"

"But that was before Clover gave her The Cabbage," Sophie said.

"Carolyn asked her where the original notebook was, and Clover told her Scarlett had taken it back. The only thing Carolyn had bothered retrieving from her dead sister's desk was her laptop."

"So she had to be wondering if the notebook was in one of those cartons in your home office," she said. "I imagine she wants nothing more than to make it disappear."

"What she didn't know was that Clover made two copies of The Cabbage before handing it over. That's one of them." I gestured toward the papers now stacked on the credenza. "Clover has the other."

The padre started collecting the detritus of our meal and shoving it into the empty takeout bag. "Carolyn hated Nolan, right? Maybe she wrote that threatening note."

"If Carolyn was our burglar," I said, "she would've seen that note right there on my desk in the open scrapbook. She'd have had good reason to grab both that and the notebook."

I thought about Carolyn's insistence on knowing why Scarlett had wanted to hire me—one of those annoying "loose ends" that so irked her. Could it be she was afraid Scarlett suspected her of killing Nolan, and that she intended to share that suspicion with me? If so, my initial meeting with Carolyn would have dispelled that fear. Plus, she'd then hired me to sift through Scarlett's belongings. Either she had nothing to hide or she was confident she'd covered her tracks.

"I'm curious." Sophie wiped crumbs off her desktop with the spare paper napkins. "Did Nolan and Ed get along?"

"I don't know anything about their relationship," I said, "but you'd think if Ed had something against Nolan, he'd have warned him to stay away from Scarlett." I punctuated this statement with a little gasp.

Martin read my mind. "Maybe he did."

"I'm not follow—Oh." Sophie straightened. "'Leave Scarlett alone or you'll be sorry.'"

He said, "Did Ed die before or after Scarlett got friendly with Nolan?"

"It was a full month after," I said, "so yeah, he probably knew Scarlett had met Nolan and that she was helping him with his day-to-day needs. And I'm willing to bet Ed and Nolan knew each other from their college days and possibly after."

"So maybe it wasn't Hal *or* Carolyn who wrote that threatening note," she said. "Maybe it was Ed."

"If Nolan's long-ago college cheating became known," he said, "would he even care?"

"I don't see why he would," I said. "He literally had nothing to lose. His life was… well, we know what his life was.

So even if Ed hated him—and we still don't know the answer to that—Nolan had nothing to fear from that notebook. Unless I'm missing something."

Sophie tossed fortune cookies at us. We sat and tore open the plastic wrappers, a sound that would normally bring my dog running, but SB lay curled up in a corner of the sofa, belly full of treats, quietly snoring.

I snapped my cookie in two and read the message aloud. "'The key to multitasking is to complete each task before starting the next one.' Umm…"

Martin said, "I don't think that word means what they think it means."

I shrugged and popped half the cookie into my mouth. There was something irresistible about fortune cookies even though they were never—let's be honest—all that tasty.

Sophie read her fortune. "'Don't let good enough get in the way of perfect.' Yeah, yeah." She tossed the trite message onto the desktop.

"Wait a minute," he said. "Are you sure that's what it says?"

She looked blank for a moment, then suddenly snatched up the little paper and peered closely at it. "That's what it says, all right. Isn't it supposed to be—?"

We said it in unison. "Don't let *perfect* get in the way of *good enough*."

"My turn." The padre plucked his fortune out of his folded cookie and recited, "'Giving up is the most efficient way to solve a problem.' And I mean really, who can argue with that?"

Sexy Beast roused himself, leapt off the sofa, and sauntered to the closed door, where he stood staring at us, patiently waiting for someone to notice he had a pressing need.

"I'll do it." Martin got up and retrieved the leash and a plastic poo bag from the tote, prompting the little dog to do his happy going-outside dance. "Let's see what's happening on Main Street, SB."

Once the door had closed behind them, Sophie said, "So I have to ask, Jane. Have you shared all this with the cops?"

"Of course. I scanned The Cabbage and sent Howie and Cookie the digital file, plus I shared everything else I've learned. I don't know how much credence they'll give it, though. They still seem to think both deaths were purely accidental. At least that's the official line. Hard to tell what they really believe. Especially Howie."

"Did you tell them what the kids said?" she asked. "About seeing the guy on the roof in the middle of the night?"

"Better," I said. "The detectives heard about it from their own mouths."

Her eyebrows rose. "How'd you manage that?"

"Howie and Cookie wanted to go back up on the roof yesterday," I said, "to look around and see if they might've missed anything. They hadn't been up there since the day Scarlett fell."

"Well, that's a good sign. Did you jimmy the lock with a credit card again?"

I made a face. "Howie borrowed the key from the super. I really wanted to show off my new skill."

"I'm sure they'd have been impressed," she said. "Let me guess. The kids just happened to be up there waiting for you."

I smiled. "Naturally, I had to introduce them. It was the polite thing to do."

"And the detectives are willing to leave their parents out of it?" she asked.

"For now," I said. "I know the kids are worried their folks will find out they've been sneaking out at night to hang on the roof. Cookie assured them that as of now, they have no intention of getting their parents involved. That might change if it turns out there's a case worth pursuing, but yesterday it was just a casual conversation."

"But they told the detectives what they saw?" she asked. "The guy who fled after they showed up?"

I nodded. "Howie and Cookie doubt it was a burglar. No thefts have been reported in the building recently, and why would a burglar be up on the roof, wearing all black? If he was there to rob an apartment, he'd want to get in and out as quickly and unobtrusively as possible."

"On the other hand," she said, "black clothing makes perfect sense if your aim is to avoid being spotted on the rooftop in the dead of night while you sabotage the railing. I'm surprised the kids didn't report it to the cops—especially after Scarlett fell off that roof the next day."

"Remember, her death was assumed to be an accident."

"Which," she said, "if I may remind you—"

"I know, I know," I said, without conviction. "It probably *was* an accident. But that's my point. The kids wouldn't necessarily have made the connection. Also, they were worried about their parents finding out they were up there at three a.m. Especially Jasmine. I take it her folks are really strict. Those kids are loyal to one another. The boys weren't about to get her in trouble without a darn good reason."

"So where does the whole thing stand now?"

"Unfortunately," I said, "there's no physical evidence, no way to tell whether someone messed with the railing's bolts and anchors."

"And the kids can't identify the man in black," she said.

"Or woman in black. It was too dark up there, and it all happened very fast. On the plus side, Howie and Cookie seem impressed by how bright and articulate the kids are. I don't think they were expecting that. They really listened to them. Unless I'm reading them wrong, the detectives are intrigued."

"If the person they saw up there did weaken that railing…" Sophie looked grim. "I'm thinking of the kids."

"Elliott mentioned that the four of them sometimes hang out in the very spot Scarlett fell from." A shudder ripped through me. "I can't even…"

After I'd seen Nolan's photo of the teens on the roof, I'd realized the loose railing could have resulted in four deaths instead of one. Now that I actually knew Elliott and his friends, I couldn't bear to imagine what might have happened.

16

Show and Tell

"SCARLETT PROCTOR WAS a pathetic hoarder who used to go *dumpster-diving* in the middle of the night! Everything in her apartment came out of her neighbors' garbage. Have you ever heard of anything more *revolting?*"

Miranda Daniels was in fine form that Friday evening, yowling into living rooms across America from the Manhattan studio of her live television program, *Ramrod News*. The show's title was a misnomer, unless your idea of news is sensationalist drivel delivered in the inflammatory, hyperbolic style Miranda's legions of adoring fans couldn't get enough of.

And no, Martin and I did not number ourselves among her fans. We took pains to avoid her show, unless she was covering a story that involved Crystal Harbor. Such was the case that evening when her guests were none other than Carolyn Bailey, Bob Jernigan, and Hal Kazarian. She'd introduced them as the three individuals who'd been closest to Scarlett. The four of them sat behind the show's curved rectangular table, crafted of frosted glass with jagged edges—kind of the furniture version of Miranda herself.

After Howie and Cookie had spoken with the resident nerds on the roof five days earlier, the detectives had begun to question anyone who knew Scarlett and/or Nolan, effectively jump-starting the Crystal Harbor rumor mill. The whole town was now talking about the kinda sorta police investigation into, not one, but two possible homicides. Needless to say, everyone had a theory as to whodunit and why, including how the items that had been snatched from my home during the burglary were connected to the murders.

It had been only a matter of time before the loathsome Miranda Daniels sank her fangs into the story. Anything to boost viewership and increase advertising revenue.

Sexy Beast took one look at Miranda's larger-than-life visage on the family room's gigundo TV screen—the troweled-on makeup, the stiff helmet of bleached platinum hair, the grotesque grimace—and sprang onto my lap for cuddles. Layla, comfortably ensconced in her plush dog bed, simply raised her big head and treated the show's host to a low, warning growl.

Martin and I snuggled on the sprawling ivory leather sofa, sipping añejo tequila from tiny ceramic cups. SB attempted to wriggle in between us, but there was no *in between* to be had, and when he finally realized we weren't going to create a gap for him, he settled atop our entwined legs with an indignant huff.

The padre tipped the half-full bottle of tequila. "I don't think there's enough booze in here to blunt the skull-crushing agony of listening to that woman for an hour."

Bob Jernigan, sitting with Carolyn on Miranda's left, took exception to the host's characterization of Scarlett. With his signature indulgent smile, he said, "I've been in her apartment, Miranda, and I can assure you there was no hoarding going on. Scarlett had a keen artist's eye for unique and surprising—"

"You want to know what's *surprising*, Bob?" Miranda said.

"The fact that it took a full month for the Crystal Harbor Keystone Kops to pull their heads out of their you-know-whats and figure out that the poor girl was viciously *murdered*."

"Well, we don't actually know—"

"Murdered in the most gruesome way imaginable," she shrieked. "Thrown off the top of a high-rise building. *Splat!*"

Carolyn raised her hand, as if she were in school. "Um, the Americana isn't a high-rise, Miranda. It's only four stories."

Miranda pretended not to hear her. "Two people were right there when she fell. They *witnessed* her horrible death. We tried to get them to come on the show and share their observations with you, our loyal viewers, but they *refused*. I'll let you decide what they're trying to hide. One of them is Jane Delaney, the self-described Death Diva. You know all about that weirdo. She'll do anything with a dead body, *for money*."

I smiled. "Well, not *anything*. But please, Miranda, do tell us more." Her audience did indeed know all about me, because she trashed me on-air with tedious regularity. Not only had Miranda and I experienced several nasty run-ins, but she resented the fact I'd always refused to come on her show.

The first time she'd told her viewers about that disgraceful Jane Delaney and the appalling things she was willing to do, *for money*, I'd been convinced the negative publicity would spell the end of my career. As it happened, nothing could've been further from the truth. Once people realized there was this strange lady who you could hire to do all kinds of icky death-related stuff, my dance card, as they say, was filled. After that, every time Miranda roasted me on-air, I sat back and waited for the jobs to roll in. The more wacky and outrageous she made me sound, the more offers of work I received. As Hal would say: *Ka-ching, ka-ching*, baby!

I'd alerted Amy to be on the lookout for calls from the *Ramrod News* producers and to refuse their invitation "to speak for your dead friend, to help the American public understand what made Scarlett tick," yadda yadda.

Apparently Carolyn, Bob, and Hal thought they could handle the pugnacious host. Either that or they believed the lies about how respectfully they'd be treated.

It was clear Miranda had a lot more to offer on the subject of yours truly, but Hal, sitting to her right, interrupted. "I have firsthand knowledge of just how depraved Jane Delaney is, Miranda," he said. "We dated for a short while."

Martin's jovial expression was at odds with his words. "Okay, I'm going to take that guy apart."

"You should be thanking him, Padre. *Ka-ching, ka-ching.*" I held out my little cup for a refill.

Miranda turned her lurid grin on Hal. "Really? You and Jane? Just how depraved is she? Don't hold back. Our viewers have a right to know."

"Let's just say, the Death Diva's macabre tastes extend to her private life," he said, with a leer. "Her *very* private life if you catch my drift."

Carolyn leaned around Miranda to snap at her former beau. "You're one to talk about depraved behavior. Who knows how many women you cheated with while we were together."

He gave a nonchalant shrug. "It's not cheating if you never made promises."

Bob placed a calming hand on Carolyn's arm and leaned toward her. Softly—but not too softly for his mic to pick up— he said, "This is not the place to discuss this, hon. You're only making things worse for yourself."

She shook off Bob's hand and turned her ire on him, at full volume. "You knew Hal was sleeping with that Margaret person. She's your fiancée's best friend, for crying out loud. Why didn't you tell me? You always said I was like a daughter. Where's your family loyalty?"

Miranda pounced on that. "Family loyalty, huh? Funny you should bring that up, Carolyn. Aren't you the woman who shamelessly *seduced* her sister's boyfriend?"

"I didn't—What?" she stammered. "'Seduce'? It wasn't like that. What do you take me for?"

"She *lied* to get me into bed!" Hal rose half out of his seat, stabbing his finger toward her. "Caro told me Scarlett was getting it on with old Nolan. She made it all up, just to steal me from her sister."

"I shouldn't have bothered!" Carolyn said. "You never stopped pleading with her to take you back, like some whiny little puppy."

Sexy Beast lifted his head, his dark eyes fixed on the TV. Someone had said, "puppy," a word he associated with treats, scritches, or at the very least, lavish praise. I offered the scritches and he settled back down with a sigh that said he'd been hoping for a Vienna sausage.

"You *hounded* Scarlett," Carolyn continued. "Always following her. Wouldn't leave her alone. You even tried to get into her apartment. Nolan told me all about it. He said your stalking got so bad, she threatened to report you to the cops."

Before Hal could respond, Miranda said, "Sounds like your new boyfriend was still hung up on your sister. Just how *desperate* were you to hold on to him?"

Carolyn blinked. "What do you mean? I wasn't... I wasn't desperate. I just..."

"You just what?" Miranda asked. "You just thought it might be a good idea to eliminate the competition?"

"Whoa," the padre said. "Did she just go there?"

Bob addressed the show's host in a calm, dignified manner. "Unfounded accusations like that are less than helpful, Miranda. They only serve to inflame the situation."

Which, hello, was kind of the point of her unfounded accusations. Did he really not get what this show was about?

"We're here to uncover the *truth*, Bob!" Miranda squawked. "If you have some objection to that, I have to wonder what *you're* hiding."

He looked like he was rethinking his decision to appear on the show. *Yeah, it's a little late for that*, I wanted to tell him. He'd probably assumed that as an experienced, successful lawyer, he could handle anything the combative TV host could throw at him. There was a reason I refused to be a guest on *Ramrod News*, where the deplorable Miranda Daniels called the shots.

Bob leaned toward Carolyn again, urging her to keep her mouth shut, as any good lawyer would. She was too full of resentment to heed the sensible advice. "Why should I listen to you?" she barked. "You don't care about me. You never did."

Miranda wasn't finished with her. "You were also counting on a nice little *payday* from your sister's death, weren't you?"

"Payday?" Carolyn's eyes bulged. "What are you talking about?"

"I'm talking about the wrongful-death suit you threatened to file."

"I—I can't—They won't let me—"

"Right," Miranda said, "because you're ineligible. Only, you didn't know that when you... well, let's just say, when your sister died under *suspicious circumstances.*"

The padre said, "It wouldn't be the first time greed resulted in homicide."

"As if Carolyn needed another motive," I said, "in addition to jealousy and, oh yeah, convincing herself that Scarlett was responsible for their father's suicide and her own divorce."

"Okay," Hal said, "I need to make one thing clear right now. I was not stalking Scarlett. There's a world of difference between stalking and…and… Well, you can't call it stalking. Did I love her? Sure. Was I desperate to make her understand *how much* I loved her? To explain our, uh, misunderstandings so we could be together again? Hell yeah. And anyway, how can you believe anything that demented old freak Nolan said? Even if he didn't get into Scarlett's pants, you think he didn't try? Wake up."

"Nolan Whitehouse," Miranda informed her viewers, "was the other resident of the Americana House of Horrors who died under mysterious circumstances in the past few weeks. They're dropping like flies! You couldn't *pay* me to spend a night in that creepy old building. Nolan fell in his kitchen, supposedly 'by accident,' and split his skull *wide open.*"

Martin and I sighed in unison. Layla rolled over and turned her back to the TV.

Miranda wasn't finished. "The cops seem to be the only ones who believe he slipped on a wet floor. So here's the question I have for all my guests. Were you ever in Nolan's apartment, for any reason? Bob, we'll start with you."

Bob was already shaking his head. "I never had any reason to enter that man's apartment, Miranda. The two of us had nothing whatsoever to do with each other."

She said, "Carolyn?"

"Same," she said. "I never went in there."

"Even though he lived right next door to you? Even though your sister visited him every day?"

"So what?" she said. "Scarlett ran her own life. Nolan meant nothing to me."

Miranda turned to her other side. "Hal? What about you?"

"Oh, sure, we used to get together for tea parties all the time." His expression morphed from mocking to surly. "I never set foot in that guy's place. Why would I?"

"That's a lie!" Carolyn cried. "A couple of weeks before Nolan died, I was getting off the elevator and I saw Hal knock on his door and shove his way inside. Even through the closed door I heard him screaming at the old guy, telling him to stop bothering Scarlett if he knew what was good for him. He sounded enraged. Like a crazy person."

Martin and I looked at each other. He said what I was thinking. "'Leave Scarlett alone or you'll be sorry.'"

I pressed Pause on the remote, causing Miranda's face to freeze in a venomous snarl that, on her, was actually kind of an improvement. I said, "So that answers one question I had."

"About who wrote the note?" he asked.

"No, we still can't say whether that was the work of Carolyn, Hal, or Ed Proctor. I was referring to whether Hal was ever in Nolan's apartment. He described it as a pigsty that day we had our so-called date, and I wondered how he knew what the place looked like."

"Well, now we know. If what Carolyn says is true, he was in there a couple of weeks before Nolan died."

"It's possible that wasn't the only time," I said. "The footage from the hallway's security camera has been erased, but I told you what Elliott and Liam heard the day he died."

"They heard him yelling inside his apartment," he said. "Early that morning, right?"

"Right," I said. "Of course, Nolan could've been alone. That wouldn't have been out of character."

"What was he saying again?"

"They heard him shout, 'You think you're so special,' stuff like that. Oh, and the one that really made me sit up and take notice? 'You think *I'm* a waste of space? Wait till she finds out about you.' That happened to be Carolyn's little term of endearment for him—'a waste of space.' Coincidence?"

"Well, let's think about this." Martin took a sip of tequila and set his cup on the coffee table. "Let's say he *was* yelling at Carolyn. What could he have meant by that? Wait till *who* finds out about her?"

I pondered that. "He could've been threatening to tell Scarlett that Carolyn caused their father's suicide."

"That's one possibility," he said. "But how would Nolan know about Carolyn's involvement in the whole embezzling-suicide thing?"

I shrugged. "He lived right next to her and he was a real snoop. You saw his scrapbook, all those photos. Who knows what he might've been able to find out, just by lurking about, keeping his ears open. But what if it wasn't Carolyn he was yelling at? What if it was Bob?"

"That's easy," Martin said. "We know Nolan participated in the Winner's Circle cheating scheme. Even if he wasn't the ringleader, I'm betting he knew that Bob was involved, too. Nolan could've been threatening to tell April all about it."

"And if Nolan was yelling at Hal that morning, it could mean what?" The answer came to me right away. "If Hal was the one who sent him that nasty note, Nolan might've threatened to show it to Scarlett."

"At which point she'd learn that her creepy stalker of an ex was threatening the harmless old guy she'd taken under her wing," he said. "There goes any hope Hal had of getting back together with her."

"Maybe," I said. "Or try this one on for size. 'Wait till she finds out about you' means wait till I tell Carolyn that you've been cheating with Margaret. What do you think?"

Martin gave a thoughtful nod. "That works. So any one of them—Carolyn, Bob, or Hal—could've been the person Nolan was arguing with that morning."

"An argument that might've ended with his head slamming into something—"

"Or something slamming into his head," he said. "I'm wondering about the timing, though. You said Elliott and Liam were on their way to school when they heard Nolan hollering?"

I nodded. "The boys left extra early that day for concert choir practice. They heard the ruckus at around six-thirty."

"Which would leave more than enough time for Hal to make his shift at the sporting-goods store, if he was the one in Nolan's apartment that morning."

"Carolyn and Bob both work in the city," I said. "That's a long commute, whether by car or train, but I'm thinking they could probably leave home by seven or so and not be late for work."

"So the timing checks out for all of them. If Nolan was arguing with one of Miranda's guests—" he flung his hand toward the paused television "—that person would've had time to finish him off, drag out the mop and bucket and stage an accident, and still get to work on time."

I thumbed the Play button on the remote, and *Ramrod News* picked up where we'd left off. Carolyn had just accused Hal of barging into Nolan's apartment to threaten him. Now it was Hal's turn.

"She killed Nolan!" He was red in the face, jabbing his finger toward Carolyn as if it could fire bullets. "She used to go on about him, how much she hated him, how he was the lowest kind of parasite. She tried to get the building's owners to evict him, and when they refused, she took matters into her own hands."

Carolyn tried to rise, but Bob pressed her back into her seat. He looked at Miranda as if expecting her to defuse the situation. Seriously? *Defuse* is the polar opposite of what Miranda Daniels does every weeknight from six to seven p.m. She simply sat there taking it all in, with a smile that could only be called viperous.

"That's not true!" Carolyn screamed. "How can you say that? I admit I hated that old loser. You have no idea what it's like living next door to someone like that. I used to have the bug guy come and spray my place every week just to make sure nothing crawled over to my apartment from his. But I didn't do anything to him."

Now she was the one pointing, as tears of rage streaked her face. I vowed then and there to buy this woman a tube of waterproof mascara. "I know it was you that did it, Hal," she said. "You killed that old man because of your precious Scarlett. She loved him more than she ever loved you."

Sheesh. That was going to get tongues wagging. I knew she didn't mean her sister *loved* Nolan, not in that way, but I could see how the viewing public might misinterpret her words.

Hal said, "No one believes your nonsense, Caro. Everyone

knows how unhinged you are. You need help. That's why I was gonna keep your secret, about offing Nolan, until you made up that crap just now about me threatening the old freak."

"This is ridiculous!" she said. "I suppose you think I killed Scarlett, too."

He gave an elaborate shrug. "Feel like unburdening yourself?"

Now Bob had to physically restrain her to keep her from springing across the set and attacking her former lover.

"You did it!" she shrieked. "You killed my sister!"

Hal laughed and twirled his finger at his head in the universal symbol for stark raving bonkers.

She directed her next words to Miranda. "They think someone weakened the railing, right? Like, the night before Scarlett died? Well, Hal was staying at my place that night."

"All night?" Miranda asked, with a mean little smirk.

"Yes. So what?" Carolyn said. "Actually, not *all* night as it turned out. I woke up in the middle of the night and noticed he wasn't in bed. I assumed he was just in the bathroom or getting some water, but when he didn't come back, I went looking for him. He wasn't in the apartment."

"What did you do then?" Miranda asked.

"I threw on my robe and ran the two flights up to Scarlett's place. I figured he had to be there, that all that stalking and pleading had finally paid off and she was taking him back. At least for the night."

Hal shook his head with a little smile, ostentatiously bored.

"I pounded on her door until she opened it," she continued. "I demanded to see Hal. She swore he wasn't there, but I didn't trust her, so I pushed past her and searched every room. She was alone."

Which meant Carolyn had been lying back when she told me she'd never seen her sister's apartment until after her death. Either that or she was lying now, spinning a tale to make her detested ex-boyfriend appear guilty.

"Did you ever find him?" Miranda asked.

"No." Carolyn sent Hal a dark look. "I even went out to the parking lot and looked for his car. It was right there in its assigned space, so I knew he must still be in the building."

"Or *on* the building," Miranda said. "Meaning the rooftop. Did that occur to you?"

"Not at the time. But these last few days, with the cops asking questions, and everyone talking about that railing and how it shouldn't have failed, I put two and two together and realized what he was up to that night."

"Which is…?" Miranda was going to make her say it.

"Hal went up to the roof in the middle of the night to mess with that railing," Carolyn said. "He wanted to make sure it would break the next time my sister leaned on it."

Hal grinned directly into the camera. "You getting all this, Detectives? Taking good notes, I hope."

I had no doubt Howie and Cookie were indeed watching this show, and recording it, and yes, scribbling like mad in their little notebooks.

Carolyn said, "I can't imagine why they haven't arrested him yet. Just how guilty do you have to be before they do something about it?"

"Did Hal finally come back that night?" Miranda asked her.

"Yes. An hour or so later he slipped back into bed like nothing happened, but I wasn't having it. I demanded to know where he'd been. 'Out walking,' he says. 'Insomnia.' This man never went out walking in his life. When he can't sleep, he pours a few shots. It took me all this time to realize he murdered my sister."

"How about it, Hal?" Miranda asked. "Determined to stick with your story? Went out for a stroll in the middle of the night?"

"Okay, the truth?" Hal directed his explanation to Carolyn. "Margaret was sleeping over at Bob and April's apartment that night, like she sometimes does when she's visiting over there and is too drunk to drive home. She crashes in one of their guest rooms."

"Margaret!" Carolyn practically spat the name, clearly outraged at his mention of the "other woman." Did she even realize that's the role she herself had played not so long ago?

"Yeah, *Margaret.*" His tone was caustic. "Deal with it. Anyway, she texts me and says come over at one-thirty, but don't knock or make any noise. I should just text her when I'm there. She doesn't want to wake up Bob and April. Those two aren't exactly my biggest fans."

"Is that true?" Miranda turned to Bob. "You didn't want Hal shacking up with this Margaret at your place?"

Bob's grim expression was a far cry from his usual affable smile. "I prefer to have some say about who stays overnight in my home. I had no idea Margaret invited…" He tossed his hand in Hal's general direction, as though his very name were distasteful.

Hal said, "So that's where I was for close to an hour in the middle of the night. I left Margaret thoroughly satisfied, then went right back to Caro's place."

"More lies!" Carolyn cried.

"About leaving Margaret satisfied?" He wasn't so

handsome now with that malignant smile. "I can't help it if you're frig—"

"You were up on the roof sabotaging that railing," Carolyn said. "You can deny it all you want, but I know the truth."

"You want to know what I think?" he said. "I think you took advantage of my absence to sneak up to the roof and do what you just accused me of doing. You knew I was still in love with Scarlett and you couldn't stand it. You wanted me all to yourself. I know you have the tools to do the job. I've seen them in your closet."

I assumed the detectives would now interview Carolyn and Hal again. They'd also talk to April's friend Margaret, to find out whether he was indeed with her that night and for how long. If Hal and Margaret would be willing to show them the texts he says they exchanged, that would help to bolster his story.

"Sorry, Hal, but Carolyn didn't do it," Miranda announced. "Not by herself, at any rate. That railing was sabotaged by someone who knew what he was doing. Someone who had enough muscle power to get the job done. There's a time for sexism, and news flash—this is it. Scarlett's killer is male." She stared right into the camera. "And *spare me* the politically correct emails, people. If you're living in some la-di-da fantasy world filled with jacked-up females and *spineless sissy boys* who wouldn't know how to fix a leaky faucet if their life depended on it, all I can say is, wake up and smell the *testosterone.*"

"Don't be shy, Miranda," Martin said. "Tell us how you really feel."

The show's host turned to Bob. "So what were *you* doing in the middle of the night while these two were running around the building?"

"At the risk of boring your audience, Miranda," he said, "I spent the entire night sleeping soundly next to my fiancée. I actually asked her for one of her sleeping pills at around eleven because I was lying awake thinking about work, and I had to get up very early the next morning to make my train into the city. A few minutes after I took the pill, I was out like a light. Looks like I missed all the excitement," he added dryly.

For sure the detectives would interview April again, too, to ask whether she did indeed give her fiancé a sleeping pill.

I grabbed the remote and pressed Pause. "Okay, I don't know whether Carolyn can fix a leaky faucet, but I do know she put together most of the furniture in her apartment. She might not be a carpenter, but she knows her way around a toolbox."

"You mentioned that she goes to a gym," he said.

"The same one Bob goes to," I said. "I wonder how much upper-body strength it takes to loosen the bolts and anchors of a railing like that."

"Hard to say. Depends how tight the connections are, whether they've been painted over. There are a lot of variables."

"I've been thinking about something Carolyn said after the memorial service. I kind of talked her into giving Scarlett's ashes a green burial in accordance with her wishes, and she said… How did she put it? 'After everything, I owe her that at least.'"

"After what?" he asked. "What is 'everything'?"

"That's just it. At the time I assumed she meant the generally crappy way she'd treated Scarlett. Stealing her boyfriend. Accusing her of causing their father's suicide, all that. Now I'm wondering whether she could've meant, well…"

"Taking her life." Martin lifted the bottle of tequila and topped off his little cup. He leaned over to refill mine.

"Just a drop," I said.

"You'll be interested to know," he said, "that I found Bob's Facebook account. There are pictures of him running in the New York City Marathon last month."

I knew we were both picturing the same thing: Bob Jernigan, dressed head to toe in black, sprinting through the woods behind our house, with a teenage basketball star and a big, muscular dog on his heels.

"Did you get into Carolyn's Facebook?" I asked. "Or Hal's?"

"Carolyn's is locked down," he said. "I can't see her posts or pictures without friending her. Hal's is wide-open, but it's all pictures of him partying, usually with a hot babe clinging to him."

"Let's think about this," I said. "Why would Hal kill Scarlett if he loved her so much?"

"I've done executive protection for a couple of celebrity stalking victims," the padre said, using his preferred term for the more elite bodyguard services he offers. "These creeps might claim it's about love, but trust me. It's about control and possession, and the danger often escalates over time."

"So the stalker's attitude is, if I can't have her, nobody can?"

"Unfortunately, it does happen," he said. "Don't ask me if Hal falls into that category. We both know he's a creep, but is he a lethally dangerous creep?"

"At the time Scarlett died," I said, "Hal was convinced—thanks to Carolyn's lies—that she was sexually involved with

Nolan. He was jealous."

"Meanwhile he was getting it on with both Carolyn and Margaret," he said.

"And who knows who else. He tried with me." The padre's scowl prompted me to add, "Just to pump me for information, Padre. He wasn't actually, you know, attracted to me."

"Of course not. I mean, the very idea." Martin made a retching noise.

I grabbed the nearest object—fortunately for my boyfriend, it was a cushy throw pillow—and hurled it at him. He thanked me and tucked it behind his head. Sexy Beast jumped up and joined in the fun, grabbing another pillow and giving it the old death shake. It's at times like these I'm reminded that, contrary to appearances, my pampered, high-strung, seven-pound poodle is in fact descended from wolves.

Layla gave the three of us a look easily interpreted as *Settle down, children.*

"There's something else, though," I said. "Scarlett was trying hard to save the Americana, which, if she'd been successful, would've cost Hal a hefty relocation allowance."

"She had a plan, right?" he asked. "To get a group of investors to buy the building?"

"Right," I said. "And Hal knew about it. What he didn't know is that Dom was already working on it—without success as it turned out."

"So Hal had a financial incentive to do away with Scarlett."

"As for Bob," I said, "his motivation for murder would've been self-preservation, or more accurately, preservation of his lifestyle. His law career for starters."

"Which would be on the rocks if his college cheating came

to light," he said. "Not to mention the possibility of being dumped by April. She has serious family money, right?"

"Yep. Plus she's his entrée into the highest New York social circles."

"When Scarlett died," he said, "she was looking into Nolan's death, trying to decide whether it really was an accident. This made her a threat to whoever killed him."

"You sound like you really do believe he was murdered," I said.

"Are you going to pretend you don't?"

I shook my head. "I don't think either death was accidental—his or Scarlett's. There, I said it."

Martin reached for my hand and squeezed it, and I knew nothing more needed to be said. He picked up the remote and pressed Play.

Miranda's corrosive grin raised the hairs on my nape. It was clear she had something special planned. I did not trust this woman's idea of *special*.

She made eye contact with each of her guests. "Who's up for a little show and tell?"

When this was greeted with perplexed frowns, she reached under the table and produced two objects, which she held up, one in each hand.

"No!" I jerked upright. "How…?"

Martin shook his head, clearly dumbfounded.

Carolyn, Bob, and Hal gaped at the old scrapbook with its navy-blue leatherette cover, and the green, spiral-bound notebook adorned with the words *Winner's Circle*. Every Crystal Harbor resident watching the show would immediately comprehend their significance, since the entire gossip-loving town was now well aware that two items matching their descriptions had been burgled from my home a week earlier.

Hal and Carolyn appeared suitably shocked. Bob's eyes widened fractionally, but otherwise he controlled his reaction, like the seasoned lawyer he was.

Martin said, "Where on earth did she get those?"

It was a rhetorical question, but I answered it anyway. "Someone must've handed them over to the show. Correction. Someone *sold* them to the show. You just know *Ramrod News* would've paid top dollar for something like that."

"It had to be the burglar," he said. "Who else would've had them in their possession?"

We both knew said burglar was most likely sitting in Miranda's studio at that very moment, pretending he, or she, had no inkling how those two items had ended up there.

17

Booty Call

MIRANDA SPENT THE rest of the show attempting to get her guests to fess up. Did they know about these books? Had they seen them before? What did the gobbledygook in the green notebook mean?

Carolyn, Hal, and Bob claimed ignorance on all points, including the last one. I knew for certain that at least one of the three was lying. Carolyn had The Cabbage, courtesy of Clover Eklund. Scarlett's sister knew darn well what the Winner's Circle was, and that her father had benefited from the college cheating scheme. Yet she primly sat there, playing dumb.

Miranda was playing dumb, too, of course, pretending these intriguing items hadn't been sold to her show by one of the individuals sitting to her right or left. She appeared more interested in the weird scrapbook than the old green notebook, the contents of which were incomprehensible. Oh, she made noises about how *mysterious* and *bizarre* the notebook was, maybe even *satanic,* and how she was certain that once decoded, it was bound to take down some *president* or *movie star.* Maybe the *entire United States Government.*

But there was no denying Nolan Whitehouse's scrapbook provided juicier material: "a peek inside the *demented brain* of someone who was violently, viciously *murdered!*" as Miranda so delicately put it. I cringed as she jeeringly displayed some of the pages. No matter how troubled or antisocial Nolan had been, he didn't deserve this.

One of the pages she briefly showed was the one where Nolan had pasted the threatening note he'd received: *Leave Scarlett alone or you'll be sorry.* A tiny scrap of white paper marked the spot where it had been ripped out of the book. Whoever had sold the items to the show had taken the precaution of getting rid of the incriminating note. It was reasonable to assume that same individual had not only authored the note but had broken into my home and probably killed Nolan as well.

The next morning, Martin took Sexy Beast and Layla to the local dog park. Hounded (so to speak) by unanswered questions, I sat at the breakfast-room table with a mug of black coffee and worked the phones, starting with Elliott Epstein. He told me that yes, he'd watched *Ramrod News* the previous evening. No doubt everyone in Crystal Harbor had tuned in. He knew the two books Miranda had displayed were the items the burglar had made off with from my house that night. I asked whether he'd ever seen the scrapbook during any of his visits to Nolan's apartment.

"No, but I saw that other one," he said, excitedly, "that Winner's Circle book. The four of us were over at Nolan's place a couple of months ago—well, there were five of us including Scarlett. We were making a huge pot of split-pea soup and roasting, like, a hundred chicken legs to stock his freezer. He comes out of his bedroom with that notebook and hands it to Scarlett. Says her dad gave it to him right before he… you know."

"Before he committed suicide," I said.

"Right. Nolan said that Ed—that's her dad—Ed wanted to make sure it went to someone he trusted. I didn't even know the two of them knew each other, Nolan and Scarlett's dad."

"I suspected it," I said. So that was one question answered. It would seem Ed Proctor had been the ringleader of the Winner's Circle cheating ring since the notebook had been in his possession.

We were both silent for a moment. I had little doubt Elliott was thinking the same thing I was, that the timing was significant. Ed gave the notebook to Nolan for safekeeping immediately before ending his life last winter.

"And then Nolan gave it to Scarlett," Elliott said, "just a few weeks before *he* died. He said her dad would've wanted her to have it, that she'd know what to do with it."

"Did Nolan tell her what the Winner's Circle was?" I asked. "What the encrypted entries meant?"

"No," Elliott said. "She asked, and he just said she'd figure it out. He told her the important thing was to keep it safe. We took turns leafing through it, but I mean, it's just a bunch of columns written in some crazy code. Now that that stupid show has it, who knows if it'll ever be decoded."

"Oh, I'm confident it will be." I wasn't ready to reveal that the notebook had already been decoded and that in fact several copies of the translation were in circulation.

Elliott said, "You think Nolan knew? You know, that something bad was going to happen to him, and that's why he gave the notebook to Scarlett? I mean, I've been wondering if he maybe had some kind of, uh, premonition. Don't laugh."

"I'm not laughing," I said. "I know you're not suggesting he could predict the future. Whether or not Nolan's death was accidental, he might've had a feeling, a premonition, like you say, based on circumstances we know nothing about. Something might've happened to make him wonder if his time was near."

"I guess you know about stuff like that," he said, "'cause of what you do for a living."

It didn't really work that way, but I let it go. "Listen, Elliott, there's one other thing I want to ask you. That morning you heard Nolan shouting—when you and Liam were passing his apartment on the way to school. Are you absolutely certain you didn't hear a second voice? Maybe a softer voice, like a woman's?"

"Sorry, no. It was just Nolan. He could've been on the phone, or just, you know, yelling at no one."

"Okay, well, you've been very help—"

"But I'll tell you what I told Detective Werker last night."

"You spoke with Howie—I mean the detective last night? He called you?"

"No, I called him," he said, "after *Ramrod News*. He gave me his direct number after the break-in. I remembered something. Not about the break-in, but about when Nolan was yelling. I don't think it means anything, but Detective Werker told me nothing's too trivial and to let him and his partner decide what's relevant. And everyone knows they're kinda looking into whether someone did something to Nolan."

"So, what did you tell him?" I asked.

"Well, when we were passing Nolan's place and he was being so loud, the door next to his opened and the lady that lives there stuck her head out."

"Just to be clear," I said, "are you talking about apartment Two-J? Where Carolyn Bailey lives?"

"Yeah, it was her. Scarlett's sister. She looked real annoyed. I guess all that hollering was bothering her. She gave Nolan's door a dirty look and went back inside her apartment. I thought maybe she was planning to knock on his door and tell him to pipe down, but changed her mind when she saw Liam and me standing there."

I thanked Elliott and hung up. I'd half convinced myself Nolan had been arguing with Carolyn that morning. Apparently that was not the case.

Next I called Cookie.

She answered with, "Howie and I had a bet going about when we'd hear from you today. He said it would be after ten a.m. I said before, because you wouldn't be able to wait that long to see what information you could squeeze out of us. Thanks for costing me a pitcher at Murray's tonight—*and* a basket of Cajun curly fries."

I checked the time. it was 10:03. "Invite me along and I'll throw in an order of Larry's Nachos." The loaded nachos at Murray's Pub had recently been renamed in honor of Larry Kool, a local celebrity whose murder last summer had stunned the community. Larry could never get enough of those amazing nachos—laden with spicy meat, two kinds of cheese, beans, jalapeños, guacamole, sour cream, and anything else you can imagine piling onto a platter of warm tortilla chips.

Dang! Why did I have to start thinking about nachos? Would I be able to hold out until elevenses?

After telling me to meet them at Murray's at seven, she said, "Your first question is going to be whether we confiscated those 'show and tell' items from the *Ramrod News* studio."

"Well, you must've," I said. "I mean, it's stolen property, right?"

"We phoned the studio immediately to inform them that officers were on their way to take possession of the items, which were evidence in an active burglary investigation as well as two possible homicide investigations."

"Why do I feel like this story's not going to have a happy ending?" I asked.

"They handed over the scrapbook," she said. "The Winner's Circle notebook, however, had managed to disappear before we got there."

"It *disappeared?*" I said. "How the heck does that happen?"

"You know what I'm thinking."

"That it was one of Miranda's guests," I said. "He, or she, snatched the thing on their way out of the studio."

"Yeah, but which one of them did it?" she asked. "And why?"

"Okay, let's back up," I said. "Who sold the books to the show? I'm assuming it was a cash transaction. Did Miranda tell you that at least?"

"She *swears* they were dropped off anonymously and that no money changed hands." I could almost hear the detective rolling her eyes.

"But you have the scrapbook, right?" I said. "Did you see that the threatening note has been torn out? I noticed it when Miranda was flipping through the pages."

"That note was the first thing we looked for," she said. "Whoever sold, I mean 'dropped off' those books wanted to make sure that note was history."

"Which points to either Carolyn or Hal," I said.

"Right," Cookie agreed, "because what reason would Bob Jernigan have had to warn Nolan away from Scarlett? But don't forget, this person sold *both* books to the show."

I saw where she was going with this. "Providing *Ramrod News* with the Winner's Circle notebook basically guarantees the cheating scheme will become public knowledge. Even if Clover's decryption never gets out, as long as that notebook exists, eventually someone's going to decode it again."

"Carolyn would definitely not want to see it go public," she said. "And Bob has even more reason to keep it hush-hush."

"So that leaves Hal," I said. "Assuming he's the one who broke into my house, he grabbed the notebook on impulse along with the scrapbook, but hasn't a clue what the Winner's Circle is."

"The only thing he'd care about," Cookie said, "would be the threatening note, if he was the one who sent it to Nolan."

"And what do you know," I said. "That note was torn out before the scrapbook was handed over to Miranda. With the note gone, he had no use for either of those books, except for how much money they could bring him. Because as we know, Hal is particularly fond of money. So it's pretty clear how *Ramrod News* got the books. Is all this enough to arrest him for burglary?"

"No, and anyway, there's the bigger question of homicide. *Possible* homicide," she corrected herself.

"Why would Hal have gone to the bother of selling the mysterious Winner's Circle notebook to the show," I said, "only to turn around and snatch it back? It doesn't make sense."

"Which tells me it was either Carolyn or Bob who made off with it last night."

"What else do you have for me?" I asked.

"Well, aren't we greedy today."

"Make that an order of Larry's Nachos and some fried calamari," I said, knowing how fond Cookie was of the calamari at Murray's Pub. "Hal and Margaret's texts. Did they show them to you?"

"Yep. It all checks out. Middle-of-the-night sexting and booty call on Tuesday, November fourth, confirmed."

"Hmm… Think he would've had time to 'thoroughly satisfy' Margaret and then go up to the roof and weaken the railing?"

"That would have to be a pretty quick booty call," she said. "And don't forget, Carolyn was wide-awake and running all around looking for him. Not to mention, we're talking two changes of clothing to get into and out of the black outfit the kids told us about. I asked Margaret. Hal wasn't wearing black clothes on the booty call."

"You really like saying, 'booty call,' don't you? Tell me about the sleeping pill. The one Bob says his fiancée gave him so he could get a good night's sleep while everyone else was running around and getting into all kinds of mischief."

"April did indeed give him a pill," Cookie said, "at around eleven that night. She watched him take it and says he conked out a short while later. Didn't get up until his alarm woke him at five forty-five."

I huffed out a breath. "So where does that leave us?"

"Of our three likely suspects in Scarlett's maybe-murder," she said, "Carolyn's the only one without an alibi for what she was doing in the middle of the night. She was all by her lonesome during the critical hours."

"Because her booty call bailed on her," I said, "to go on a different booty call. Sheesh, now you have me saying it."

After we hung up, I started thinking about those nachos

again and wishing Murray's opened earlier than eleven. I couldn't decide whether to hold out until then or to scarf down the two pieces of leftover fried chicken that were winking at me from the bottom of their greasy cardboard bucket every time I opened the fridge.

I was still debating this momentous question when my phone rang—or rather, when it started playing "Tequila." The screen displayed Carolyn Bailey's name. I considered ditching the call. I was still processing my conversation with Cookie and not at all confident I could carry on a civilized conversation with Scarlett's sister without blurting, *"You did it, didn't you, Carolyn? You killed her. Admit it!"*

In the end, curiosity won out and I tapped the green button. "Hi, Caro—"

"I need to see you." She sounded frazzled, close to tears. "Now."

"Now?" I said, still obsessing over those nachos. "Right now?"

"It's an emergency."

The line went dead.

Fourteen minutes later I pulled into one of the guest slots in the Americana's parking lot. As I hurried toward the building, I passed Hal's assigned space. His aging black Tesla was noticeably absent. In its place was a brand-new Tesla that looked like it had just rolled off the dealer's lot. Not a scratch on its shiny silver paint job.

Well, whaddaya know. Looked like someone came into some *ka-ching ka-ching*, baby.

When I exited the stairwell on the second floor, I spied Carolyn in her open doorway, staring fixedly at the closed elevator, her back to me. How long had she been standing in that spot, impatiently awaiting my arrival?

She appeared startled when I approached from the other direction. She wore sweats and no makeup, her skin blotchy from crying. Her hair had been scraped back into a sloppy, off-center ponytail.

"I need to hire you," she said, once we were in her apartment. She didn't invite me to sit or offer coffee and cookies this time. "You have to help me."

"Okay, first tell me what the emergency is."

"Did you watch the show last night?" she asked. *"Ramrod News?"*

I wanted to tell her she'd be hard-pressed to find a resident of Crystal Harbor who had not seen that show. Instead I simply answered in the affirmative.

"Then you saw!" she cried. "She has my notebook. That Winner's Circle thing. She refuses to give it to me."

"*Your* notebook?"

"It belonged to my sister, so it's mine now," she said, stabbing a finger at her chest. "I asked Miranda for it the instant the show ended. She just *laughed* at me!"

"Well, that was, um, very rude of her," I said, "but I don't know what you think I can do about it."

"Get it back for me!" she shouted, as if I were impossibly dense. "You know that woman. Go see her. Explain that that book is my legal property and see if you can get her to hand it over. If not, get it any way you can. Steal it, bribe someone, I don't care. Just get it."

"All right, time out," I said. "I don't break the law."

"Oh please," she sneered, "everyone knows you bend the rules when it suits you. Just tell me what it'll cost. Only remember, I don't have a bottomless purse like some of your rich-bitch clients."

I said, "Here's why I can't get that book for you, Carolyn." She started to object, forcing me to talk over her. "Miranda doesn't have it anymore. Someone stole it from the studio last night."

She gaped at me for long seconds. "I don't believe you."

"Then take it up with Detective Kaplan. She's the one who told me."

I watched her consider the possibilities, watch them chase one another behind her bloodshot eyes. Watched her come to the same inevitable conclusion I just did.

Bob.

Carolyn avoided my eyes as she reached out to open the door. "All right, then. Sorry I made you come by for nothing."

I didn't budge. "Do you still have the papers Clover gave you? The copy of the notebook and the decryption?"

Color flooded her face as she swung back toward me. "She told you about that? I should've known that dotty old woman couldn't be trust—"

"I know you met Clover," I said, "so you know she's anything but dotty. If it weren't for her hard work, and Scarlett's, you wouldn't even know about the Winner's Circle."

Her chin came up. "My father didn't cheat his way through college, Jane. He might've fallen in with the wrong crowd for a while, might've made, um, a couple of errors in judgment, but he graduated with distinction from an Ivy League university, and for anyone to insinuate—"

"No one's *insinuating* anything." I'd had about enough of this irritating woman and her self-serving logic. "Not only did your father cheat on a bunch of tests, Carolyn, but he was the ringleader. The whole thing was his idea and—"

"No! You're wrong."

"Then why did he have the Winner's Circle notebook all these years?" I asked. "Your father gave it to Nolan just before he… before he passed, and then Nolan gave it to your sister about two months ago. Clover helped her to decode it."

"Dad had the notebook because he *stole it from Bob*!" she said.

"He…? Wait a minute. Back up."

"After Clover gave me those papers," she said, "and I realized what they were, I handed them over to Bob. I thought he should have them since his name was in there, too. He was stunned. He said the original, the notebook, was locked in a safe in his apartment. At least he'd thought it was. My dad must've snuck into the safe during his last visit to him."

"When he was trying to get Bob's help in fighting his embezzling charge, right?" I said.

"Right. They were… well, let's just say they parted on very poor terms."

So *Bob* was the ringleader?

"But how did your father get into the safe?" I asked. "How would he have known the combination?"

"Bob said the combination was some simple numerical code they'd used for the Winner's Circle way back then, a default computer password they could all remember—all the guys who helped run it. I guess Bob wanted a combination for his safe that he wasn't likely to forget."

So she was basically admitting that Ed was one of the "guys who helped run" the scheme, since he knew the computer password, while still asserting his participation amounted to "a couple of errors in judgment." Got it.

As I left her apartment, I found myself thinking about

Bob. I could see him calmly slipping the notebook inside his suit jacket last night while everyone's attention was elsewhere—most likely on Miranda as she laughed off Carolyn's insistence that the dang thing belonged to her. Bob would have strolled right past them and out of the studio well before the police arrived to take charge of the evidence.

I grabbed the stairwell door handle and paused, suddenly remembering that Nolan had planned to attend his college reunion dinner at a posh restaurant in Manhattan. Which had surprised me. I mean, talk about a fish out of water. Now, however, it occurred to me that perhaps his reason for RSVP'ing *yes* had nothing to do with rekindling old friendships.

Clover had said they'd finished decrypting the notebook by the end of September, three days before Nolan died. I have to believe Scarlett would've shared the good news with him.

I imagined Nolan rising from his seat during the dinner and securing everyone's attention. Imagined the look on Bob's and April's faces as he regaled the distinguished alumni with fond reminiscences of the Winner's Circle, the brainchild of their own Bob Jernigan. Who knew? Perhaps some of the other cheaters might even be in the room, sipping champagne and chowing down on beluga caviar and chateaubriand. They'd be practically wetting their pants for fear of being named next. What jolly fun for poor, old, forgettable Nolan Whitehouse.

I pictured his self-satisfied grin, imagined him thinking, *This one's for you, Ed.*

Sadly, he never got the chance to live out that particular fantasy.

You think I'm *a waste of space?* he'd shouted shortly before his death. *Wait till she finds out about you.*

I'd speculated that the mysterious "she" was Scarlett, or perhaps Carolyn. Now only one name came to mind.

April.

It was Bob in Nolan's apartment that morning—it had to be. Nolan had been taunting him, threatening to tell Bob's fiancée about his onetime role as the creator of, and driving force behind, the Winner's Circle college cheating scheme. And not just April. I could see Nolan making sure Bob's Wall Street law firm knew all about it. Maybe the state bar, as well.

Perhaps Nolan told Bob he was planning a big announcement at the reunion dinner they'd both be attending the next evening. I could picture Bob snapping, could picture him ensuring his old college buddy would be a no-show.

Not only had Scarlett suspected Nolan had been murdered, but she'd actually had a suspect in mind, according to Cookie. And she'd possessed some kind of clue, which at first I'd assumed was the threatening note Nolan had pasted into his scrapbook.

I now realized I'd gotten that part wrong. The clue wasn't the *Leave Scarlett alone* note, it was the Winner's Circle notebook. Once it had been decrypted, Scarlett had seen how damaging it could be to Bob Jernigan. He'd had ample reason, not only to get it back, but to keep Nolan from blabbing about the cheating scheme and Bob's role at the head of it.

I saw now that Scarlett had never intended to place the notebook in a safe-deposit box, as Clover had assumed. She'd meant to hand it over to Detective Cookie Kaplan, who would have placed it in a secure evidence locker to be used in the investigation into Nolan Whitehouse's murder. Something about her conversation with Cookie, however, had made her feel her concerns weren't being taken seriously, and the notebook had ended up in her desk, where Martin came across it five days after her death.

Had Bob known Scarlett was looking into Nolan's death? That she was calling the cops and asking all kinds of inconvenient questions? If so, what did he do about it?

A laughing male voice wrenched me out of my reverie. "Spacey Janey. That's what I'm gonna call you from now on."

I stood blinking at a grinning redheaded teen, my hand still gripping the stairwell door handle. I made a show of shaking my head to clear it. "Lost in thought there for a bit. How are you doing, Liam?"

"I'm great. Listen," he said, "I just want you to know, I wasn't kidding the other day when I asked if you can use an assistant."

"Right," I said. "For all that 'gooey corpse stuff.'"

His grin broadened. "Hey, I'm willing to pay my dues. I can start with the merely disgusting and work my way up to the revoltingly vomitous."

"If you're serious about working, there are times I could actually use a little help."

His eyes widened. "Really?"

"Don't get too excited," I said. "I'm talking about pretty boring stuff to start, like delivering flowers to veterans' gravesites on Memorial Day. Demand has grown and it's getting to be too much, even with my boyfriend pitching in. Nowadays the job's taking us to cemeteries all over the Island and in the five boroughs."

"I can do that," he said, "but Memorial Day is, what, five months away."

"I might have other jobs," I said, "but some of them wouldn't be suitable for a minor."

"I'll be eighteen on New Year's Day. Bring on the gore."

"Question. Do you own a suit?"

Liam recoiled in mock umbrage. "What kind of barbarian do you take me for, madam? But of course I own a suit. And not one, but *two* genuine polyester neckties. Need me to impersonate a funeral director? I can do that. The embalming part might be a little tricky, but I'm willing to give it a go."

"Baby steps. First let me meet your folks. I want to make sure they have no problem with you helping me to, say, scatter ashes or work a pet funeral. Why don't you ask them to give me a call." I handed him my business card.

"And now for my impression of a gentleman." He commandeered the handle and held the door open, escorting me into the stairwell with a little bow and a sweeping arm gesture. I'd assumed that, like me, he was on his way out of the building, but instead he pointed down the hallway. "I'm going to Elliott's. We're gonna study for the calculus midterm." He saluted me with the card. "So stoked, Jane. I'll be dreaming of pet funerals."

"Okay, that's kind of disturbing, Liam."

The door clanged shut and I turned toward the stairs. I didn't make it down one step before I again heard my name called. I looked up and saw Hal Kazarian leaning over the third-floor handrail.

"Thought I heard your sexy voice," he said.

18

Spare Fishing Tackle

"GIVE THE 'SEXY' thing a rest, Hal. You're not into me and I'm definitely not into you."

"Ouch." He sauntered down the steps to join me on the second-floor landing. "All alone today? What, is it Grampy's nap time?"

"Bold words from a guy who got tossed on his caboose last time he underestimated Grampy."

"A lucky sucker punch."

I couldn't help it, I laughed, the sound echoing in the deserted stairwell. "If that makes you feel better. The truth? He swatted you like a pesky mosquito. Trust me, if Martin McAuliffe ever decides to punch you, there will be no confusion on the matter."

"You like the tough guys, huh?" He leaned against the yellow-painted handrail, crossing his arms and ankles. Another of his patented cool-guy poses, which I was finding exceedingly tiresome. Something else I could do without? His spicy cologne, which seemed to gain intensity in the confines of the stairwell.

A door opened and closed overhead, followed by rapid footfalls down the stairs. We both said a quick hi to Amy

Collingwood as she passed us on her way to the first floor. She made no move to stop and chat, for which I was grateful.

When we were alone again, I said, "I saw your new ride out in the parking lot. Pretty swanky."

"Yeah, I figured it was time for a change."

"That must've set you back," I said. "Forgive my curiosity, but I can't help wondering how you could afford it. Your big relocation allowance is months away."

He shrugged. "When opportunity knocks, you've gotta answer the door."

"Of course," I said, "sometimes you have to make your own opportunity."

He frowned. "Meaning?"

"Meaning how did you come by those two books you sold to *Ramrod News*?"

His dismissive snicker was unconvincing. "I want some of what you've been smoking."

Sometimes a fib is the fastest route between point A and point B. "You know I'm good friends with Miranda Daniels, right?" I said.

Hal went very still. "Bull. The way she talked about you on the show last night? The woman hates your guts."

I laughed. "Are you kidding? She does that as a favor to me. She knows the more outrageous she makes me sound, the more her viewers will be banging down my door, just wild to hire that weirdo Death Diva broad." Naturally, if Miranda ever discovered how much her barbs were helping me, she'd never utter my name 0n-air again. "Oh, and by the way," I added, "thanks for that business about how depraved I am. Every little bit helps."

"So you and Miranda are besties," he said. "So what?"

"So I called her this morning and I said, 'Miranda honey, the curiosity is killing me. Who sold you those books?' And what do you think she told me?"

He acted nonchalant, but if his heightened color was any indication, it was just that. An act. "Are you going to get to the point sometime today?"

I mock-punched his shoulder. "Now, don't be modest. It was *you*, you little scamp! And you just sat there all innocent like you'd never seen the things before. What an actor. Your talents are wasted at Vargas Sporting Goods. I'm telling you, you should move to Hollywood."

Clearly Hal was torn between denying the accusation and preening under the fake flattery. Ah, the challenges of living with a bloated ego.

The door swung open and an older couple entered the stairwell. We all nodded greetings before they gradually made their way down to the ground level.

After we heard the door close on the first floor, Hal said, "Well, if I did sell them to the show, and I'm not saying I did, what of it? Is it against the law to make a profit? This is America. Supply and demand, baby. I had the supply, they had the demand. *If* I did it, which I'm still not—"

"Yeah, yeah, you're still not admitting it," I said. "I'll tell you what *is* against the law, Hal. Disposing of items you know darn well are evidence in a criminal investigation."

"I didn't know—"

"*Everyone* knew by the time that show aired," I said, "so don't even try that with me. You want to know what's an even worse crime? The burglary itself."

I watched the implication register. "What are you inferring?" he asked.

I bit my tongue to keep from correcting this slow learner's word choice, as April had done. "You broke into my house, Hal. You grabbed the scrapbook and that green notebook from my desk and then ran like hell through the woods so my big, strong dog and my big, strong pet sitter wouldn't catch up with you and, you know, bite you and stuff. The dog, not the pet sitter."

"What are you talking about?" He wore a perplexed frown. "I'm not the one that broke into your place."

"Hal, give it up. You had the goods. You sold them to *Ramrod News*. I know you did it, and soon enough the Crystal Harbor cops are going to know you did it."

Yeah, I know it was kind of chancy, my making that kind of veiled threat. Okay, not so veiled. But my gut told me he was no danger to me at that moment. Physically, he still appeared relaxed, plus a handful of people had seen us schmoozing in the stairwell. He had to know that if anything happened to me, there were witnesses who'd seen us together.

"Listen," he said, "I really don't need the cops getting involved."

I laughed. "No kidding."

"No, really, I didn't take that stuff from your house," he said. "It wasn't me."

"I suppose you're going to claim you found those books."

"I *did* find them."

"You're not that good a liar, Hal." Not true. He was a really good liar. His act was totally believable. Unless it wasn't an act and he was telling the truth, but I mean, what were the odds?

I said, "Okay, I'll bite. Where did you find them?"

"I'm not at liberty."

"Good-bye." I reached for the door handle. Only then did he make a move toward me. I faced him squarely with my hand inside my purse, and he backed off, palms raised in an appeasing gesture.

As I've mentioned, I don't carry a gun. I do carry a cute little object Dom had given me a year earlier for self-protection: a five-inch purple aluminum spike, enhanced with finger grooves down its length. The purpose of the grooves was to provide a secure grip while discouraging one's attacker, presumably by jabbing the pointy end at his eyes. That spike had actually helped save my life on one scary occasion, though not in the way originally intended.

If Hal imagined I was holding a more lethal type of weapon, I wasn't about to disabuse him.

He said, "Listen, just take my word—" He broke off with a muttered curse when the first-floor door opened below us. Jasmine Reddy and Richie Esparza raced up the steps, carrying takeout bags that smelled an awful lot like the darn nachos I'd been jonesing for. Life is so unfair sometimes.

They slowed to a stop when they spied us, their gazes shifting from me to Hal and back again. Hal's laid-back posture fooled precisely no one, and I was certain I mirrored his agitation.

Richie looked pointedly at my hand hidden in my purse before settling on my face. He didn't mince words. "You okay?"

Hal said, "She's fine, buddy—"

"I didn't ask you." Richie treated Hal to a menacing stare-down. Meanwhile Jasmine got right in my face and let her raised eyebrows speak for her.

"Really." I forced a smile. "I'm fine. We're just having a,

um, an enthusiastic conversation." I slid my hand out of my purse. "Thanks, guys."

The teens sent Hal a pointed look as they slowly opened the door and stepped into the second-floor hallway. I assumed they were headed for the calculus study session in Elliott's apartment.

"Okay, look," Hal said. "The truth?"

"No, I prefer the little stories you've been making up. Let's hear another one."

"I have a deal in the works," he said, "a very lucrative deal. I can't risk anything messing it up. The cops get involved and it's *adios, dinero.*"

"What kind of deal?" I asked. "You already sold the books to *Ramrod News*—for plenty of bread by the looks of that new Tesla. What else do you have to sell?"

"Listen," he said, "it's for your own good that you don't know."

"You know, Hal, whenever I hear the words 'for your own good,' I know it's not *my* own good we're talking about."

He looked away, clearly trying to decide how to deflect me.

On impulse I blurted, "I want in on your deal."

His chortle was more of a snort. "That's not gonna happen."

"Count me in or I go to the cops," I said. "They'll learn all about how you broke into my house, stole those books, and sold them to *Ramrod News*. And you know they're now questioning how Scarlett died, and Nolan, too. They're going to be looking very hard at the person who burgled my home."

I hope you know I did not in fact want in on his deal and that I had every intention of going to the cops no matter what.

But I had a bad feeling about whatever Hal was up to. I just knew it had something to do with Scarlett or Nolan or both. This might be my only chance to find out what was going on.

He shook his head. "I'm telling you, Jane, I didn't do it. You have no reason to go to the cops."

"Okay, I'm going to throw something else into the mix," I said, "a sweetener if you will. First, a fun fact about my business. If you think everything the Death Diva does is totally aboveboard and legal, then you're hopelessly naïve."

"Oh, I never thought that," he blustered. "What kind of a rube do you take me for?"

"The public has no clue about some of the jobs I do," I said. "You think I got that big house on five acres just by scattering ashes and cleaning out dead people's apartments?"

As you know, I didn't get that big house, period. Sexy Beast did, just by being the beloved pet of wealthy Irene McAuliffe, but Hal didn't need to know that.

"Yeah, I knew you were holding back." He wore a sly smile. "So what kind of stuff have you done? Anything really, you know, *special?*"

I made a show of checking our surroundings and lowering my voice. "Let me put it this way. If the authorities ever got wind of some of my more *special* jobs, I'd be in Attica right now, rocking an orange jumpsuit."

Hal barked an appreciative laugh. The idiot was buying it. Which only goes to show, people believe what they want to. Jane Delaney the bad, bad girl was a lot more exciting than Jane Delaney, scatterer of Grandma's ashes.

"So why tell *me?*" he asked. "Aren't you afraid I'll rat you out?"

"Oh, you won't rat me out," I said pleasantly. "I know

every way there is to dispose of a dead body. Without leaving a trace."

He scowled. "Are you threatening me?"

"Don't be silly." I offered a dazzling grin. "I know you'd never do anything that would necessitate such extreme measures. As for why I'm telling you all this, my business has grown by leaps and bounds, and I've been on the lookout for a partner. But it has to be someone with the right looks, temperament, and ambition."

He looked dubious. "And you thought of me?"

"Hey, you fit the bill." I forced myself to add, "Especially in the eye-candy department. I'm sure you'd have no trouble charming all those stinking-rich Crystal Harbor matrons. But you have to be willing to get your hands dirty once in a while."

"What about Grampy?" he said. "Doesn't he work with you?"

I gave him a no-nonsense stare. "I know you know his name."

After a few moments he said, "Whatever. *Martin.*"

"He's gotten involved a couple of times," I said, "but between you and me, his acting chops just aren't there. I need someone with your particular talents."

In fact, the padre routinely collaborated with me, particularly in the more bizarre assignments. My man could always be counted on to don some wackadoodle costume and play his role to the hilt.

"I think we can work something out," he said. "When do I start?"

"As soon as you let me in on this deal of yours," I said. "Fifty-fifty."

"Now, wait a min—"

"Call it a buy-in on your Death Diva partnership. And only if it turns out to be worth my while. If you're BS'ing me about how lucrative this thing is, you can forget about becoming part of the organization." When he hesitated, I added, "And as a bonus, I won't report your activities to my friends in the Crystal Harbor Police Department."

"Not fifty-fifty," he said. "No way. I'll give you thirty percent. Take it or leave it."

"Thirty-five." I had to make it look good. "And you'll get thirty-five percent of any jobs you do for me. Once you prove yourself, I'll raise it. Eventually we could be splitting everything. Full partners."

He stuck out his hand and we shook on it.

At that instant the door swung open and all four resident nerds crowded onto the landing with us. Elliott alone seemed to take up half the square footage. The kids just stood there staring at us. Hal wisely kept his mouth shut this time.

I said, "I thought you guys were studying."

"Decided to take a break," Richie said.

"You're still here," Jasmine observed.

"Still here," I said. "Still chatting."

Elliott addressed me, but his flat gaze was on Hal. "We thought you might like some company walking back to your car."

"Or you can hang with us if you'd like," Liam said. "We have some nachos left."

My stomach squealed. Liam's laugh turned into a grunt when Jasmine elbowed him.

"I really appreciate it, guys," I said. "Tell you what. I'll come by and check in with you before I leave. How's that? What's your apartment number, Elliott?"

"Two-A," he said.

"I'll swing by in a few minutes. Promise."

After they left, Hal said, "That's a relief. I thought those kids might be headed up to the roof."

"So what if they were?" I asked.

"We don't need the company. Come on." He started up the stairs, taking them two at a time.

I hurried after him. "Wait, we're going to the *roof*? Why?"

"Why do you think? It's private," he said. "This place is like Grand Central."

I was about to remind him that his apartment was also private, not to mention warm. But then I asked myself if I really wanted to be alone with Hal Kazarian in his personal domain, and I'm sure you can guess my very sensible answer. Not that I sensed I was in danger. At this point I felt I had little to fear from him.

I was out of breath by the time we reached the locked door to the roof. I watched Hal stab his credit card between the door and jamb repeatedly, his frustration mounting. It was clear he'd never done this before. Finally I snatched the card out of his hand, deftly wiggled it just so in precisely the right spot, and held the door open for him.

"Guess you have more experience with illegal stuff like this," he grumbled as he led the way up the stairs.

Once we were on the roof, he started to let the door slam shut. I caught it and toed the nearby brick into place to hold it open, as the kids had done. "The door sticks," I explained. I saw him wonder how I knew that, but he made no comment.

The day was cold but not crushingly so, the sun hiding behind cloud cover the color of dirty gym socks. I wrapped my pink wool scarf around my throat and tucked the ends into my suede jacket. Hal turned up the collar of his navy-blue pea coat, gazing around the space in a way that made it clear he'd never been up there before—which made me wonder what had made him choose the roof for our private convo. He briefly pulled out his phone to check the time.

My breath was visible in the frigid air as I said, "This way." I headed toward the far end where the kids liked to hang out, with its wraparound brick parapet walls. I chose a position at the rear corner of the building.

"Why here?" he asked, following me.

"It's pretty busy down there on a Saturday." I gestured toward the front of the building four stories below. "From here, we can't see your neighbors coming and going, which means they can't see us."

His approving expression was replaced in the next instant by a leering grin and the lamest line in the history of lame lines. "Come here often?"

"Spill," I commanded. "You tell me everything or our deal's off. And don't even think of holding back. I'll know it and I won't be happy."

I experienced an unaccustomed thrill playing the heavy. Not that I was tempted to make it a permanent thing, but it was nice to know I could intimidate a sexist, self-absorbed jerk like Hal Kazarian when the need arose.

"But first," I said, "I need you to verify something for me. You sent Nolan that threatening note, didn't you? The one you ripped out of the scrapbook before you sold it to *Ramrod News*."

"Yeah, that note was from me," he said. "And before you ask, no, I didn't kill the old freak. I never laid a finger on him."

"What about Scarlett? Are you the one who weakened that

railing?" I nodded toward the spot where she'd smoked her last cigar.

Hal glared at me, breathing hard, making me wonder if I'd gone too far. At last he said, "I might not be boyfriend of the year, Jane, but I'm no murderer."

"So about the burglary," I said. "If you *are* the one who broke into my house, just come right out and say so. I won't call off our deal over it. If anything, a skill like that increases your value to the organization."

"Thanks for the vote of confidence, but it really wasn't me. When I found those books, I knew right away where they came from, though. I mean, everyone's been talking about that weird scrapbook and the old green notebook filled with a bizarre code."

"Which brings me back to the big question," I said. "Where did you find them?"

His lengthy exhalation formed a misty cloud. "Okay, I found them in Bob's apartment. I hooked up with Margaret again a couple of days before the *Ramrod News* show. Same deal as before—she was staying over at Bob's place and she snuck me in in the middle of the night after the other two were asleep. Once Margaret and me were finished, I started searching the place."

"She didn't notice you prowling around the apartment?"

He gave a dismissive wave. "I left her in a sex coma. She was out for the count."

I said, "Where were the books? I know Bob wouldn't have left them just lying around."

"Three guesses." Hal's puckish smile, complete with a puppy-dog head tilt, was clearly meant to be boyishly disarming. Did this really work on women?

"You're really getting on my nerves," I said through gritted teeth. "I know he has a safe."

"How do you know about the safe?"

"Answer the question, Hal. Is that where they were?"

"No," he said. "I'm no safe cracker. Sorry if that's one of those skills that are so valuable to the organization."

I wasn't surprised Bob had found a different hiding spot for the books. By that point he'd already learned his home safe wasn't exactly Fort Knox. "Where, then?"

"There's this carton on the floor of his coat closet. It showed up a week ago. The writing on it says, 'Spare Fishing Tackle,' and it's sealed with packing tape."

"Probably storing it there until he and April move into that big new house they're buying," I said.

"Which might make sense if he didn't have tons of stuff from his old place sitting in a storage facility, just waiting till they close on the new house. I saw the bill once. Why keep this one box of fishing tackle—*spare* fishing tackle—in his apartment?"

"Not bad, Sherlock." *Gee, maybe I* should *hire this guy.* "So you, what, decided to take a peek at Bob's lures and rubber worms in the middle of the night?"

"And sure enough, I found plenty of lures and rubber worms. But at the very bottom of the box, in a plastic bag…" He spread his arms wide. "Am I good or what?"

"Weren't you afraid he'd notice the books were missing?" I asked.

"I retaped it really neatly, left the box exactly where I found it. And he *didn't* notice they were missing, not until he saw Miranda waving those things on-air." He mimed the action, his arms upraised.

"But why snoop around the apartment in the first place?" I asked. "Were you looking for stuff to steal?"

"If I was looking to steal," he said, "I wouldn't have had to look hard. Those two, they keep cash and valuables lying around everywhere. Margaret, too. What is it about these rich idiots?"

"What *were* you searching for, then?"

Hal looked more serious than I'd ever seen him. "Proof that Bob killed Scarlett."

19

It's a Self-Defense Thingy, I Swear!

HIS WORDS WERE so unexpected, it took me a moment to process them. Finally I said, "What makes you think he did it?"

Hal pulled out his phone again, glanced at it, put it back in his pocket. "It goes back to that first time Margaret snuck me into Bob's apartment in the middle of the night."

"The night before Scarlett died," I said.

"Right. Bob and April had no idea I was there, like I said, not until I mentioned it on that show. Margaret and me did the deed and then she was out like a light. That's her thing. Anyway, it was maybe two-fifteen, two-thirty at that point. I needed to get back to Carolyn's before she realized I was gone."

"Oops," I said. She'd already pounded on her sister's door looking for him.

He made a face. "Yeah, well. Anyway, it was real dark in Bob's apartment, just a little moonlight coming in the windows. I was tiptoeing down the hall when I saw movement in the living room. I flattened myself against the wall and held my breath."

"Was it Bob?" I asked.

Hal nodded. "At first I thought it was a burglar, 'cause he was dressed all in black—jeans, jacket, gloves, knapsack. Then he moved near the window and I could see it was Bob and that he was holding a ski mask. It was one of those thin, superexpensive ones made out of, I don't know, whatever they make astronauts' jockstraps out of. With just a slit for the eyes."

"I assume the ski mask was black, too?" I said.

"Yep. He opened the door and looked up and down the hall, then slipped out of the apartment."

"Where did you think he was going?" I asked.

"At the time?" Hal shrugged. "A woman, what else?"

"With a ski mask?"

There was that smarmy grin again. "Hey, people are into all kinds of kink, Jane. I'm guessing you and Grampy are strictly vanilla."

"One more 'Grampy' and our deal is off," I said.

"Hey, I'm just having a little fun here. Lighten up."

I said, "Any idea how long Bob was gone from the apartment?"

"Nope. As soon as the coast was clear, I went back to Carolyn's place."

"And you didn't make the connection after Scarlett died?" I asked. "Didn't wonder if Bob's little nocturnal excursion had anything to do with her death?"

"Why would I?" he said. "I mean, everyone was saying it was an accident. Carolyn was even talking about suing the building's owners. But then a few days ago the cops started asking questions, and that's when I put two and two together. I mean, I always knew Scarlett didn't get along with Bob. Something to do with her dad's suicide."

"So when you found those two books under the fishing tackle," I said, "you were actually looking for proof that Bob killed Scarlett. What kind of proof?"

"Those black clothes," he said. "And the knapsack, which I figured is where he put the tools. The ones he used to loosen that railing."

"You could've gone to the cops even without that stuff," I said. "It's their job to gather evidence, not yours."

"Well, anyway," he said, "I found those books instead, the ones everyone was talking about."

"At which point you definitely should've gone to the cops," I said, "instead of selling them to that horrible show." I thought I knew where this was going. I hoped I was wrong.

"What do you care?" he said. "You just told me how you skirt the law, do all this illegal stuff."

"Tell me about this deal of yours," I said.

"This deal of *ours* now," he said. "It's perfect. You're gonna love it. Bob is gonna cough up big bucks to keep me quiet."

My stomach dropped. I was right. He was trying to blackmail a murderer.

"How do you know he'll go for it?" I asked.

Hal grinned. "He already did. We hashed it out last night, after the show. I'm gonna end up a hundred grand richer. Well, sixty-five grand after you get your cut, but I'll make that back and more once you and me are partners. *Ka-ching, ka-ching*, baby."

On *Ramrod News* last night, Hal had publicly accused Carolyn of killing her sister, though by then he'd known full well that Bob had done it. He must've already been planning to blackmail the man who'd murdered his former girlfriend, the woman he'd described as the love of his life.

Hey, the guy never claimed to be boyfriend of the year, right?

"So he's paying you to keep quiet about seeing him slip out of his apartment in the middle of the night," I asked, "with a knapsack full of wrenches or whatever he needed to sabotage that railing?"

"Plus I promised never to tell where I found those books."

I said, "What if Miranda blabs to the cops that they came from you?"

He shrugged. "I'll say I found them in Carolyn's apartment."

Which would lead the authorities to deduce that she'd burgled my house when in reality it was Bob who'd pried open the window of my home office, grabbed those books off my desk, and upended the cartons looking for additional evidence of his guilt—before all the barking and yelling clued him in that he wasn't alone.

I had asked Hal what else he had to sell, besides the books. The answer? His silence.

"Listen to me, Hal." I looked him in the eye and spoke very slowly and clearly. "Bob is never going to pay you."

He waved that away. "We have a deal—a verbal contract. He's not going to go back on it. He's a lawyer."

"He's a killer," I said. "You made a deal with a killer, Hal. He murdered Scarlett and he probably murdered Nolan, too. You really think he's going to let you just walk away, a hundred grand richer?"

I knew I'd failed to make my point when he said, "A hundred grand is pocket change to a guy that rich. He'll pay." He looked at his phone again.

"Why do you keep checking the time?" I asked, annoyed.

In the next instant my heart did its jackhammer impersonation as I belatedly answered my own question. "Hal, we've got to get out of here." I grabbed his sleeve and turned toward the stairway bulkhead…

…just as Bob kicked the brick aside and let the door bang closed behind him.

Hal greeted him with a wide smile. "Right on time! What's that for?" he asked, as Bob picked up a tapered scrap of wood and firmly wedged it under the door to keep it shut.

"It wouldn't do to be interrupted," Bob said, "while we conclude our business."

"Oh, right," Hal said. "Makes sense."

Bob had a black knapsack slung over one shoulder. As he strolled toward us, he exhibited no curiosity about his surroundings. Well, why would he? We all knew this wasn't his first visit to the roof.

"And Jane has decided to join us, I see." His familiar gentle smile, which at one time had put me at ease, now sent a ripple of terror through me.

"I brought her in on our deal," Hal explained. "Jane and me, we're in business together now, so everything gets shared."

"I suppose you'll be demanding more money."

"No way, man," Hal said. "I know better than that. A straight hundred grand, like we agreed."

Having joined us in our secluded location at the rear corner of the parapet wall (why had that seemed like such a good idea?), Bob finally did look around, no doubt to ensure privacy.

I looked around, too, hoping the Devines had decided to install security cameras up there, following Scarlett's death. No such luck.

Finally he turned to me. "Jane, I assume your new business partner has told you about the agreement he and I reached, including all the pertinent details."

I was quick to say, "Nope, we didn't get into details," even as Hal blurted, "I sure did, got her up to speed on all of it. You don't need to worry about Jane. She's cool, knows how to keep her mouth shut. She does this sort of thing all the time."

I squirmed as Bob, whose success as a lawyer required him to read the subtleties of body language, stared unblinkingly at me. And trust me, my body language at that moment was anything but subtle. My breath was smoking like a steam locomotive, and I struggled to make eye contact.

"So you're aware," he said affably, "that I weakened that piece of the railing, right over there—" here he helpfully pointed toward the front of the building "—in the middle of the night. All that was left for me to do was wait. Knowing Scarlett and her habits, I was confident it would just be a matter of time. And sure enough, it was all over by six the next evening."

Briefly I considered hightailing it to the bulkhead, prying out the wooden shim, and fleeing down the stairs. I had no doubt that if I tried it, Bob Jernigan, regular gym-goer and marathon runner, would subdue me before I'd made it halfway to the door.

He couldn't possibly mean to pay us the promised blackmail money and let us go. Every nerve in my body screamed that I was in mortal danger.

Hal, on the other hand, was his usual uncomplicated, overconfident self, a man driven by two things: money and sex. As far as his love life went, currently he was using that second thing to get more of the first. Eventually Margaret would learn an important life lesson, but not before paying dearly for the education.

If, that is, Hal made it off that roof alive.

"And yet," I told Bob, "you hired me to organize a memorial service for Scarlett. Was that simply to deflect suspicion from yourself?"

He shook his head. "At the time, I was confident her death would continue to be regarded as accidental. You might not believe this, but it didn't sit right with me that Carolyn felt no need to honor her sister's passing. As a longtime friend of the family, I felt it was my duty to step in."

Yeah, I know, it didn't make sense to me either, but I wasn't in a position to argue with the guy.

"So you brought the money, right?" Hal eyed Bob's knapsack as he thrust his hands in his pockets to warm them. "I mean, maybe we should just, you know, get down to it."

Bob pretended not to have heard him. "It all goes back to the Winner's Circle. My critical mistake was in holding on to that notebook all these years. It represented so much work, with such significant rewards. Quite frankly, I couldn't bear to part with it." His smile turned self-deprecating. "'Pride goeth before a fall.'"

"Did it occur to you," I said, "that if you'd applied all that work to studying instead of cheating, you might've aced those courses legitimately?"

My sensible, self-protective side asked my reckless, mouthy side how long she'd had this death wish. Fortunately for me, Bob was simply amused. I got the feeling he was exceedingly proud of the Winner's Circle, his brainchild, and welcomed this rare opportunity to brag about it.

"I had little doubt I would indeed have aced my course load," he said, "and graduated summa cum laude on my own merits, but once I'd gotten the idea for the Winner's Circle, the challenge became irresistible. And as I'm sure you're aware, the scheme turned out to be quite lucrative. I wasn't nearly as well off as most of my classmates, and if they were too stupid or lazy to earn the grades their parents demanded of them—not to mention the med schools and law schools and MBA programs they hoped to get into—then I was more than happy to charge them exorbitant fees to ensure their academic success."

I said, "You must've freaked when Carolyn handed you The Cabbage—I mean the copy of your notebook and the decrypted translation."

"I'm not one to 'freak,'" he said, "but I admit I was… disconcerted, shall we say. I'd kept that old notebook in a cigar box in my home safe. I hadn't opened that box in close to a year. I had no idea it had been looted—and by Ed Proctor of all people. I'd underestimated him."

Of course, if Bob hadn't been so careless with the combination to his safe, Ed never would've been able to get into it.

Hal checked the time on his phone again. "Okay, fascinating stuff, guys, but can we wrap it up? Do what we came here for?" Again he stared longingly at Bob's knapsack, obviously imagining it stuffed with hundred-dollar bills—his promised payoff.

I suspected I knew what that bag contained, and it wasn't a thousand pictures of Benjamin Franklin.

Bob and I both ignored him. I said, "I understand why you felt the need to get your hands on that notebook again, but how could you be so sure it was at my place?"

"Well, the thing was just too intriguing," Bob said. "An old relic like that, written in code? I couldn't imagine you tossing something like that into a dumpster. And was I wrong?"

"No," I said, "you had that part figured out. However, you broke into a house that was occupied—and one of the occupants was a big, protective dog. Rookie mistake, Bob."

He actually laughed. Pressing a gloved hand to his heart, he said, "You wound me, Jane. That was my first foray into burglary, and with any luck, also my last. Carolyn had mentioned that you and Martin would be going out that night, so I chose a spot where I could observe without *being* observed, and waited for you to leave."

"Did Carolyn also tell you where I'd stored the boxes from Scarlett's apartment?"

"She did. That girl turns into quite the chatterbox when you get a glass of wine into her. I was prepared for little Sexy Beast to be in the house, of course. He knows me, but I'd also taken the precaution of bringing some dog treats."

As much as I hated to admit it, SB would've been thrilled to see this particular burglar, treats or no treats. He'd warmed to Bob the first time they'd met. Well, so had Martin and I, for that matter.

"But when the barking started," Bob added, "I heard a second dog, and I immediately knew this animal was no harmless little poodle. I managed to turn the lock on the door just in the nick of time."

"And then you grabbed the books and scrambled out the window," I said.

"'Scrambled' paints such a vulgar picture."

"Burglary is pretty vulgar, Bob," I said. "Sorry, but there's just no getting around it."

He appeared to consider that before tipping his head in reluctant agreement.

"When you ran into Clover and me last week," I said,

"outside the building, and I mentioned Layla, you pretended not to know I had another dog." Even though said dog had chased him behind my house not twenty-four hours before.

"I also pretended not to know that Clover's lawyer is Sten Jakobsen, who practices right here in Crystal Harbor. You made up that story about the package you had with you, saying you'd offered to overnight it to her lawyer, but of course it would have been quicker and easier to drive five minutes to Sten's office and drop it off."

Dang. "So you kinda knew it wasn't legal papers in that envelope," I said.

"Carolyn had told me the decryption came from Clover," he said, "so when I saw the two of you together with a package identical to the one I'd been given, what else could I infer except that the old woman had made a copy?"

Somehow his correct use of "infer" made me despise him all the more.

I didn't say it made sense. Ask me if I care.

He said, "So how many copies are floating around? Do the police have one?" When I didn't answer, his psycho smile widened. "But of course they do."

Watching Bob, I saw him come to grips with the fact that soon the whole world would know about the Winner's Circle. His wealthy, well-connected fiancée was certain to dump him. His law career, too, was history. Only one thing mattered now.

"I will not go to prison for murder," he said.

"No problem, man," Hal said. "The three of us, we're the only ones that know, and—" He mimed zipping his lip. "Jane thinks you killed Nolan, too, but my money's on Carolyn."

Bob looked at him with disdain. "Can you seriously picture Carolyn wrestling Nolan to his kitchen floor and slamming his head into the tiles with enough force to kill him? Not to mention having the forethought to drag out his bucket and mop, and slosh water onto the floor?"

Clearly that wasn't the response Hal had been expecting. "You must've, you know, had a good reason."

"Those of us who were involved with the Winner's Circle had long ago been sworn to secrecy. Nolan was about to violate that promise. We were both planning to attend our university's fortieth-reunion dinner the next evening. He made it clear he intended to tell our fellow alumni, and my fiancée, all about the Winner's Circle, with special emphasis on my role at the head of it. You understand why I could not let that happen."

"Well, uh, I guess so. Sure," Hal said. I watched as it belatedly dawned on him that he'd gotten himself into a very dangerous situation.

"What I did not know at the time," Bob said, "is that Nolan was not in the habit of cleaning his own floors. That parasite let Scarlett wait on him hand and foot while he collected undeserved disability payments. A waste of space in every sense of the word."

Parasite. Waste of space. It suddenly occurred to me that Carolyn had probably picked up those terms—and perhaps her hatred for her next-door neighbor, as well—from the man she'd considered a father figure.

"I'm telling you," Hal said, "that old freak was messed up."

"I would have liked to search the place for any physical evidence regarding the Winner's Circle," Bob said, "but it wouldn't do to linger at the scene of the 'accident,' and in any event, I had little hope of finding anything in that apartment."

Hal's head bobbed up and down. "I've seen it. The place was a pigsty."

"For a full month," Bob said, "no one questioned that he'd simply slipped on a wet floor, resulting in a fatal head injury. But I knew Scarlett had spent weeks cleaning out his apartment, and there was no telling what incriminating items she might have come across. So I put out feelers and discovered that she'd spoken with a police detective that very day about her suspicions regarding Nolan's death. She had a culprit in mind, though she had yet to name him."

"Think she knew about the Winner's Circle thing?" Hal asked.

"Without a doubt," Bob said. "She would have learned about it from her father, or perhaps Nolan. They both resented me. I didn't know at that point that Scarlett actually had the notebook in her possession, of course, or that it had been decoded. I thought it was still in that cigar box in my safe."

"Yeah, about her old man," Hal said. "When Scarlett and me were together, she told me you're the reason he offed himself. Like you drove him to it or something."

"That is not true," Bob said.

"Yeah, I figured it was a load of crap," Hal said.

"I didn't drive him to suicide," Bob said. "I strangled the man with my bare hands."

I gulped air against a sudden wave of dizziness. *Hold it together!* I commanded myself.

"Whoa." Hal's gaze bounced between Bob and me. "That's, uh, hard-core, man."

"More hard-core," Bob asked, mildly, "than my rigging that railing over there to collapse the next time your girlfriend leaned against it?" He waited for an answer.

"Uh..." Something seemed to catch in Hal's throat. He cleared it and mumbled, "Ex-girlfriend. She didn't really mean that much to me by then, you know?"

Liar. Hal had stopped ogling the knapsack. Now he seemed more interested in the closed door to the stairwell.

Bob plucked one of Boss Lady's black hairs off the sleeve of his brown leather jacket. He wore dark-red lambskin gloves. "The difficult part wasn't killing Ed, it was dragging his body two flights up to the attic, locating some rope, and hanging him from a cross beam. Needless to say, I skipped the gym that day."

I heard myself ask the obvious question. "Why did you do it?"

"Ed was incensed when I refused to represent him on the embezzlement charge. He'd been stupid and he'd gotten caught. I had no intention of associating myself with such a sordid case. That's when he brought up the Winner's Circle, how tight we'd been back then, how we'd always been there for each other, trusted each other one hundred percent. He baldly stated that if all that had changed, he saw no reason to continue keeping our secret. I suppose he thought that would sway me. He learned I don't take kindly to threats."

Hal said, "I saw this thing on one of those true-crime shows where this guy strangled his wife and tried to make it look like she hanged herself. But the cops figured it out with, you know, forensics and stuff."

"By the time Ed died," Bob said, "it was well known that he'd stolen money from his employer and was panicking at the thought of going to prison. No one questioned that he'd committed suicide, not even his daughters. There was no investigation."

What Bob hadn't known when he'd murdered his old friend is that Ed had already swiped the Winner's Circle notebook from Bob's safe and passed it to their former classmate Nolan Whitehouse. I hoped that secret knowledge had given Ed some small measure of comfort at the end.

"I'm curious about something," I said. "You asked April for a sleeping pill that night. She told Detective Kaplan that she watched you take it and that it knocked you out."

"I foresaw the possibility that we might eventually be questioned," he said, "so I let April *think* I took the pill. I palmed it, of course. She, however, did take one, and slept soundly through all the comings and goings that night."

"I figured it was something like that," I said.

"So, Jane, it seems you've been talking to the detectives about all this," he said. "Well, of course you have. No matter. They might have their suspicions, but they can't prove anything."

Hal said, "And you know you can count on me to keep my mouth shut, right? I mean, we have a deal, right, Bob? And I take that very seriously. You have my word. Right?"

Bob's tone was arid. "And your word means so very much to me, Hal. We all know how truthful you are in all things."

"Yeah, so, uh…" Hal's jittery gaze kept sliding toward the bulkhead door. He took a tentative step in that direction. "Listen, man, why don't we finish up later. It's cold and, uh… you know, I'll catch you later."

"Aren't you forgetting something?" Bob asked pleasantly, as he slid the knapsack off his shoulder and opened it.

I tensed even as Hal hesitated, his greedy gaze once more focused on the knapsack.

Bob reached into the bag and extracted a black semiautomatic pistol, with a silencer already attached to the barrel. He dropped the knapsack and held the gun loosely at his side, but there was no question he could drop either of us if we made a run for the bulkhead or screamed for help.

"What's that for?" Hal whined, as his palms rose in a defensive gesture. "Listen, man, I told you, you can trust me. I'm not gonna—"

"Shut up," Bob said, and thankfully, Hal obeyed.

I managed to keep my voice from quavering as I said, "Killing us will only make things worse for you, Bob. The cops have more evidence than you think, enough to connect you to Scarlett's death, and Nolan's, too." I didn't know whether this was true, but I was working the only angle I had. "And once they have you for those, it's a sure bet they'll exhume Ed's body and discover he was strangled prior to hanging. And you're the man with the motive for all three killings."

If Ed had been cremated, there would've been no chance to reexamine the body. I happened to know he'd been buried because of something Carolyn had mentioned the day of her sister's memorial service. Scarlett had told her she didn't want to be interred next to their parents, preferring a green, eco-friendly burial when her time came.

"It isn't three killings," he calmly said, "it's four. So far. The first one was quite a long time ago. It was my third year at Yale Law and I'd fallen in love with a fellow student, a lovely girl named Cassandra. I was young and besotted, and somewhat naïve, I suppose. Cassie was the outdoorsy type, and we were enjoying a beautiful spring day, gathering morels in the woods. It was the first and only time I violated the secrecy of the Winner's Circle. I was so proud of my accomplishment, you see, and I assumed she'd be just as impressed. Well, you can guess the rest."

"Cassandra wasn't impressed," I said. "She was appalled."

He sighed. "Gone was the vibrant, loving girl I'd lost my heart to. Cassie insisted I come clean with both universities and take responsibility for my ethical violations. She seemed to believe I wouldn't have been admitted to Yale without having cheated at Columbia, which was as insulting as it was inaccurate."

And I'd thought *Hal* had a bloated ego. Bob was simply better at concealing it on a day-to-day basis. Let's face it, he was a master at concealing a lot of things. "I'm assuming you didn't take her advice and come clean," I said.

"After all the work I'd put in to get where I was?" he asked. "When I told Cassie I had no intention of ratting myself out, she informed me she had no choice but to report me herself. I saw it all going out the window in that instant, everything I'd worked so hard for, all my dreams of an illustrious law career. That's when I discovered the truth in that saying. Given the right circumstances, one is capable of anything."

Hal breathed a panicked curse. He kept scanning our surroundings, obviously trying to discern a way out of his predicament that didn't involve leaping off a four-story building.

"A hiker found Cassie hours later," he continued. "Her head had been caved in with a large rock. I'd had just enough presence of mind to take her wallet so it would look like a robbery. No one had seen us together that day. Dumb luck on my part. It's not as if I'd planned it out in advance. That kind of organized thinking would come later."

My God, the man was a serial killer. And Hal and I were about to become victims five and six.

"Someone must've spotted you coming up here," I said.

"Do you really believe I'd be that careless?" he asked. "And if you're thinking April is twiddling her thumbs in the apartment, wondering where I am, you would be mistaken. She's spending the weekend in Manhattan with her mother and the bridesmaids. A wedding-gown fitting followed by clothes shopping, dinner at Eleven Madison Park, and rooms at the Pierre. Brunch at Perrine tomorrow, then some Broadway revival. *Cabaret? Candide?*" He wagged his free hand. "Something with a *C*. Followed by more clothes shopping. As far as my fiancée is concerned, I shall be holed up in my home office all weekend, working on a tricky legal brief. Poor me."

"You can't be meaning to just shoot us and leave our bodies here," I said. "And I hope you know there's no way we're going to go anywhere with you."

"You seem to forget I'm the one with the gun." He gestured with it as if to say, *See? Gun.* "Hal, are you having some sort of seizure?"

I turned to look at Hal, standing a few feet away. He was apparently trying to send me some sort of unspoken message, repeatedly jerking his head toward my purse.

Before I could interpret this bizarre behavior, Bob reached for the strap and hauled my bag off my shoulder.

"Dammit, Jane!" Hal cried, as Bob opened my purse and upended it. "Why didn't you shoot him?"

"With what?" I asked, as my personal belongings bounced across the gravel: wallet, cell phone, keys, hairbrush, two little bottles of hand sanitizer, three lip balms, four rolls of mints, five packets of tissues, six pens, a dozen hair ties, a full bottle of ibuprofen, an empty bottle of ibuprofen, a broken necklace (so *that's* where it was), a year's worth of crumpled store receipts, now floating on the breeze, and the aforementioned purple self-defense spike.

"What happened to your gun?" Hal demanded.

"What gun? I never *had* a gun."

He said, "Then what were you reaching for in your purse earlier? When you acted like you were about to blow my brains out."

"Oh. That." I pointed to the spike, which Bob had lifted and was closely examining.

"You carry a sex toy around with you?" Hal said. "Cool."

Bob stopped fondling the spike and let it dangle by the little loop attached to the fat end. "Do I need to ask where this object has been?"

"It's not a sex toy!" I said. "Jeez. Don't you guys know a self-defense thingy when you see one?"

"As a matter of fact, I do," Bob said, indicating his pistol. He tossed the spike onto the gravel. "We've wasted enough time. Hal, I trusted you to keep your mouth shut. That was our deal, for which you were to be paid handsomely. Instead, you told your new 'business partner' everything."

"But she won't—"

"How stupid are you? Of course she'll go running to the police. Those detectives are her *friends*. She has a history of collaborating with them."

Before I could object to this entirely accurate statement, Bob moved like a cobra, immobilizing me from behind and pressing the gun's muzzle against my temple.

Hal was wide-eyed. "What—What are you gonna do?"

"I'm going to take care of your stupid mistake, and then you and I will proceed as planned. I have your money right here." Bob nodded toward the knapsack, which in my opinion looked a little too flat to hold all that cash. "*If* you can manage to keep your mouth shut from now on."

"I will!" Hal said. "I messed up, man, I admit it, but it won't happen again. I promise."

"Are you kidding me?" I said. "Hal, he's not going to let you go. And even if he does—"

"Shut up," Bob growled, jamming the gun hard against my head.

"Even if he does," I continued, "plenty of people saw you and me together in the stairwell. Who do you think is going to go down for my murder? You or the guy who's about to pull the trigger?"

"Don't worry, Hal," Bob said, "I have it all figured out. Her body will never be found."

He chose not to elaborate on how he intended to accomplish this miracle. There was no place on the roof to conceal a dead body, even temporarily, and hauling one through the Americana apartment building, even in pieces (yeah, I went there), was certain to garner a bit of attention on a busy Saturday.

Hal, however, being at the moment both gullible and terrified, was more than ready to believe the older man. He nodded vigorously. "Yeah, okay, you do what you have to do. We'll go back to Plan A."

"I need you to do something first," Bob told him. He pointed to a spot on the gravel a few feet away. "You're going to lie facedown right there, hands linked behind your head. Don't get up until I instruct you to."

Hal looked alarmed. "Why?"

"I don't want you to watch," Bob said. "You're new to all this and you might reflexively try to intervene."

"No, I won't do that, I swear."

"This is nonnegotiable," Bob said. I couldn't see his face

since he was holding a gun to my temple and all, but I had no doubt that silky little smile was firmly in place.

And I mean, his reasoning was so sound, his tone so reassuring, who could argue?

Me, that's who. I could argue.

"Hal, don't you see what he's doing?" I said, as Hal knelt on the gravel. "After he shoots me, he's going to shoot you point-blank and put the gun in your hand—to make it look like murder-suicide. Like you killed me because I found out you murdered Scarlett, but then you're so guilt-ridden over killing both of us that you can no longer live with yourself."

Bob chuckled. "That's some imagination you have, Jane."

And okay, so I was making it all up on the fly, but so was Bob, and I was pretty sure I'd described the gist of his plan. Either that or I'd just provided one. Which, if that was true, well, my bad.

"I'm waiting," Bob said, in his most soothing voice, and Hal finally lowered himself to the gravel, facing away from us so he wouldn't have to watch Jane Delaney turn into the late Jane Delaney.

"Hal, you're making a huge mistake," I said.

"Your hands," Bob reminded him.

Hal looked up momentarily. "Just one thing. I mean, I'm not trying to nitpick or anything, but how are you gonna move her, uh, her body without anyone seeing?"

"You just leave that to me," Bob crooned. "I have it all worked out. Your hands?"

Hal lowered his head again and linked his trembling fingers behind his head, my cue to become The Most Uncooperative Murder Victim Ever. I struggled against Bob's hold and hollered at the top of my lungs. I mean, what could he do about it at this point? Shoot me?

"Help!" I stomped on his feet, kicked back against his shins, squirmed like an eel as I tried to pry his arm off me. *"Murder! Call nine-one-one!"* Surely someone down below would hear me.

My efforts caused the gun to shift slightly, giving me an opening to slam my head backward with punishing force. I both felt and heard the satisfying crunch of nasal cartilage, followed by a startled yelp of pain.

It was a sweet sound, but just then I heard something even sweeter: loud banging on the other side of the bulkhead door, fists at first, followed by more resounding blows. The door shuddered under the force of shoulders and feet, which only caused the wooden wedge to tighten its grip. Multiple voices shouted my name.

The resident nerds.

With Bob momentarily distracted, I was able to twist just far enough to bring his gun-wielding hand within reach of my teeth. I did not squander this opportunity but chomped as if my life depended on it (yeah, I know), resulting in a louder, shriller, more agonized howl.

My ferocious bite caused Bob to drop the pistol. He lunged for it, but I managed to give the gun a solid kick just as his fingertips touched it. The weapon spun across the gravel and came to rest against the new section of railing at the front of the building.

As he started to chase it, I launched myself on his back, targeting every tender part within reach of my fingers and feet, and screaming for Hal. Where the heck was he? Bob was surprisingly strong and agile for a man his age, and it didn't take him long to throw me off. The air fled my lungs as I made a hard landing on the roof.

He'd almost reached the gun when Hal suddenly tackled him, having apparently decided that Jane Delaney might actually have a point and perhaps he shouldn't be taking this particular serial killer at his word. Bob grunted from the body blow but held his own as the two men wrestled, moving ever closer to the pistol.

I raced toward them, my initial objective being to either grab the gun or kick it off the roof, anything to keep it out of Bob's hands. Just as my foot was about to connect with the weapon, he yanked my leg out from under me, pitching me onto the gravel for the second time.

Dang! That hurt.

The bulkhead door flew open with a bang, and the four teens spilled onto the roof. They immediately took in the scene and started racing toward us across the expanse of gravel.

I was still struggling to rise. *"No!"* I hollered at them. *"Gun! Go back!"*

Just then, Bob slipped out of Hal's grasp and grabbed the pistol. The next part happened with breathtaking speed. Hal hooked his arm under Bob's opposite arm and swiftly turned and ducked, flipping him onto his shoulder and catapulting him over the railing in one smooth motion.

20

Where Are They Today?

"THAT'S NOT A *real* Lichtenstein." Martin squinted over his shoulder at the painting hanging behind Clover Eklund's space-age burnt-orange sofa. "Is it?"

Sophie answered for their hostess. "It's real. Clover's friend Evelyn gave it to her as a housewarming gift five decades ago."

"And if you ask me whether it's insured," Clover said, "you'll be wearing this." She gestured with the pitcher of eggnog she'd just carried in from the kitchen.

I said, "I see you went ahead and had the drawing framed. It looks perfect there." The pen-and-ink drawing Scarlett had done of Clover was positioned next to the Roy Lichtenstein painting of a woman applying lipstick.

Clover filled our cups with eggnog and served herself a couple of cookies—shaped like a Christmas tree and a reindeer—before giving herself over to the buttery-soft embrace of her Eames lounge chair. "I'll never get over Scarlett's senseless death, but it gives me a measure of peace to look at that drawing and remember what a wonderful, talented young woman she was."

It was the afternoon of December 24, Christmas Eve, and Clover had invited the three of us over for a casual holiday get-together. Well, the five of us—she included Sexy Beast and Layla in the invitation. The dogs had sniffed their way around the living room, scarfed down the gourmet dog treats their hostess kept on hand for canine visitors, and were now playing tug-of-war with a rope toy.

Sophie had brought a big box of decorated cookies from Patisserie Susanne, Christmas-themed for the most part, with a few blue-and-white Hanukkah cookies thrown in since it was the last day of the eight-day Festival of Lights.

The week before, I'd taken Clover to a performance of the play that featured the antique sewing machine she'd sold to Scarlett. I'd alerted the director in advance, and before the curtain went up, she'd thanked Clover from the stage and asked her to stand and accept the audience's applause. Appreciative hoots and whistles followed as the old woman, thrilled with the attention, waved and blew kisses.

Okay, I hear you. Enough about cookies and sewing machines. You want to know about Bob. It had been two and a half weeks since Hal had exhibited surprising heroism by hurling the killer off the roof of the Americana apartment building.

Bob had regained consciousness as the paramedics worked on him, preparing to transport him to the hospital. Hal and I stood nearby, speaking with a pair of police officers, while other cops held back the crowd that had gathered.

I watched Bob's gaze sharpen, watched him take in the frenzied activity around him and realize what had happened— that he'd experienced the same horrific fall that his victim Scarlett Proctor had.

After a few moments I saw his facial muscles go slack and his eyes lose focus. I knew what had happened even before one of the paramedics searched in vain for a heartbeat, while another aimed a small flashlight at his pupils.

Some might say he'd gotten off too easily. I consider judgments like that to be above my pay grade. On the other hand, I'd be lying if I claimed to feel pity for Robert Jernigan, who'd murdered four people in cold blood and had every intention of adding Hal and me to the body count. I considered myself lucky to have survived with nothing more serious than a few bruises and scrapes.

Clover said, "I still don't know how Hal managed to throw Bob over that railing. Is he that strong?"

"It wasn't a matter of strength," I said, as I reached for a cookie shaped like a Hanukkah menorah, "or not *just* strength. I mean, sure, Hal is young and fit, but I heard him tell the cops he was on the wrestling team in high school. He said the adrenaline rush caused his old training to kick in. It was reflex. He didn't stop and think, gee, this situation calls for a one-arm shoulder throw. It was more a matter of muscle memory."

Martin stroked the back of my neck. "Well, I for one will forever be grateful Hal's muscles remembered that particular move."

"But he was willing to sacrifice you," Sophie said, "when he thought he could save his own skin and end up a hundred grand richer."

"True," I said. "He'll never be my best bud, but I'm glad he chose wrestling in high school. A wicked fastball wouldn't have been much help under the circumstances. What I think? That adrenaline rush of his was prompted by more than self-preservation. Hal was well aware of his failings where Scarlett was concerned, but he never stopped loving her. Yes, he tried to blackmail Bob, but you can't tell me that negotiating with her murderer wasn't eating away at him. In the end, he got his vengeance."

Sophie examined the cookies, finally settling on a snowman with a carroty orange nose and a red-and-green-striped necktie. "I heard that April's friend Margaret cut Hal loose."

I nodded. "Once all the facts came out—the stalking, the blackmail attempt, et cetera—she finally wised up and realized she might be better off without him."

Clover adjusted her perky brown wig, which had started to shift to one side. "I understand she and April took off for… Was it the South of France?"

"Yep," I said. "April took a leave of absence from the museum. I don't think Margaret has a job. The two of them are staying in a villa in Provence owned by April's parents."

"Maybe they'll meet a couple of French hotties," Clover said. "Anything would be an improvement over their last boyfriends."

Sophie bit the head off her snowman cookie and washed it down with eggnog. "Did I hear something about an exhumation?" She directed this question to me, knowing I had the inside track on the goings-on at Whispering Willows Cemetery.

"Carolyn insisted on a thorough forensic examination of her father's body," I said, "since Bob claimed to have killed him. Sure enough, they found definitive evidence that Ed Proctor had been manually strangled. He was dead before Bob strung him up."

"Carolyn can now let herself off the hook for his death," I said. "I think she felt responsible because she gave him the idea to steal from his employer. She's started therapy, and I heard she and her ex-husband are talking about getting back together."

"Those girls had already lost their mother." Clover set down her Santa cookie, half-eaten. "First Bob Jernigan took their father from them, then he killed Scarlett and left her sister all alone. How evil do you have to be to do something like that?"

"His murder streak started thirty-seven years ago," Sophie said, "way back in law school. Our Crystal Harbor detectives got in touch with the NYPD. Gave them the name of Bob's first victim, Cassandra, and the few details Bob had mentioned. They ID'd her right away and let her family know what really happened to her. All these years they'd thought it was a robbery that got out of hand, when in reality she was murdered by her boyfriend, Bob Jernigan, a man she knew and trusted."

Layla roused herself to come over and investigate the cookie platter, with Sexy Beast on her heels.

"Not for puppy," I singsonged, which they both knew meant better luck next time. The dogs looked at each other as if to say, *I hate it when she does that.* They turned to Clover, who they'd already learned was the keeper of the doggie treats. She obligingly pulled a baggie out of her cardigan pocket and gave them each one.

"Now, go on." She made a shooing gesture. "If you're good, you'll get another one later."

They trotted into the kitchen, where she'd set out a water bowl for them.

Sophie said, "I've been thinking about those four kids."

"The resident nerds?" I asked.

"I thought *I* was the resident nerd," Clover said.

"You're the queen nerd," Sophie said. "These kids can only

hope to aspire to your exalted level of nerditude."

"Is that a word?" Martin asked.

"It is now," Sophie said. "I'm curious about how their parents took the news that they've been sneaking up to the roof in the middle of the night. Did they freak?"

"Not as much as you'd think," I said. "Howie and Cookie did their best to take the heat off them. They were effusive in their praise of the kids, insisted they were instrumental in helping to solve Scarlett's murder. Which might be overstating their contribution, but it seems to have worked. Even Jasmine's folks couldn't stay outraged. She's decided she wants to become an FBI agent, by the way."

"Elliott is pet-sitting for us," the padre said. "We were afraid his parents would put the kibosh on that after the break-in, but they were pretty chill about the whole thing—after lecturing him on the right way and the wrong way to respond to a burglary."

"And Liam just started working with me," I said. "He assisted with his first pet funeral a few days ago—a gerbil belonging to Veronica Sheffield's sister-in-law's seven-year-old stepdaughter, Amelia." Veronica was the source of a ridiculously large percentage of my business.

"A *gerbil?*" Sophie rolled her eyes. "Talk about people who have more money than sense."

"Amelia's parents bought a plot in the Best Friend Pet Cemetery, if you can believe it," I said. "A tiny bronze casket, granite headstone, massive floral arrangements, the whole nine yards."

"Good heavens," Clover said. "In my day it was a shoebox, a hole in the backyard, a quick prayer, and a new gerbil. I'll bet all that fuss only made it worse for the little girl."

"It did," I said. "Amelia was inconsolable. Well, until Liam gently took her aside and discussed the demise of Mr. Wigglebottom in simple, straightforward terms a child could comprehend. No one had bothered to do that. Liam told her about losing his bunny, Snowflake, when he was her age. He assured her the pain would recede with time and that it didn't mean she loved Mr. Wigglebottom any less. I was pleasantly surprised because his normal attitude is rather flippant. But he handled the situation with great sensitivity."

"This Liam sounds like a keeper," Clover said.

"I think he shows great promise," I agreed. "I was afraid his parents would object to his working for someone called the Death Diva, but once I'd made it clear what kind of work he'd be doing, that I'd be paying him fairly, that it wouldn't interfere with his schoolwork, *and* that he'd be required to wear a suit, they were all for it."

"Do any of these nerds of yours play chess?" Clover asked. "You wouldn't believe how difficult it is drumming up a game among my neighbors. Or maybe you would."

"As a matter of fact," I said, "Richie Esparza is in the chess club at school, and I understand he's really good. Wins all kinds of tournaments. He used to play with Nolan. I'll bet he's just as eager as you to find a worthy opponent in the building. I'll put you two in touch."

"Please do," she said. "How exciting."

Martin lifted the eggnog pitcher and refilled everyone's cups. "I'll tell you what I'm curious about. All those other people who participated in the Winner's Circle scheme, besides the three we were focused on. Where are they today?"

"Oh, I can shed a little light on that," Clover said. "I Googled some of the cheaters listed in the notebook, the ones whose names crop up most often. As you might expect, most have been quite successful in business and politics. A handful of Fortune Five Hundred types, of course, plus a congresswoman, a federal judge, a pastor, and several physicians."

"Physicians?" Sophie made a face. "If they cheated in their undergrad years, there's a good chance they cheated in med school. Is that the guy you want operating on your brain?"

"They didn't all come out ahead," Clover continued. "A few ended up on the lowest rungs of the ladder, like poor Nolan. One guy made a quick fortune and is now doing time for insider trading. And then there's this one woman who became a professional ethicist."

"Oh, for the love of—" Sophie slammed her palms on the arms of her chair. "An *ethicist*? Someone who cheated her way through college is instructing other people on what's right and wrong?"

Before the mayor could build up a full head of steam in Yiddish, Clover said, "I was just as outraged as you, but then I watched a TED Talk she gave in which she actually brought up her college cheating history. No details, of course—she didn't name the Winner's Circle or anyone else who was involved. She talked about how it became a turning point in her life. She found she couldn't live with her choices, and it prompted a serious self-examination. She dropped out of Columbia and took some time to consider the kind of human being she wanted to be. Eventually she earned several advanced degrees, with an emphasis on the philosophical study of morality. So I'd say this particular cheater managed to turn lemons into lemonade, as the old saying goes."

There was a knock at the door. I told Clover to stay put

and got up to answer it. Dom Faso, my ex-husband, stood on the threshold, looking just as surprised to see me as I was to see him.

SB and Layla immediately raced over, since Dom wasn't alone. His dog, Flower, whom he'd recently adopted from the local animal shelter, was by his side. Flower's short hair and tricolor body—including a black saddle and floppy tan ears—stamped her as part beagle. But those spooky blue eyes positively screamed Siberian husky. She was a medium-size mix with a sweet and frisky disposition.

The leash flew out of Dom's grasp as Flower made a mad dash to join her dog-park pals in the living room. They commenced play-wrestling and chasing one another into and out of the kitchen.

Clover said, "Flower, tell your daddy to get inside so we can close that door. I'm too old to chase three ridiculous dogs through the corridors of the Americana."

As Dom entered the living room, he took in our small gathering, offering a warm smile to Sophie and a curt nod to Martin before turning to Clover. "Looks like I timed it wrong. I can come back later."

"Don't you dare leave," she said. "I assume you have news for me. But first, sit. Eat a cookie. And don't give me that health-food nonsense. A little sugar won't kill you."

He sat on a sleek, vintage armchair from the previous century and selected a snowflake-shaped cookie while I looked questioningly from him to Clover. What kind of news? What was going on?

I was about to ask just that when Dom turned to Martin. "I'm glad I ran into you."

"Let me guess," the padre said, as he plucked a dreidelshaped cookie off the platter. "It's about your daughter and my nephew."

"They've been seeing quite a lot of each other."

"Boys," Clover warned, "if this is going to devolve into some tiresome male dominance display, then you can just take it outside. But leave your dogs here. They know how to be good guests."

The good guests were at that moment settling into a fluffy cuddle puddle on the carpet.

"Have you actually met Nate?" Martin asked Dom.

"I have. He came in and introduced himself the first time he picked up Kari."

Well! A display of old-school dating etiquette from Martin's seventeen-year-old nephew. I wondered if it was an indication of how serious he was about Kari. It might simply mean his parents had raised him right.

"We've had a few conversations since then," Dom added.

"And what do you think of him?" Martin asked him.

"He seems like a good kid," Dom said. "Kari likes him, and I trust her judgment."

I said, "Did you know that Suzanne Travert just hired Nate to work part-time at the patisserie next summer?"

"Really?" Dom said. "Did anyone tell him he'll need to get there before dawn?"

"He knows and he's cool with it," Martin said. "The kid's pumped, raring to get started."

I had to believe Nate reminded my ex of himself at that age: not just the boy's work ethic, but his interest in a food-related career.

Dom let his gaze wander to the Lichtenstein. "You know, I've always wondered. Is that a real—"

"It's real!" four voices chorused.

"Clover my dear," he said, "you're just full of surprises."

She cackled. "You don't know the half of it."

"I just might have a surprise of my own," he said with a sly smile.

She sat forward, suddenly excited. "Don't tease us, Dom. Out with it!"

"Okay," I said, "what the heck is going on?" I looked at the mayor. Nothing happened in Crystal Harbor that she didn't know about.

Sophie shrugged. "Beats me."

"Okay, I've played it real close to the vest with this," Dom said. "Didn't want the rumors to start flying. You know Scarlett had this idea to save the Americana, right?"

"Right," I said. "She wanted some local business leaders to band together and buy the building so it could remain standing and no one would be evicted. You told me you couldn't drum up interest in that plan."

"That's right," he said. "No one else considered it a decent investment. That's why I decided to simplify things and make it a solo project."

I stared at him, certain I must've misheard. "You mean… You don't mean you…"

"I'm buying the Americana," he said. "I outbid the developer who planned to tear it down and slap up a mansion. The Devines happily accepted my offer, and we just signed the contract."

Clover let out a whoop of sheer joy. Three canine heads jerked up, three pairs of doggy eyes focused on the human who might or might not have just emitted a howl of agony. I could swear I saw little worry lines crease Layla's forehead. It's nice to imagine she was concerned for the old woman's health, but let's face it. Clover was the one with the treats.

"Obviously *you* knew this was in the works," I told her.

"I was hopeful," Clover said. "I knew how Scarlett felt about saving the Americana and that she'd spoken with Dom about it. When I saw him at the memorial service, I made him promise to try and find a way, and to keep me in the loop."

Dom was probably the wealthiest business owner in Crystal Harbor. If anyone had the resources to pull this off solo, it was him.

Martin set his cup and plate on the coffee table and crossed to where Dom sat. He held out his hand. "Respect, man. Good for you for stepping up."

Dom's expression barely changed, but I knew my ex, and it was clear he hadn't anticipated the gracious gesture. He stood and shook Martin's hand. "Thanks."

"I'm proud of you, Dom," I said. "I have to admit, I thought the Americana was a lost cause."

His smile turned crooked as he resumed his seat. "Ask me in a few months how I feel about being a landlord."

"Well, I assume you'll be hiring a manager," I said. "I mean, I know you're used to being a hands-on boss, but this one's a little outside your wheelhouse."

"The Devines recommended a couple of managers," he said, "and I'm planning to hire one of them. But the fact is, I'm actually looking forward to getting involved."

"Hal won't be happy," Sophie said. "There goes his relocation allowance."

"And no more stolen items for him to sell to *Ramrod News*," I said. "No rich girlfriend to sponge off of. No blackmail prospects. Hal might actually have to learn to live within his means."

Clover pushed out of her chair, marched right over to Dom, grabbed his ears, and gave him a big, smacking kiss on the lips. "Dominic Faso, you are a genuine white knight. Scarlett knew just what she was doing when she asked you to work your magic. Now, let's get you some eggnog."

About the Author

Pamela Burford comes from a funny family. You may take that any way you want. She was raised in a household that valued laughter above all, so of course the first thing she looked for in a husband was a sense of humor. Is it any wonder their grown kids are into stand-up comedy and improv? Oh, and here's another fun fact: Pamela's identical twin sister, Patricia Ryan, aka P.B. Ryan, is also a published novelist. Patricia is the Good Twin, and yeah, Pamela knows what that makes her. But hey, Evil Twins have more fun!

It should come as no surprise that everything Pamela writes is infused with her own quirky brand of humor, from her feel-good contemporary romance and romantic suspense novels to her popular Jane Delaney mystery series, featuring snarky "Death Diva" Jane, her canine sidekick Sexy Beast, and a fun love-triangle subplot. Pamela's own beloved poodle, Murray, wants you to know that any similarities between himself and neurotic, high-strung Sexy Beast are purely coincidental.

Pamela is the proud founder and past president of Long Island Romance Writers. Her books have won awards and sold millions of copies, but what excites her most is hearing from readers. Swing by and say hi at pamelaburford.com.

www.ingramcontent.com/pod-product-compliance
Lightning Source LLC
Chambersburg PA
CBHW051248210726
48287CB00002B/398